PENGUIN

F.I.R.

Monabi Mitra teaches English literature at the Scottish Church College, Calcutta. *F.I.R.*, the first of the DSP Bikram series, is the result of a continuing interest in the working of the Indian police force.

# F.I.R.

## MONABI MITRA

Penguin
metro reads

PENGUIN METRO READS

Published by the Penguin Group

Penguin Books India Pvt. Ltd, 11 Community Centre, Panchsheel Park,
New Delhi 110 017, India

Penguin Group (USA) Inc., 375 Hudson Street, New York, New York
10014, USA

Penguin Group (Canada), 90 Eglinton Avenue East, Suite 700, Toronto,
Ontario, M4P 2Y3, Canada (a division of Pearson Penguin Canada Inc.)

Penguin Books Ltd, 80 Strand, London WC2R 0RL, England

Penguin Ireland, 25 St Stephen's Green, Dublin 2, Ireland (a division of
Penguin Books Ltd)

Penguin Group (Australia), 250 Camberwell Road, Camberwell,
Victoria 3124, Australia (a division of Pearson Australia Group Pty Ltd)

Penguin Group (NZ), 67 Apollo Drive, Rosedale, Auckland 0632,
New Zealand (a division of Pearson New Zealand Ltd)

Penguin Group (South Africa) (Pty) Ltd, 24 Sturdee Avenue, Rosebank,
Johannesburg 2196, South Africa

Penguin Books Ltd, Registered Offices: 80 Strand, London WC2R 0RL,
England

First published in Penguin Metro Reads by Penguin Books India 2012

Copyright © Monabi Mitra 2012

ISBN 9780143417545

Typeset in Adobe Garamond by Guru Typograph Technology, New Delhi
Printed at Manipal Technologies Ltd, Manipal

F.I.R.

# 1

'There's a new cop in town,' Nikki Kumar said as she straightened up from her toe touches. She flopped down on the grey non-slip gym mat, panting from her exertions. 'I met him at the club yesterday. Seemed quite our kind, you know. He actually stood up when I was introduced to him.'

There was silence at the fitness clinic. The other two women were so wrapped up in their own reflections, Nikki Kumar could very well have been talking to the gym equipment. An Indian blonde was eyeing herself critically in the mirror and casting envious glances at Nisha Bose, the third member of the club. The mirror in front of which Nisha was standing seemed to recognize the radiance of her beauty as it returned her steady gaze.

'Now stop it, you two.' Nikki Kumar looked annoyed. 'Come here, catch your breath, and I'll tell you all about him.'

'All you know about him. It's not the same, you know.' Nisha raised a finger to her chin and surveyed herself dreamily.

'It will be, once I get my hands on him. All I need are two parties and one club night. I got twenty-five per cent of his life history last evening; the rest should be easy.'

'What you mean is twenty-five per cent of what the man wants to be known around town,' said Nisha Bose, still annoyingly disdainful of Nikki Kumar's gym bulletin for the day. 'But do tell us all the same.' She sat down before Nikki, assumed position for sit-ups, and waited for Nikki to begin.

'His name is Toofan Kumar and he was in Delhi before this. With the Information Bureau, before he took a transfer to Cal. He . . .'

'Intelligence Bureau,' said the third girl, Anjali, her voice breaking from exertion. She was standing before a mirror, lifting weights, watching each muscle go taut as her arms went up and each sinew relax as the arms came down. A cousin had recently got married to someone in the police and Anjali felt a correction was a matter of family duty.

'How does it matter?' snapped Nikki. She was beginning to lose her temper.

As Nikki puffed on the treadmill, her overwrought imagination created a cosy little conversation with Toofan Kumar out of what, in reality, had been a few minutes of hurried greetings and half a stolen conversation over a glass of beer. But now, Anjali and Nisha were paying her no attention at all!

'He seems to be promising. All the other policemen I know have stopped answering my calls.'

'How you frighten them, Nikki dear!' Nisha Bose stared languidly at her painted toenails.

'I don't, but my drivers do. Is it my fault if the traffic lights turn red just when my car reaches the intersection? We usually squeeze through but sometimes these drivers are so slow, soon there's a traffic constable peeping through the window.' Nikki Kumar sniffed.

A man, lean and energetic, entered, balancing a tray with three glasses of lemonade and wet towels. He deposited the tray in a corner and fiddled with a CD player. The gym was flooded with a mechanical voice repeating words in a nasal tone over a background of hectic drumbeats. The man looked at Nisha Bose out of the corner of his eye and hesitated. She ignored his presence and he left. The other two women were absorbed in themselves and they did not notice this quick exchange.

Nikki said brightly, 'But now I've met Toofan Kumar and will be safe for the next year or so. Should we have a cosy dinner at the club first, followed by a bigger do, or should I burst him in on to the party scene and then ask DP to follow it up with a round of golf?'

'Don't go overboard, Nikki, I beg you. One thing at a time! A cop's a good thing, but in small doses. In spite of everything, they do handle dead bodies.' This was Anjali, who had finished her toning for the day and was ready to join the conversation in a fuller way.

'Cops and corpses! Not anymore!' Nisha laughed a silvery laugh and stood up with a swift fluid movement. 'They're too busy knocking around processions and demonstrations to worry about the public any longer. And in the evenings they are with us!'

A road wound towards the horizon through a patchwork of paddy fields. The black metalled sharpness of its surface was highlighted against the coppery terracotta of earthen embankments that flanked it. A straggling line of tired-looking casuarinas, their thin barks painted white in a brief, energetic spurt of activity by the Forest Department, tried ineffectually to beat back the tangle of weeds that grew happily at their feet. Down below, the verdant rice, separated by aisles of piled mud into chessboard symmetry, stretched limitless and infinite in its perfection.

Deputy Superintendent of Police Bikram Chatterjee alighted from his mud-spattered Tata Sumo and surveyed the scene without enthusiasm. He had been running a low fever for the last two days. And having been awake the night before, he was exhausted. He had dozed off in the car, occasionally awakening to answer phone calls with the practised ease of a person who has learnt through long experience how to switch quickly between sleep and alert awakening.

It was almost dark, about 6 p.m., when the sky takes on that indeterminate colour between pale orange and grey. All nature seemed to Bikram to be in a restless, last-minute bustle before settling down for the night. For someone who hadn't slept well, such energetic preparations seemed annoying. A koel trilled insistently from a tree, crows hopped back and forth busily while, high up above, a flock of kites wheeled lazily in perfect circles. When Bikram sniffed the air he smelt the raw earth, the green leaves and, above all, the sharp heady tang of ripening mango flowers. Another two weeks and the small green mangoes would begin to form.

A man who had been rummaging around in the glove compartment now creaked open the front door and heaved himself out. Inspector Ghosh, with greying hair and melancholy eyes, yawned, coughed and cleared his throat before looking dispiritedly at his surroundings. Because he was tired, sick and unwashed, Bikram looked disapprovingly at the belt stretched impossibly over Ghosh's bulging stomach.

'If you eat another chicken roll or even look at another bottle of McDowell's, I'll send you for a week of advanced firearms training.'

'I try, Sir, but it's the wife. She gives me Maggi for breakfast and instant pasta when I'm working late.'

'Oh yes! And what does the owner of Bengal Bar give you for the weekend? Boiled vegetables and a glass of lemonade, I suppose.'

Ghosh, Bikram's second-in-command, knew better than to indulge in idle backchat with his boss, especially before an unpromising raid on a small village a hundred kilometres from Calcutta. Most of the inhabitants of the village were pickpockets, peddlers of crack and makers of crude bombs that fetched good prices before government elections. A few graduated to kidnapping, extortion and robbery. Bikram and Ghosh's mission today was to try to catch a man suspected to have a finger in all the pies.

'I hope that excitable informer of yours got it right this time,' said Bikram testily.

'Oh yes, Sir! Babul's the man. He boasted to a whore that he's moving in for a big kill. He'll buy her Scotch from Calcutta wine shops soon. Maybe a newfangled cell phone as well.'

'Have we come all this way on the testimony of a Bowbazar slut or does your guy have other information as well?'

Ghosh took out a violently coloured handkerchief moist with sweat and passed it around his neck. 'He's positive, Sir. This is it! Nothing can go wrong tonight.'

The two men surveyed the road, the fields, and the clump of date and palm trees in the distance that marked the entrance to the village. Bikram measured the distance to it from where they stood by counting the electric posts that loomed over the fields. A red and black bus, listing to one side, its roof piled high with sacks and suitcases and two cycles, sounded a loud do-re-mi horn as it rounded a corner of the road.

'Mistry!'

Mistry, the driver, languidly zipping his fly after urinating over the embankment near the rear side of the car, trotted to the door and held it open for the two.

'Back to the thana, quickly. Where's my flask? And wipe your hands before you touch it.'

The policemen came back at midnight. The bushes and trees buzzed with the sound of crickets, and glow-worms flickered tantalizingly.

First, two dirty white Ambassador cars, long curling scratches on their bonnets, POLICE lettered in red-and-white Bookman Old Style font at the back, came to a stop a little away from where the road drove into a meandering twist. A few minutes later, two more vehicles arrived, not Ambassadors but ugly Jeeps, almost as high as buses, a black iron collapsible gate built into each rear door. All four cars squatted impossibly by the road, clinging crazily to the edge of the embankment. Doors creaked open, the collapsible gate was folded back jerkily, and lines of men climbed down unsteadily, weighted under a strange assortment of goods. There were ancient muskets strapped to their shoulders and knobbly wooden canes in their hands. One or two wore helmets of fading green and incredible weight. Their brown uniforms were speckled with grease stains and clotted dal, and the buttons that held in place their WBP (West Bengal Police) shoulder badges hung askew. Their faces were dispirited and uninspired. Most of them were thinking of the night ahead of them: the endless tramping and running with nothing to look forward to except a breakfast of a loaf of bread and four bananas washed down with some bitter-sweet tea. One or two hitched the heavy rifles uncomfortably on to their shoulders as they walked a little way off for a quick pee. Another stopped to blow his nose and spit into the tangled undergrowth. Then, when a tubby man in a dirty uniform shouted something in a cracked voice, the men shuffled themselves into untidy rows and columns.

Bikram left Ghosh to brief the men. Usually, during muster, a tangle of emotions swept over him: they ranged from sadness for this pathetic group of sullen, dirty men to anger against the authorities who did nothing for them. When the instructions were complete, he roused himself from his thoughts, gulped down great draughts of ice-cold water from his flask, and led the way.

The bunch turned off the road, slithered down the scrubby embankment and on to the paddy fields. They walked on the mud banks that separated each field, feeling the mud sink beneath their boots. They began walking in a single file but, soon, the faster walkers beat their way through the paddy, feet sinking into the soft earth slushy and treacherous from the day's watering. In the darkness, Bikram could just make out the shadowy steel of the gigantic electric pylons and kept track of the distance by counting them.

'Turn off your torch, you bastard!'

A light had bobbed somewhere behind them and there was a whimper as Ghosh rammed his cane into someone's butt.

'Something slithered past, Sir; this area is full of . . .'

'Shut up,' grumbled the others.

There was more muttering and cursing towards the back of the line. An elderly constable, his moustache damp with misery as he tried to manoeuvre his huge form through the fields, slipped an inch into a patch of slush and cried out for help. In the end, it took them an hour to cover just three quarters of the distance to the village. Bikram looked briefly at his fancy watch, bought in celebration after another, hugely successful raid, and wondered if he would be equally lucky this time.

As they reached the edge of the village, Ghosh abruptly stopped. The wind was blowing towards them and, over the smell of mud and leaves, came the sharp, unmistakable smell of burning tobacco.

'Stay here,' he whispered to the constable behind him.

Ghosh and Bikram crept forward stealthily, occasionally halting and listening. The smell of the tobacco smoke was getting stronger. A straggly copse of banana trees, long leaves trailing irregularly on the ground, loomed in front of them. Someone was crouched under one of the banana trees.

Except for the red tip glowing intermittently in the darkness, nothing was visible.

Ghosh jumped first. As he hurtled all his ninety kilograms at the midnight smoker, the cigarette shot into the air and landed a foot away. At the same time, an all-too-familiar smell came to Ghosh and he gabbled in misery, 'Oh no! He's been shitting.'

Bikram switched on his torch and blinked as the pale beam of light illuminated the scene. Ghosh was wrestling with a bare-chested man in a checked lungi which was now slipping open, occasionally allowing glimpses of his private parts. Fresh shit was smeared on Ghosh's trousers.

The man, in one quick movement, shot out an arm and hit Ghosh across the mouth even as the latter looked down at the mess on his shoes. As he turned to run, lungi flying, Bikram threw his torch at his head. There was a dull thud and the torch rolled on to the ground, casting crazy shafts of light on the foliage. Without waiting to retrieve it, Bikram wrenched out his revolver and pressed it to the stomach of the fallen figure, even as Ghosh flung himself on him again.

The waiting troop, sensing trouble and guided by the tilting shafts of light, scrambled up and joined the jumble. Someone picked up the lungi and covered the naked man. At the same time, frenzied barking rang out in the distance, followed by another howl, and yet another, until a perfect orchestra of full-bodied, angry barks rent the air. Bikram sighed. If Babul was anywhere around, he would be well warned and was, perhaps even now, slipping out of his house and into the safety of whichever secret hideout he had chosen. Stealth was now rendered useless, so the party abandoned its furtive march and swept into the village. Their torches bobbed down dusty meandering lanes on which two people could hardly walk abreast. Scraggy dogs yammered and howled and pursued the policemen. Owls screeched, and crows, disturbed by the sound of tramping feet, hopped angrily from branch to branch. Ghosh, seething from the humiliation of the shit on his trousers, pushed forward, revolver in hand. As he drove on, six of his men tried to keep up with his sudden pace. Bikram dropped back, switched off his torch, slowed down and stopped. He sniffed the air. A light rustling breeze brought to him the delicate smell of night flowers. Laced through the perfume was the unmistakable smell of water. Bikram closed his eyes and tried to recreate the map Ghosh's source had sketched. Babul's house stood exactly at the centre of the village, fortified by a dense clot of mud huts with thatched tops and asbestos-roofed cottages. His house was the only double-storeyed structure and it had a narrow driveway in front and a boundary wall all around. If Bikram left the house and its adjacent areas to Ghosh's brigade and waited quietly beyond, along the rear side of the pond, he might still be able to track Babul as he crept away.

They waited along the water's edge, Bikram and his men— the three from his team to whom he was closest, and whom he had handpicked. Mosquitoes fed greedily on their bare arms and foreheads and buzzed about in clouds above their heads. The three guards stirred now and then, slapped at their noses and hair. Only one man stood still, hardly breathing, his eyes narrowed in the darkness, watching and waiting.

Behind the house, shadows crept along the boundary wall. Something seemed to detach itself from the darkness. There was a hiss and a scratching sound as a larger darkness hoisted itself over the wall. Bikram pursed his lips and waited for the policeman who had climbed over the wall into Babul's compound to open the front gate and let Ghosh in. Soon, Ghosh's voice could be heard, harsh and grating against the silence of the night.

'Open the door! Open the door immediately!'

Silence.

More hammering and banging; this time with the butt end of a rifle. 'Open up, you bastards!'

A light came on in a back room, a faltering reddish glow in the erratic voltage of the rural electric supply. A voice sharp with apprehension rang out. 'Who's there?'

'Open up and we'll let you know.'

'No way! Not until you identify yourself.'

Bikram waited, motionless. Something was bound to happen now. The people inside had guessed what was going on and were simply buying time.

Something, or someone, moved at the side of the house and crept out from under the tangled stems of a tree. The three men at the back of the house, intent on guarding the rear wall, had not noticed. Perhaps it was chance or some deep rooted instinct, honed over years of waiting, which caused Bikram to switch his torch on. A beam of white light skittering over the trees and bushes picked out a man, bare-chested and wearing only a lungi, scuttling away from the house.

'Catch him!'

There was a flash and a bang. Someone had fired a shot. Even as he ran, Bikram realized that one of the guards at the back of the house was slowly sinking to the ground, hands flailing, rifle dangling incongruously from his shoulder.

'He's been shot. Come quick.'

Ghosh appeared from around the house, five policemen flapping behind him, their rifles raised, even as Bikram and his men ran towards the path.

Trapped, the fugitive stood for a moment at the edge of the pond, low groans rising above the clamour behind him, his revolver useless against the array of weapons around. He raised his arms above his head, looked around once and plunged into the water.

'Light, quickly.'

'Aaaeee, I'm dying.'

'He'll get away, Sir, shall I jump in after him?'

Above it all rang Bikram's voice. 'Don't shoot, anybody! And quiet. He's here somewhere and he's got a gun.'

A sudden hush fell on the gathering; even the wounded policeman stifled his cries. Bikram could hear Ghosh muttering expletives under his breath and the short gasps of the breathless men. Torches scoured the water but could pick out only blackness and the dark hoods of water hyacinths.

'Keep watch on the water. He'll make a dash for it soon.'

Seven or eight of the men were already running up and down the bank, two scrambled down to the edge and began to circle from opposite sides.

Ghosh touched Bikram on the shoulder. 'The guard, he's hurt, Sir. He's been shot in the leg and he's losing blood.'

Bikram sighed and walked back wearily to where the man lay writhing on the ground, forehead damp with sweat, sweat stains spreading across his armpits and chest, the useless leg tilted awkwardly. Someone had unstrapped his rifle which lay behind. Bikram leaned beside him.

'You'll be all right. Do you know your blood group?'

'No.' The man's face had turned pallid with fear. 'I saw him creeping away. I tried to spring on him from behind but I didn't realize . . .'

Bikram looked up at the moonless sky in anger. Should they have waited for the full moon and the chance of light? Should he call off the raid and retreat? But something told him to push on with the ambush. Lately, he had got into this habit of feeling oddly apprehensive, he who had once been so sure of his own success. He also had odd moments of divination; brief flashes in which he felt that what he was doing now would be of some great import later.

They were hammering again at the door and, this time,

someone opened it. The injured man was now groaning loudly, his body limp. One of the constables came out with a rectangular piece of dirty cotton that looked like a vest, savagely ripped it up and tied a rough bandage around the leg. Ghosh's walkie-talkie had come alive in a series of staccato bursts as he shouted for a car to take the main village road to the house. 'Come double quick, you oaf, there's been a bullet injury, yes, turn left from the Shib Mandir and past the old Rajbari where one of the guys will take over and bring you here. Over.'

Faces peered cautiously out of the house as the women jostled for a better view, faded saris wound tightly round their breasts and heads.

All this while, a group of men ceaselessly darted round the pond and the back of the house, torches criss-crossing the dark water and the bushes around it. But the pond was large and only the front portion of it was used, the rest of the water was covered in slime and the clustering water hyacinths.

'Turn off your torches, everybody.'

Ghosh looked up in surprise.

'I have a plan,' said Bikram. 'Let him think we're giving up and letting go. If he's hiding somewhere, he'll try and make a dash for it.'

'Everybody be quiet,' hissed Ghosh. 'And listen . . .'

They were back in darkness. An owl swooped low with a shrill screech. The light in the house had vanished and the waiting policemen could feel, rather than see, the inmates pressed against the window bars, watching them. The dogs were still barking furiously. From far away, came the low wails of jackals, rising and falling in perfect horror-movie fashion. Motionless, they waited for something to happen— but nothing did.

Bikram, biting his lips in vexation, waited impatiently. Do something, he begged the fugitive. Don't send me back to headquarters empty-handed. A face rose in his mind with its look of mockery and pleasure as Bikram returned in failure.

Then suddenly, someone screamed. 'Help, help! I'm dying. For god's sake, help.'

Everyone darted towards the pond as the still, foetid waters churned to reveal a man scrabbling and scratching at the water's edge, trying to climb out. The beams of light showed the man, long weeds draping his chest, hair plastered in wispy tendrils of root and scum, collapse on the mud path bordering the pond. Around his thighs and arms were four or five rubbery shapes, ten inches long, plump with blood and glistening in the light. As the man lay tearing at something around his waist, screaming all the time, they could see his eyes turn white with fear.

'Leeches,' said a terrified voice from amongst the gathered men. It was the young constable who had switched on his torch in the paddy field for fear of snakes.

'Leeches, Sir, leeches,' he gabbled, 'they're a special kind, we call them the greedy leeches, they grow a foot long after sucking blood, they hide beneath the weeds of old unused ponds. Oh, this man will die; we'll all die if they crawl to us.'

They ran back to the house to get common salt as the fugitive lay writhing beside the pond, his shrieks rising higher and higher. This time, all the inhabitants of the house joined them—a group of limping old men and hunchbacked women, vigorous young girls and one gangling youth of fifteen or sixteen—all shouting and cursing the police: they've killed him, how will we live, see what they've done. In a while, the leeches fell off and lay in satisfied curls on the bank, five in all, while long snaking rivulets of blood oozed lazily down the man's legs and arms and even his groin, for one leech had feasted on his private parts. All the while, the policeman with the gunshot wound groaned and gasped at the back, temporarily deserted by his mates as they crowded round the man with the leech bites. Amidst all this stood Bikram Chatterjee, implacable and grave, saddled with two 'seriously wounded cases', as the indefatigable Ghosh informed him, requiring immediate medical attention in a village from which the nearest hospital was seventy kilometres away and liable to be deserted at this hour, the doctor in charge snoring in his quarters and no medicines available anyway.

In the end, they returned to the thana with the policeman and the thief. An ambulance had been summoned and the two men were packed into it, sharing a makeshift bed on the ambulance floor.

Bikram made quick phone calls to colleagues and friends in hospitals and police outposts along the way. Dawn was breaking as they reached Calcutta, trucks carrying the day's vegetables unloading their wares outside markets, milk vans trundling along the roads, as Bikram and his men burst into the city and made for Medical College and Hospital at great speed.

## 2

'Tara, I wish you would take the trouble to visit Robi today. He's been rather fretful lately and wants you over.' There was silence at the breakfast table. Tara's mother dipped her toast in her tea and swallowed quickly. Her father filled his soup bowl with more milk and muri, added two spoons of sugar, and stirred vigorously. Tara buttered her third piece of toast and layered it carefully with a spoonful of honey. The only sign that she had heard her father at all was that her hands trembled slightly.

'What's the matter? Didn't you hear what I said?'

'Of course she did,' said Tara's mother soothingly. 'She's just trying to work out her timings.'

'Must you interfere with everything I say? She's not dumb that she can't answer for herself! Did you hear me, Tara? Robi wants you to visit him today.'

'It's Thursday. Not today.'

It promised to be a stormy meal but Tara's voice was calm.

'I don't care if it's Thursday or Friday. A promise is a promise. I told Robi you would go and that's that.'

'I'm sorry, but I can't. I have an art class today.'

Tara rose decisively with her plate and went towards the kitchen. As she had half-expected her mother to come in after her while she was doing the dishes, it didn't surprise her when she did. Yet her mother's customary pleading annoyed her and annoyance soon turned to anger.

She replied wearily, 'Help me, Ma. I can't stand this life

any longer. What have we got out of our relationship with Robi and Nisha except unhappiness?'

'I know. But Robi's father was kind to us at a time when nobody else was. Do this for our sake. Or for mine,' Tara's mother added hastily on seeing her daughter's expression.

'What about the classes at the club?'

Since Tara had capitulated—as her mother knew she would—they put the rest of the plan together. Tara's mother would telephone the club and tell the secretary that Tara would be late because of her father's blood test reports that had to be shown to a specialist. And Tara would go to Robi and Nisha's stately house, with its shaded garden and expensive drapes, to maintain family peace.

Tara was thirty-three, unmarried, living with her parents on the top floor of a three-storeyed house in a shabby neighbourhood that had once been genteel. The pavements, once wide and clean, were now overrun by snack bars on wheels, ugly aluminium carts that sold street-side chowmein in a fierce sauce.

The two bedrooms in their house had three varying states of mind. Tara's father was a strong-willed bully, frequently moody and feverish, intolerant of others, often abusive, living only for his own sake and needs. Tara's mother had, over the years, dulled her hopes and simply existed, timid and submissive. By the time she entered her teens, Tara realized she needed to get away from this sad household if she were to survive. At that time, she had inhabited two worlds: the world of school and friends, bubbling with the assurance of youth, and the quiet despondence of home. At the same time, she had been buoyed by the certainty of escape. But when it was finally time to escape, to apply to some university abroad and never come back, Tara found a strange reluctance within her. Perhaps she was timid, or apathetic, or hopeless, or, as she suspected, a combination of all. Tara's dissatisfaction was soon dulled to passivity and a resigned endurance of the status quo.

In the dusty begrimed offices of Wisdom Press, Tara finished her day's work—ploughing through piles of submitted manuscripts. At 5.00 p.m., as the roar of traffic outside the window reached a frenzy, Tara washed her hands in the cracked basin of the office lavatory, brushed and tied her hair into a ponytail and prepared to leave.

'Going somewhere?'

As usual, Anju had sensed something.

'It's the weekly visit to Robi.'

'Was it your father's orders or mother's?'

'Both, I suppose. They must have worked it out together.'

'Don't you think you should change into something better?' Anju looked her up and down with a look of dissatisfaction. 'Not coarse cotton for a tea party at the Boses'.'

'If there's a tea party you may be sure I'm going to be kept out of it. I'll be babysitting Robi while his wife dazzles the guests.'

'Then you may as well have some tea before you go. Or maybe some coffee. How about a cappuccino at Café Coffee Day? The answer is yes. My treat.'

Tara sighed. It was useless arguing with Anju. So they left the smell of books behind them and made for the new café that had opened just a month ago.

Inside, it was cool and smelt of chocolate and coffee. They sat on the tiny round wooden chairs with iron fluting, and Anju ordered. There was a noisy group of college students in a corner, arguing loudly and harassing the waiter. In another corner, two good-looking men were smoking and whispering between themselves. When Anju and Tara entered, the two turned around to look them up and down.

'The one on the left looks like Aryan, doesn't he?'

Tara said nothing.

'Why didn't you marry him?' Anju persisted.

'You are determined to play the agony aunt today, aren't you?'

'I was just curious. He was a good catch. I wish I had such a chance myself.'

'You would have fared quite badly. His family was completely traditional. Rajasthani. Vegetarian, money-minded and anti-Bengali. They would never have allowed it. Aryan was only fooling me and himself, of course, when he thought they would accept me.'

'But there are no Bengali boys in Calcutta anymore. They've all left for Mumbai and Delhi and Bangalore and beyond. What are we to do, Tara? Marry some liverish loser earning ten thousand a month or remain spinsters all our lives! At least you have your sister-in-law.'

'She's a bitch!' said Tara tightly.

The coffee was served and she buried her face in it. Anju, sensing trouble, kept quiet. The boys from the college group started singing a song by a popular Bengali rock band and the girls clapped and giggled. The two men in the other corner hailed the waiter for another round of coffee and looked slyly at Anju, who met their eyes and saw they were looking appreciatively at Tara.

'I could give you a lift in a cab. I need to shop for a birthday gift and I'll go right past your cousin's house.'

'I'll take the Metro. Might as well get it over with.'

Tara finished her coffee, carefully patted her mouth, and prepared to leave.

Anju hesitated, then said, 'Look at those guys in the corner there, Tara. Ever since we've been here, they have kept looking at you. I received only a casual, non-starter of a glance. Maybe it's not always that bad, Tara. Even if your cousin and his wife don't care for you, and have you over only for their own convenience, you can make something out of it.'

'Such as?'

'Oh, come on! I don't need to spell it out for you. Use your instinct. Join the party under some pretext or hang around until you're introduced to some of the young guests. If you dress right they can't exclude you. You might just meet someone.'

'If I could have done it that way, Anju, I could have done a lot of things in life. Beginning with one of those two in the corner there. Or perhaps with both!'

'But you just don't try. I'm not telling you to throw yourself at men but please, at least explore possibilities. It is as if you make yourself plain and unattractive on purpose. You're only cheating yourself of the chance of a better life.'

'I wish you'd pick a better time for your lecture. And don't say you are trying to help me.'

'One day . . .'

'. . . I'll remember your words of wisdom, and repent. And you'll play with your grandchildren and think about peevish Tara who sulked in a corner of the Bose mansion while delicious men buzzed all around her.'

'Oh, all right, have it your own way. Enjoy the food at least!'

'The food is not worth the price,' said Tara with finality and got up to leave.

Robi and Nisha Bose lived in a spacious bungalow in a fashionable part of the town. Once, the street had been lined with mansions with dark, imperious gates and large gardens in which squawking parrots announced the fortunes of their owners. Most of the bungalows had made way for high- rises with exteriors done up in pink-and-black, and car parks filled with shining cars. Even now, one such mansion was being bludgeoned into oblivion.

Tara stood at the gate for a moment or two, hesitating. She then squared her shoulders and reached out for the gate. It swung open on its own. A durwan stood inside, his face a careful combination of contempt and insolence. The man stood aside to let her in, leaving the smallest space possible so that Tara had to brush against his body to enter.

'Memsahib has been waiting for a long time,' he said and then added brightly, 'very crowded buses, I know. I told Babuji, we need to buy Tara didi a car. Then she'll be here on time and I won't have to keep craning my neck to hear her come.'

Tara ignored the durwan's insults. She reasoned to herself: a poor relation—the unmarried daughter of a greedy, parasitical father—is meant to be teased and despised and made the butt of servant-room ridicule. Should she have married Aryan? But that would have made her Mrs Jain, with a diamond nose stud and sequinned sari and, perhaps she might have been kept from seeing her parents had she not borne her in-laws a male heir within the first two years of marriage. Tara's thoughts thus ran around in circles of self abuse. In the meanwhile, she had crossed the lawn, run up the porch steps and rung the bell under the patterned shadows thrown down by the woven cane lamp. On her left, she could see, through the tall French windows, a room cosy and glowing with flowers and lace cushions and comfortable sofas. Nisha's guests had not yet arrived.

Robi was waiting in his wheelchair for Tara, his walking stick standing upright beside him. His left hand hung nerveless by his side while the right moved and clenched and fidgeted with irritated energy. Nowhere was this energy more apparent than in his eyes—bulging and wild—that darted restlessly around the room. When Tara entered, he was concentrating on scratching his left shoulder and, as his fingers scrabbled stiffly on his shirt, there came into his eyes a disorderly, almost menacing, look.

'You're actually on time today.'

When he spoke, Robi's low nasal drawl masked the fact that some of his speech was slurred.

'I got an early train.'

He would never realize, thought Tara, that she came early on such days to avoid the speculative looks of guests. Robi had always been self-absorbed and uninterested in the subtler shades of human thought. But now in his illness he was almost brutish in his self-centredness.

'You're looking nice, though. Almost pretty. I didn't know you could look nice in such a plain dress. Better than all the tight dresses youngsters seem to be wearing these days. At least that's what I find in the newspapers. By the way, there's an article on coping with terminal illness that Nisha said you should read out to me. Fairly representative of my situation.'

Tara settled herself in a chair and propped her back, already aching with the rigours of a ten-hour workday, with two cushions borrowed from a chaise longue in the corner. The room was dimly lit and airless. The slatted windows were bolted, the curtains were drawn. Only the bathroom door was open and through it came the smell of liquid antiseptic and the faint smell of urine. Robi Bose prattled on. 'I wonder what Nisha is wearing tonight. I asked her in the morning but she said she hadn't decided. Maybe it's the new sari she bought last week. What's the name of that store near Kowloon, the one which sells imported silk? I think it's from that one. Soli's, I think, or was it Chawla's? Used to buy her one every time the company bagged a fresh contract!'

A fat maid waddled into the room, ignored Tara, set down a tray with biscuits and tea before Robi and attempted to escape. Robi, however, stopped mid-sentence to call her back. 'Where's Memsahib? And where's Buro? Tell him I want to go to the bathroom. Get me a napkin from the table there. Has the party begun?' The maid, endeavouring to leave without replying, shot a quick look at Tara, who was looking at the floor. Robi's voice, no longer a slow drawl, rose to a high-pitched whine. 'Where's Buro? He's supposed to be my attendant, not enjoy himself at the party. It's my house. Nisha! Nisha!'

Tara rose to close the door and caught a glimpse of the maid laughing to herself as she fled down the stairs. In the room, Robi carefully picked up a biscuit and began to eat it hungrily. His eyes darted back and forth from his teacup to the plate of biscuits. Crumbs began to cluster round his lips. Still he ate and Tara, watching him from her chair, wondered at the insatiable appetite, the unfed urges, of her cousin. When he had finished eating, Robi leaned back in his wheelchair and closed his eyes. His right hand lay on his lap, swollen and white, like his feet, the fingers moving spasmodically. He spoke after a minute and his voice was once again controlled. 'I know how hard it must be for Nisha to have me laid up here like a burden. She's borne it all so wonderfully. Never complaining, not even for a minute.'

A car reversed in the driveway. Tara figured this from the tinny Hindu devotional song the vehicle belted out as it did so. She wondered which of Nisha's guests would be inelegant enough to have such a tune.

'She's had to work harder too, ever since I've been laid up. Poor thing! Something or the other always seems to be going wrong at work. Organizing, making all those idiots work, and putting together prints and stuff for all those interiors she has to design. There are times when she has to stay out late, very late. She says she can't bear to leave me alone, untended, in Buro's hands, but I explained to her that there's no option. Money runs out so fast.'

Robi stopped for a moment to survey the imagined effects of his dwindling assets. Tara, too, looked around the room. The large, teakwood four-poster, the flowery bedcover thrown carelessly over it, the dark, polished cupboard that ran the whole length of one wall, the handy marble-topped tables in corners, the expensive Tibetan rug—all so expensive, exclusive. Unbidden, there came into her mind a picture of her parents' bedroom and its worn furniture, the cheap bedcover, the steel almirah, the State Bank of India calendar on the wall. Impatiently, Tara cut Robi short. 'Baba said you wanted me over for something important.'

'Did I?'

Robi appeared to think, shuffled his feet and reached for the walking stick. 'I do wish Buro would come up.'

He's treading cautiously, thought Tara, which means he wants me to do something and not tell Nisha about it. I wonder what it is that he doesn't want Nisha to know. She looked at her cousin with renewed interest. Robi was digging into his pockets for something. He pulled out an enormous silk handkerchief, blew his nose, sniffled, then put the handkerchief back in his pocket. He looked at Tara keenly and began: 'Nothing important, maybe it's nothing, really. I just wanted to look at some old photographs with you. Out of the old album.'

Tara sat back in relief. The moment had passed and she was safe. There was no need to exert herself to negotiate some impossible demand that would require her to cross swords with Nisha. Deep in her heart, Tara was terrified of her sister-in-law's self-assurance.

Robi continued to talk, his pace increasing, and he became increasingly difficult to understand. 'Nobody understands my feelings anymore. Nobody cares. Nisha's not even interested in digging out the album. You're the only one left who still understands the importance of memories.'

Tara sighed. 'Where are the albums?'

'Will you find it tedious? You look tired already.'

'I work, and I've come here after a hard day. If it was just a matter of family photographs you could have kept it for the weekend. The way Baba put it, it sounded as if you wanted me here for something terribly important.'

'Well, actually, there is something else, but we can discuss it after tea.'

'We can talk about it now,' said Tara quietly. So there *was* something else!

'I don't know how to begin.' Robi looked awkward. 'Look, Tara, there was a time when you and I were friends, really good friends. Remember those fabulous holidays we had, dad and mum and uncle and aunt and you and I going to Puri and Darjeeling?'

Tara remembered. They travelled by first-class coach, which meant non-air-conditioned compartments with two kinds of windows which were slid up and down according to need, a glass one inside and a slatted wooden one on the outside. They drank water out of an enormous round flask and lurched up and down the corridor while their fathers played cards and their mothers gossiped. At least, Tara's mother gossiped while Robi's mother listened with an indulgent smile on her face. She had been pretty and stylish and had studied in a convent run by missionaries while Tara's mother went to a suburban Bengali-medium school.

'Remember the joint birthday parties we had? Your mum dressed you and put jasmine garlands in your hair and small garlands on your wrists. We had payesh for lunch and went out to Park Street to buy cakes for the evening.'

'Where your mother looked resplendent and perfectly in place in her close-cut sleeveless blouse with her hair piled high in a coiffure while my mother stood nervously behind, sweating faintly and looking ugly in her cotton sari.'

Robi was quick to catch the bitterness in Tara. 'Your mother is a good lady. Simple and good.'

'You mean naïve and trusting.'

'Why do you say that? Has anyone ever broken her trust in any way?'

Tara wanted to say, yes, your parents did, but the fools didn't understand and pretend not to even now, but stayed silent. A chill had crept into the room that had nothing to do with the AC.

'Mum adored her. She always said that your mother had taught her more about life and how to face it than anyone else. Apart from teaching her how to fry luchis and make shukto.' Robi seemed bent on mining as many fond memories as he could. Tara grew restless. 'I keep thinking of our childhood and those happy days. We weren't very well off but at least we were contented. Much more than we are now, when we've got all this and much more, more than we could ever imagine when we were children.'

Tara ran her fingers over the luxurious velvet cushion. 'Not we, but you. Both of us dreamt, but only you made it. I haven't had it as good as you!'

'I know. That's why I'm making you an offer you can't refuse. I'll buy you a small flat. Near the airport, if you want, so that you can watch the planes take off and think of the places you can go to and the wonderful holidays you can have. Singapore, even Thailand.'

Tara stared in disbelief. She wondered if Robi had gone

mad, perhaps due to the interminable months—almost five years now—he'd spent as an invalid. Robi understood her silence to be assent. Words tripped out in a near-intoxicated rush. 'Think of it, Tara. A place of your own, a beautiful modern flat! Your bedroom would look over a walking track and a landscaped garden. There might even be a swimming pool. You can sit by the pool on a full moon night and sing.'

Oblivious of the comic potential of the scene he had just described, Robi rattled on. Finally, Tara found her voice. 'But why?'

'So that you can lead a decent life.' Robi looked crafty. 'We only need to work out the deal. Fine-tune the situation.'

'How?'

'It's quite simple. Your father and I have worked it out. We settle his claim to this house by buying you a flat somewhere around . . .' Here, Robi named a neighbourhood in a part of suburban Calcutta where retired commoners bought dreary flats with impossible names like Cosy Nook and Walden Estate.

'It would be good for them,' continued Robi enthusiastically. 'Fresh air and tranquillity. No worries.'

Tara thought of the advertisements for apartments she had seen on billboards along the roads and on the backs of buses. Happy families—husband, wife, their two children and a grandparent or two—clustered around a swimming pool or a park, reading newspapers and laughing delightedly while the apartment blocks rose benignly behind them.

Robi continued blithely. 'Think of the benefits. You get a whole flat free of cost.'

'And gift all the rights we have on this one to you!' Tara got up and picking her purse, stood before him. She hoped he wouldn't notice her trembling hands. 'It won't work. In any case, it was silly of you to hope that I'd agree to this preposterous suggestion.'

She could see Robi's jaw twitch and a vein stick out on his forehead. His right hand had begun its incessant fidgeting again, the fingers curling and uncurling shakily. He looked both pathetic and malignant. Were he to die now, a part of her mind thought, it would serve him right for underestimating her intelligence.

'You'll be shorry for thish,' said Robi, his words slurring in rage. 'Your fathersh agreed so you can't have any objection.'

'You can enter into any agreement with my father without my consent, legally,' said Tara. 'You can make sneaky deals behind my back with an unworldly and ignorant old man. But you'll have to deal with me first.'

'No wonder you've never had a boyfriend!' Robi stretched out a shaking hand towards the calling bell. 'You'll never get married either, at this rate. Poor Tara! Prim Tara! Sitting alone in a poky room in the dead of night because all the men have passed you by!'

Tears pricked Tara's eyes and rolled unbidden down her cheek. 'Clean up the mess inside your own house before taunting others. Do you know what your wife does for quick money? But perhaps you do know and yet can't do anything about it.'

They stopped at that and sudden silence filled the room. Tara could hear noises from the street. A truck roared past and the floor shuddered for an instant. Robi could hear quick steps up the wooden stairs. His eyes hurt and there was a ringing in his ears. The desire to urinate was overwhelming and he contained himself with an effort bordering on pain.

When Nisha Bose entered the room she guessed at once that something terrible had happened. The two figures in the room seemed graven in stone. Fear shot through Nisha's heart. What rash thing had Robi said that would undo months and years of careful design and hard work? Calling out to Buro and leaving Robi in his hands, she gave herself up to Tara and set about repairing the damage.

They withdrew to the adjoining room and stayed there for half an hour. A lesser woman might have failed but Nisha was as intelligent as she was beautiful. She shed her queenly manner and begged Tara for forgiveness and understanding. After a while Tara, too, surrendered, not just to Nisha and her charm but to the spell of money and plenty that the house cast. Tara was too hard-headed not to understand Nisha's act but was exhausted in body and spirit. For a while, it felt good to be deceived by her.

'Let's be friends, Tara,' Nisha ended. 'Don't let Robi's madness come between us. What he said and did today is the kind of thing I have to put up with daily, now, since his illness. Sometimes I feel I'll lose myself in his insane world. That's why I party and have men friends and occasional flings. You and I are the same age, so you'll understand. But you have a whole lifetime ahead of you, why, you haven't even begun. People say I'm beautiful but where has my beauty got me? Come out with me more often, Tara, and see what the day brings. I'm scared of pushing you because you're so much more intelligent than I am and I keep thinking you'll snub me. Nikki's having a party on Thursday, just a small and informal group. I wish you'd come with us. Some of Nikki's friends have seen you here and find you alluring; you're so different from all the silly girls on the party scene. You will come, won't you?' Nisha's glib words washed over Tara and soothed her. She looked into Nisha's clear deep eyes and decided to lose herself in them. In that great moment of weakness, Tara agreed.

A man, coiled on a motorcycle, his face partially covered with a black scarf, roared up to another man's house, pulled out a revolver, fired five shots that sounded like crackers after a triumphant India–Pakistan cricket match and roared away.

Siddique Ali, who had stepped out of his front door to say goodbye to his in-laws, staggered to the ground as blood spurted crazily out of him. As the women screamed and passers-by stumbled for cover, Siddique Ali felt his nerves numbing and the walls dancing. A sensation of terrible blackness, almost solid in its density, descended upon him. The last thing he saw was the orange evening sky with a single wispy star that seemed to beckon to him before the darkness took him away.

Ghosh had plotted and planned all morning to go home early because his wife had a cousin visiting from USA for a long-awaited family reunion. Mrs Ghosh had tormented Ghosh all morning and noon with her ceaseless reminders.

The call came through just as Ghosh reached his front door. The door had a Ganesha sticker and a nameplate that said 'Moloyendu Kumar Ghosh, Inspector of Police, Crime Branch'. 'Ullo,' he managed, still breathing hard.

'It's me, Kabir. I've got some bad news.'

'I've taken a half-day's casual leave after two years. I'm not going anywhere.'

'You don't have to.'

The door opened and a frowning Mrs Ghosh, dressed in a starched cotton sari that had elaborate gold zari work all along the border, stood shaking her head and pointing at her watch.

'Siddique Ali is dead.'

Since the connection went fuzzy, all Ghosh heard was 'is dead'. A spasm of fear shot through him. Had the chief minister copped it? Mrs Ghosh was in a sufficiently military mood today to say no to his going even for that. He sat down on the sofa and felt for his boots over the vast expanse of his stomach. 'Who is dead? I can't hear you, who did you say?'

'Siddique Ali, your source. The guy who was giving you information about Babul. Someone on a motorbike pumped bullets into him this evening at around 5.30 or six.'

'Where was this?'

'Outside his house. He had gone there last night to meet his family. Some kind of get-together.'

One shoe had been clawed off but the other remained. Ghosh had been pulling off his sock, now he sat back and abandoned his work. The pest, the bastard, the prick! Hadn't he told Siddique a million times not to be seen around his house, his neighbourhood, or anywhere near that place?

'Is he dead?'

He knew the answer even before it came. 'Yes, brought in dead to hospital.'

Ghosh remembered Siddique Ali's vacant staring face as he had explained to him the dangers confronting him. He had hoped he had not overstated the problem, since no one would ever turn up to give information to the police if he had, but Siddique Ali had been trusting to a maddening degree. 'No one will ever get at me, now that you have taken over my life. You'll look after me, I know.'

'I will, but you will have to help me. Stay away from your girl in Sonagachi and, whatever you do, DON'T GO NEAR YOUR FAMILY.' Ghosh had shouted so hard he had had a coughing fit and Siddique Ali had produced a menthol lozenge to calm him.

Now he was dead. His first-class source! He had been sure of slowly getting at Babul through him and making some inroads into the gang smuggling drugs and counterfeit currency along the Indo–Bangladesh border. And all because a man who had slit open throats, done drugs, stolen, killed and maimed couldn't say no to his in-laws! What the hell was he supposed to do now?

Mrs Ghosh hovered in the background, looking suspicious. 'I hope we are going.'

'We are, but . . .'

'But?' Her voice was harsh.

Ghosh grimaced. 'Nothing, let's go.'

'Don't make it sound like you are doing me a big favour. After all the nonsense I've swallowed all these years, you think you're doing me a favour!' Her voice became shriller. 'If this had been your mother or your sister, would you have . . .'

'Listen, cut it out. Not in front of the guards, they'll report everything.'

'Let them, is it a crime?'

'Is there anything to eat?'

'No. I said we'd be in time for an early dinner.'

Ghosh limped to his bedroom and hunted for a towel, then suddenly slumped down on the bed and put a pillow over his eyes. His ears buzzed and his eyes stung. He was a veteran of many sudden deaths, but Siddique Ali's passing was painful. Was he getting old? Would they ever be able to get Babul now? Was it his fault that he hadn't been able to give adequate protection to Siddique Ali? Had someone from the local thana ratted on him?

'Are you ready? It's getting late!'

Ghosh groaned and raised himself. He would go up to the rooftop at his sister-in-law's house under the pretext of admiring her potted plants and report everything to Bikram.

# 3

A t every party there is a corner to which the out-of-place invitee slowly drifts. Tara found her little spot between a showcase and a corner lamp. All around her shimmered shades of black and brilliant blue. Men and women trotted around the room in little eddies, greeting, exclaiming, their faces flushed. Some of the better-known guests were ushered in from the door and they entered, bobbing and nodding, shaking hands even as their eyes looked over the shoulder for the next guest. The conversations picked up threads discarded at previous parties. Tara was miserable. And with reason.

'She wouldn't fit in, my dear,' Nikki Kumar, the hostess, had said with characteristic bluntness when discussing the guest list with Nisha. 'She doesn't drink and can't dance. Besides, she can't even dress right.' But Nisha was insistent. 'I suppose I need to do something for her now and then,' she said piously. 'Let her meet some men. She's quite attractive in her own way. Some men like this kind of unsophisticated innocence.'

'I don't believe she hasn't had a fling with someone. Some obliging guy next door or perhaps someone from college about whom you don't know.'

Nisha, pushing a coaster idly round the table, head tilted at an angle as she cradled the cordless receiver, smiled. The image of Tara sitting, almost mortified by embarrassment, in the company of strange men, sprang to her mind. Nisha's hand unconsciously strayed to her hair, traced the lines of her cheek, her lips, and reminded herself of her own beauty. 'Well anyway, you must invite Tara. Robi too would like that. Sometimes he feels a little put out by all the noise and dazzle. Says it draws too much attention to him.'

'Oh, all right. But I'm still not sure that we should.' And in a moment of unwitting prophecy, added, 'Perhaps Tara's coming to this party will lead to all kinds of complications and upsets.'

'Don't be silly, Nikki. I hope you're inviting Parry Prakash and Co.?' The conversation then moved on to other topics and Tara was forgotten.

Tara, Nisha and Robi had arrived at 9 p.m., suitably late, only to find that no one else had arrived. Tara and Nisha entered and Robi was wheeled in behind them by Buro. Robi was wearing an expensive shirt and a perfume that smelt agreeably spicy. Tara noticed a subtle change come over him as he entered the room. Gone were the sagging shoulders and the nagging, dissatisfied look. His eyes darted gleefully all around and he greeted Nikki with a swaggering, flirtatious air.

'Robi darling, how are you? You smell delicious. Umm, I could eat you up.' Nikki bent over and planted a kiss on him.

'Fit as a fiddle.'

'And you, Tara? Welcome to my humble parlour.' Nikki Kumar swept her hand modestly over the drawing room.

Nisha had flung herself on to a sofa, her large ornate handbag tossed carelessly aside. She fiddled with the silver necklace at her throat and looked up at the ceiling. Buro helped Robi over and arranged him beside Nisha.

'Put the wheelchair away,' said Nisha to Buro in a low voice. 'There, in the corner.'

'It feels good to be back in your house, Nikki. Feels good to smell the wine and the women. I suppose they'll be here shortly.' Robi was in high spirits.

Tara looked around for a place to sit.

'Come here, Tara.' Nisha beckoned Buro and a round basket chair was drawn up beside Robi. 'Yes, sit beside me, Tara. I'll introduce you to all our friends. They all adore me. You'll see how popular I am.' Robi laughed again.

Nikki Kumar came up with glasses. Robi made a face at his lime and soda and sighed. 'Can I have one shot, a small one, Nisha?'

'No.'

Nisha looked down at her drink and took a languid sip.

'What'll you have, Tara darling?'

Tara wondered what to say.

'Wine? Cognac? A Bloody Mary?'

'Coke, I think. She can try the wine later on.'

'How do you know she wouldn't like a proper drink, Nisha?' Nikki scolded lightly, smiling all the while.

'Would you, Tara dear?' Nisha paused.

'No,' said Tara shortly. Why had she ever come?

Guests began drifting into the room in little batches of ones and twos at about ten. Till then, Nikki Kumar tried to entertain Tara. And where was she working now, she asked Tara. How interesting! The Leeds Press, perhaps, or was it the OUP? No, something smaller, a local publishing house. And where was her office? Beyond Dharamtala? Wasn't that where the old Anglo-Indian tailors lived, the ones who could still sew duster coats and gingham aprons? It was obvious to Tara that Nikki Kumar's world ended at the dingy roads that skirted the old English and Anglo-Indian havens with their Chinese beauty parlours and second-hand piano shops. Beyond, lay the frontiers of unspeakable Bengali squalor to which the inhabitants of her world rarely journeyed. With such bitter thoughts, Tara passed the time.

When the ten o'clock rush began, Nikki Kumar became

very busy, handing out glasses of wine and chicken drumsticks wrapped in silver foil. Tara was absurdly hungry but noticed that others were not, accepting only the first of the kebab sticks their hostess pressed upon them. Nisha floated along from guest to guest breaking effortlessly into groups.

'Hi Gaurav, hi Zeeshan, hi Puja!' The room was buzzing. A shrill voice rose above the clamour.

'Hi Bunty Baby! What've you been doing? You're looking fantastic!' It was Robi. Bunty Baby, a young man of indeterminate age and nationality, approached Robi.

'What a surprise! Haven't seen you for quite some time!' His hair was arranged in the fashionable spikes of the day and he looked at Robi with some inner amusement. Quite a few young women detached themselves from their groups to greet him.

'Where's Nisha?' asked Bunty.

'I'm here.'

Nisha put her face up to be kissed. Under the kohl, her eyes glowed and her skin was luminous, with glitter sparkling tantalizingly on her cheeks. Bunty put his hand on her shoulder and squeezed it a little as he pecked at her cheek.

'She's getting better and better with age,' said Robi. 'Isn't she, Bunty?'

'And you haven't changed at all, Robi,' replied Bunty, still looking at Nisha.

'Bunty's getting younger,' said one of the young women around him. The others tittered.

'But I'm still the same,' said Nikki Kumar, unexpectedly joining them. She had a glass of whisky in her hand and was swaying a little.

Tara, still sitting beside Robi, watched the exchange with interest. She hadn't ever seen Bunty at Robi's house and wondered how old he was. Nisha usually went for older men. Bunty must be providing variety, she concluded. At this moment, a well-toned, wolfish woman bore down on Tara.

'Hello,' she said in a loud, husky voice. 'Are you the newspaper lady?' She wore a grey silk sari with sequinned parrots and a closely-cut sleeveless blouse.

'I'm afraid not,' said Tara humbly and then added in a banal way, 'I'm not part of any newspaper.'

The woman looked Tara up and down, shifting her gaze, rapidly estimating value and social worth. Tara shifted uneasily, and quite unnecessarily took two rapid sips from her glass. Remembering party protocol, she said, 'My name is Tara.'

'I'm Anjali. What do you do, Tara?'

'I, well I, I do a few things here and there. A bit of teaching and so on.'

'Really! How interesting! Where is your school? I suppose it is a school, isn't it . . . oh, hi Vicks! Long time no see.' Anjali turned away in mid-sentence.

'Come with me, Tara. Come and meet some of my friends. My chanting-group ones. We have chanting sessions every week.' Nisha had seen Tara's forlorn expression and decided it was time to pay her some attention.

'Yes, take her with you; she must be bored to death babysitting me.' Robi, demonstrating physiotherapy movements to a man with a goatee and a serious expression, stopped to say his part. 'Even nurses need to be aired now and then.'

'He usually gets like this in the middle of a party,' said Nisha. 'First the weepy invalid, then gradually, as he warms up, the old sarcastic returns.'

For a while Tara tried to be a part of the amiable buzzing around her, but somehow the little knots of people remained difficult to penetrate. Nikki Kumar flapped in and out, looking,

in her white trousers and maroon raw silk blouse like an old
hen in borrowed feathers.

A little old lady with cropped hair dyed black and white
in zebra stripes sat meditatively in a corner. Tara noticed
a vacant place on the sofa beside her and moved resolutely
towards it. 'May I sit here, please?' Tara wasn't quite sure what
to expect in answer. The old lady tilted her head just once.
Tara was left wondering: Did she mean yes or no? The lady
said nothing, merely went on looking at the guests. Tara
hesitated for a moment and then sat down while the old
lady carried on as if Tara didn't exist. Should I, wondered
Tara, dare to  start a conversation with her? She looked
down cautiously, pretending to arrange her sari and trying
to size up her companion. Shoes, she remembered Anju
telling her, were the best indication of personality. Tara
stole a look at the old lady's shoes, a delicate affair in silver
with a one-inch heel and then at her own low-heeled pair.
Plain and unexciting. Just like me, she added to herself.
She decided to abandon another potentially unfulfilling
attempt at party chatter. Exhaustion was now creeping up
her tired ankles, up through her aching knees and elbows,
right up to her neck and shoulders. Why ever did I come,
she thought again.

A group of three men sitting on a sofa near Tara was steadily
working its way through a series of large drinks. One had
a shaven head and a small diamond in his left ear and a pair
of goggles that made him look exactly like a certain Bollywood
villain. Another was short, bald and bespectacled with an oily,
ingratiating smile. The third was tall and well built with curling
lips that gave an arrogant sneer to whatever expression his
features composed themselves into. A heavily built man in
his fifties, wearing a somewhat incongruous combination of
white shoes, white suit set off by a maroon tie, appeared in the

doorway. The man with the oily smile jumped up and ran across the room to greet him.

'What the hell is he doing here anyway, Mr Prakash?' said the man with the sneer.

'Haven't you heard, Mr Kumar? Nikki's very close to him. Good for the husband's business, or so I've heard.' The gentleman with the earring winked.

'I don't mean Dr Geo Sen.' Toofan Kumar indicated the new arrival in white. 'We all know about him. I mean this bloody oaf here.' He rolled his eyes at the oily, bald man now clasping Geo Sen's hands in a glad handshake.

'I would have thought Nikki had more sense in her than to invite that annoying Mr De. Nasty social climber. Hello, hello, excuse me,' Toofan Kumar bellowed at a passing waiter. 'Get me a refill. And more kebabs. Chicken, not paneer.'

In time, the conversation turned to politics.

'Crime is increasing, Mr Kumar. What are your men doing about it?'

'In a city with a population of about a hundred lakhs, you call two burglaries and four suicides crime? Come on, Mr Prakash!'

'But the police need to have an effective intelligence system; you must admit you're failing there.'

'Your ideas are being fed by the morning newspapers.'

Nikki Kumar walked up, balancing a cigarette and two glasses. 'Failure? Who's discussing failures and sad things at my party? Oh dear Toofan, talk about something else. Here you are, Parry!'

She nimbly exchanged Mr Prakash's near-empty glass with the one in her hand.

'Where's the music, Nikki? We all feel the need for some dancing now.'

'Now?'

Nikki looked at her watch in horror.

'At eleven! The night is young, Parry darling. Plenty more excitement to follow!'

Tara decided to move. She looked around for another secluded perch. There was a comfortable-looking nook in the hall that led off the main drawing room. This hall was the entrance to the dining room and would be later converted into a dance floor. As of now, it was empty save for two men earnestly discussing something in low tones. Tara strolled towards the corner. As she paused to make way for a couple, she looked up. The woman was wearing a red chiffon sari that hung in perfect folds over her symmetrical figure. There was an arresting beauty about the face that seemed familiar till Tara remembered she had seen it on television. 'Shona Chowdhury,' her mother's voice rang in her head, 'the most beautiful and the most talented woman in the industry. Did you see her play Bankim's heroine last week? It was as if he had written the character with her in mind.' Behind her followed a man as tall as the woman and as striking but in a completely different way. Shona Chowdhury looked like a marble statue that had come to life and acquired a human sheen. The man who walked behind her was handsome but with the comfortable good looks of the real world. In a few years he would be putting on weight and the hair at the back of his head would be thinning. Now, he had dark hair cut very short and walked with his hands behind his back which accentuated his lean, well-chiselled frame. A slight frown and pursed lips indicated that he was not looking forward to the evening at all. His grey eyes had an unfathomable expression in them as they swept round the room.

As Tara made her way to an empty chair, she noticed that the new arrivals had caused a titter of excitement in the room. Nikki Kumar, flushed with whisky and success, hurried over to the door. 'Hello hello! I was afraid you'd forget. Do come in. Welcome, Mr Chatterjee. I was afraid you wouldn't come even if you were able to! Shona has told me about how shy you are.'

Men and women walked up to the new couple. The marble goddess returned all compliments and questions with a dignified smile and an occasional word. Once, Shona Chowdhury turned around to introduce her partner and Tara, from her vantage point in the corner, noticed how the actress paused for an instant as she looked up at his face. She adores him, thought Tara, and suddenly felt a rush of envy. She found it impossible to take her eyes off him. He seemed distant from everyone in the room and Tara could feel a kinship with him. She longed to be introduced. Would Nisha give her a chance? But she realized that Nisha herself hadn't been introduced to him at all. Shona Chowdhury had simply smiled and said a few words and walked away.

The two men sitting near Tara had stopped whispering and were looking with undisguised curiosity at the new couple.

'Ah, this is the woman Satish wanted to sign up for his new movie. Sexy chick, huh? Who's behind her?'

'Some policewallah she's engaged to. Bikram Chatterjee. Not IPS, I think.'

'Inspector or something? That's strange. She could have anyone she wanted.'

'I wonder how Toofan sa'ab is taking it. To socialize with an underling and that, too, a good-looking one! He wants to be the only police chap with beautiful girls.'

Tara looked at Toofan Kumar. The man was heroically trying to avoid noticing the stir of excitement caused by his subordinate.

Just then Nisha caught sight of Tara and walked over to her. 'So you're here. Robi's been looking all over for you.'

Tara couldn't resist the question. 'Nisha, who's the man in black behind me?'

Nisha looked over her shoulder. 'Toofan Kumar, from the police. Good you drew my attention to him. I'd better have a word with him. Keep him in good humour and all that.'

'And the other man, the one with the beautiful girl. Isn't he also a policeman?'

Nisha looked searchingly at Tara. 'Yes, he is, but of a lower rank. What makes you so interested?'

Tara blushed. 'Just like that!'

Nisha took a sip from the ever-present glass in her hand. 'Haven't you met any young guys here? You can't sit mooching in a corner and expect to be spoken to!'

'This isn't a pub or a disco that I can pick men up,' said Tara edgily.

'But you can make a beginning.'

Nisha brushed her hands over Tara's sari and shifted the pallu lower on her chest. Then, smiling, she moved over to the group behind her.

Toofan Kumar, elated at Nisha's attention and the diversion it afforded him, got up to wish her. Tara looked back with interest at Toofan Kumar. A young cousin had spent the last two years cramming for the Civil Services exam, and he was full of information regarding the Indian Police Service. He'd told her of the rank divide and how the twain never met, at least not on an equal social footing. And to circumvent a potentially embarrassing situation for him, Toofan Kumar pulled out his cell phone and began a conversation, putting on an air of deep distraction. So, Shona Chowdhury took the first step. She walked to Toofan Kumar and waited for him to finish. Toofan took his time, finished his call and looked up. Then, pretending to be pleasantly surprised, he rose and made a deep namaste. 'So good to see you again, ma'am! How are you?'

Behind Shona stood Bikram Chatterjee. The expression on his face was unfathomable. He stiffened his arms and clicked his heels. The room was as noisy as ever but Tara could sense people shifting position for a better look at the scene.

'I hope you are enjoying yourself. Would you like a refill of whatever you're having?'

Tara turned around with a start. An old man stood at her elbow. He was wearing a shirt with brilliant red poinsettias printed on it. A gnarled hand clutched a mahogany cane with a silver eagle head. His white hair was brushed back to reveal a wide brow from under which twinkled a shrewd pair of eyes. He looked like the kind of person who would not bother with pretension. He was old but looked fit and carried a powerful sense of presence. The old man sat down by her side and leaned forward to look at her glass. 'Wine, is it, or champagne?'

'Just a soda,' said Tara apologetically.

'Really! That's brave.' The old man looked kind. 'Not many around here would be plucky enough to do that. Ah, but perhaps it's a new trend that you're setting. Like vegetarianism and yoga.'

Tara laughed. 'No, it's just that I've been brought up humbly middle class. Girls didn't touch alcohol in my mother's world.'

The old man exclaimed. He'd seen Shona and her fiancé. He fumbled for his cane and half rose from his seat. As if by coincidence, Bikram Chatterjee's gaze swept across the room to where they were sitting. He strode across to the inner room. He reached their chairs and Tara stood up in confusion. Automatically, without thinking, she smoothed her hair and immediately regretted the gaucherie of her action.

'Bikram, Bikram. I hoped you would come.' There was real joy on the old man's face. He rose unsteadily and straightened slowly, waving aside the proffered hand. 'No, no, there is life in me yet.' He stretched out his arms and embraced the young man. As he did so, Tara noticed the gnarled hands with the blue veins which contrasted sharply with the pale skin.

'I was looking around for you, too. Shona told me you might be here.' As Bikram spoke, Tara noticed how his smile had lit up his whole face, giving him an innocent, boyish look. She looked at him closely. A man of perhaps thirty or thirty-five. A long straight nose and a delicate chin, uncommon amongst flat-nosed, usually be-whiskered, Bengalis. A pair of incredible eyes. Shona Chowdhury evidently knew how to choose.

Tara gathered her bag and prepared to go. Another haven gone! Would they never serve dinner, or was eating an unsophisticated and unnecessary thing to do? In any case, she could easily slip out. No one, she thought ruefully, would miss her.

But the old man seemed to have divined her thoughts. 'Preparing to leave? But not without a meal! What would your mother say?'

A waiter had been hovering around the next room. He now sprang to their side.

'Is there some kind of soup on today's menu?'

'Yes, Sir, we have spicy chicken and pepper soup. And for vegetarians . . .'

'Get us three bowls of the chicken soup on a trolley,' the old man interrupted. 'And proper round spoons, not the drop-shaped Chinese variety.'

There was now a power about the old man that made Tara restless. She suddenly felt very silly. And this authority was so different from the mildness of his former manner; it was as if the arrival of the young officer had stirred him up.

'Bikram, allow me to introduce a very charming lady who has been keeping an old man company and whose name I have most distractedly not asked. But she is more intelligent than most here and more genuine than some of them will ever be. Also,' here he looked at Bikram Chatterjee, 'like you, she's uncomfortable in Nikki's monthly interlude of shallow affectation.'

Tara gave her name somewhat blushingly, elated by the old man's compliments. Nikki Kumar noisily entered the room. 'You can't go without having a bite, dinner has already been served. No, no, I won't hear of it.' This was addressed to Bikram and the other man, though Tara, in a moment's confusion, thought Nikki meant her. Tara rose, grabbed her bag, and walked quickly towards the door. Beyond, the gaiety had reached a crescendo. As she made her exit, Tara caught sight of Toofan Kumar looking slyly at Shona Chowdhury and then irritably at Bikram Chatterjee as he helped the old man in.

Outside, the garden was cool and fragrant. As Tara stumbled towards the gate, she caught the spicy smell of champak and passed a few low shrubs of the lily-like flowers that bloomed only at night. The smell, redolent of childhood nights on the terrace, seemed to make her present humiliation more piercing. Somewhere, a gate opened and a durwan, looking curiously at her as she wiped the first few tears that came down, asked for the car number. Tara shook her head and began to walk down the road. A taxi drew up and she managed to mumble her address as the driver hooked his left arm over the seat and opened her door. As Tara fell back on the seat, she noticed that her right hand still clutched a paper napkin now crumpled into a ball. Rolling down the window, Tara flung the torn napkin out. When Tara looked back, a dog was sniffing at the napkin and trying to paw it open.

# 4

'**B**ikram!'
  'Sir!'
  'Where in bloody hell have you been? Your phone's been engaged for the last ten minutes. Girlfriend or what?'

It was the morning after the party and Bikram Chatterjee expected Toofan Kumar to be his rudest.

'I'm sorry, Sir,' said Bikram as blandly as he could. 'Actually, I was checking up with Ghosh about the Sunny Sharma affair. There have been complaints from one of their customers about a certain financial irregularity.'

'Oh, damn the Sharma cheating case. I don't suppose Ghosh has managed to get anything on them. No need to arrange any papers. In any case we shouldn't be too hasty.'

'Sir.'

Bikram permitted himself a smile. The Hermes Travel Agency advertised unbelievable tour offers for South-East Asian countries from its prim offices on Camac Street. However, what it really specialized in was quick weekends for middle-aged men with suitable escorts at discreet guesthouses. The proprietor, Sunny Sharma, was known to be close to Jojo Verma, who played tennis with Toofan Kumar and sent him a bottle of the best Scotch now and then. The need to get Bikram off the Sharma front and distract him was, therefore, imperative.

'I've got more important things for you to do.' The telephone spluttered for another minute or so as Toofan Kumar barked out his orders. Bikram listened patiently, his long fingers tracing out complicated circles on the paper before him. From the window of his flat he could see, far below, the chaotic 9 a.m. rush of life.

Half an hour after his conversation with Toofan Kumar, Bikram set out on an assortment of tasks ranging from serious police work to the utterly laughable. There was a testimonial to be given in court in the matter of a well-bred junior executive swindling his firm with amazing alacrity for a whole year. There was the delicate matter of scouting round for a picnic site for the Police Wives' Association Annual Picnic. Lastly, there was Toofan Kumar's order to be complied with. This involved a visit to a plush part of the town and Bikram kept it for the last.

Mistry, his driver, defiantly gunned the car through a sea of three-wheelers, hand carts and battered passenger buses. Beside Bikram sat Ghosh, now belching over his breakfast of onion omelette and five pieces of buttered toast. Ghosh had somewhat recovered from Siddique Ali's death. Bikram had spent fifteen minutes counselling him.

'It was my fault.'

'Don't be absurd. He should have listened to you.'

'How can I blame him? I suppose his wife was like mine, whining on and on about her mother wanting to see Siddique. If only he had told me, I could have . . .'

'Done what? Sent the Special Protection Group around with him?'

'Well, anyway, what do we do now?'

'Remember to see his widow now and then and send some clothes to her children. I'll keep some money aside from the Source Fund.'

'And what do we do about Babul and the border?'

'When the lord closes a door, he opens a window!'

Ghosh blinked and wished Bikram would stop quoting the Bible at him. This infuriating habit came from attending a convent school and having a professor for a father and a schoolteacher for a mother.

Bikram smiled. 'What I mean is that we have the guy we picked up during the raid. Has he said anything yet?'

'Uh huh. We'll have to take him apart at the PS.'

'Do you think he actually knows anything? He'll probably sham for attention.'

'That, only you can find out, Sir. But I think he'll be a valuable contact. We don't have too many people giving us info on dope, women, fake currency and border crossovers all at one go, now that Siddique's gone. This fellow's quite a catch. Buy one, get three free.' Ghosh was so pleased with his metaphor that he laughed wheezily for a moment. Since this was the first time he had smiled in two days, Bikram let him.

'Mistry, take us to Angel,' Bikram said. 'There's time to look him up and find out how he's doing. The wounds should have healed by now.'

Angel Nursing Home was nothing more than a four-storeyed residential building—it once housed a large Bengali joint family—that had been converted into a shabby medical centre. The tiny rooms and kitchens of the original building had been broken down and reassembled into wards, doctors' chambers and operation theatres. At the end of a cramped corridor, Bikram and his men arrived at a lift only to find a throng of nurses, slovenly ward boys and paan-chewing ayahs blocking the entrance. Ghosh tried to batter his way through but Bikram started climbing the stairs. A panting Ghosh tried to keep pace. When they eventually reached their destination, he sat down on a chair and wheezed, unable to utter a word.

'Maybe you too should be admitted here. For a treadmill test.' Bikram sounded testy but there was concern in his eyes.

A doctor came bustling up to meet them. He had an

ingratiating smile on his face. He looked young but was already beginning to bald. The doctor performed abortions for ten thousand rupees each and had a steady stream of clients from the small towns surrounding Calcutta. He was anxious to keep policemen happy. 'Oh dear, oh dear, what have we here.' The doctor spoke in English with a BBC accent. 'Should we get you a glass of water? Take your time, no hurry.'

Ghosh rose huffily from the chair. 'I'm all right now. Let's get on with it. Have you killed the patient or has he survived your attention?'

'Such wit!' The doctor continued to smile. 'Is that all the thanks we get for admitting your guy early in the morning, no questions asked?'

'May we see him now?'

Like Ghosh, Bikram did not like the doctor, the nursing home and the way its affairs were managed. But they had had no alternative. The injured constable had taken up all the resources of the public hospital to which Bikram and Ghosh had rushed him. To find a bed for him; to test him for his blood group and procure pouches of blood from a blood bank halfway across town; to convince the sleepy and disinterested doctor in charge to make preparations for an emergency operation—all this and much more had sapped their strength. In the confusion, the other man, the fugitive bleeding from leech bites, had been taken by an overzealous police inspector to the nursing home.

Outside the ward, the fat constable on guard had arranged for himself a plastic chair and a lurid Bengali newspaper and was nodding his way through it. The doctor clapped his hands to wake him up. 'Get up, get up, your superiors are here.'

The constable attempted a belated salute and trotted in after them.

'Out,' said Bikram. 'And I don't want to see the newspaper when I leave.'

The man was lying in a mid-sized room crammed with six beds. An intravenous needle was pushed in near his wrist, its plastic tube snaking up to the bottle hanging from the iron stand above, a bedpan stood under the iron cot, and assorted parts of his body were swathed in bandages. The man, lying on his back with his eyes fixed on the ceiling, seemed strong but, in his present condition, was wiped out and helpless.

The doctor stood by his bed with his hands behind his back. 'Here's someone to see you.' He had raised his voice to a shout, quite unnecessarily, and woken all the others in the room. Two patients struggled to an upright position; one began to moan for the doctor's attention.

The young man turned his head and looked fleetingly at Ghosh, then at Bikram. He raised one arm and tried to reach out towards them and then let his hand drop. 'You've saved my life, Sir,' he quavered.

'Cut out the drama,' said Ghosh distastefully as he mopped his forehead and looked around the room.

The ward was full and the doctor busied himself, pretending to check pulse beats or fiddle with bandages, all the while tracking the situation with one curious ear.

'No one dies from leech bites,' said Bikram briskly. 'You could have suffocated yourself though in that dirty water.'

'In our line of work we can die from anything at any time,' said the young man dramatically. 'I was driven to this world out of hunger but now I'm addicted to it.'

His name had been registered in the nursing home ledger as Raja Das but he was known simply as Border Raja in his sphere of influence. The police had been looking for Babul who, it now transpired, had not been in the village at all for the last few months, but had unaccountably netted Raja.

Bikram was now sure that the unfortunate Siddique had had some score to settle with Raja and had sent the police on his trail using Babul as a decoy.

Raja was still looking at him. 'Don't arrest me as yet, Sir. I can give you information, lots of it. About . . .'

'We'll discuss this later,' said Bikram, aware that the whole room was listening. 'I haven't come here for information. I wanted to make sure you were all right. You lost a lot of blood, and there were other complications, but fortunately things have got better.'

The man turned his head away. His voice shook a little. 'I've heard about you. And I was always scared that you would catch me one day. But now that I've seen you, perhaps things might go differently for me.'

Bikram led Ghosh out of the ward and into the corridor outside. The smells of formalin, antiseptics, urine, sweat, fear and death mingled in a heady cocktail. 'What have we booked him under?'

'307, Sir.'

Attempt to murder. An idea stirred in Bikram's mind. Charge-sheet him under Section 308. No, wait, 326.'

Ghosh looked at him keenly from under his beetling eyebrows and nodded. 'That's a good one.'

Section 326 of the Indian Penal Code states that causing grievous hurt by a dangerous weapon can be punished by life imprisonment or by a lighter, ten-year sentence with a fine. This had the advantage of keeping the offender on tenterhooks. The trial would drag on and the man would be out on bail and nothing would ever be proved anyway. But Bikram and Ghosh would thereby have created an informer for whom it would be easier to supply bits of information and keep the cops happy than run the trouble of going underground and putting his business at risk. And in the long run, Raja might even get a chance to terminate some enemies by setting the police on them.

'I'll explain it to him once he's released.'

'I doubt if you'll have to explain at all. He's probably worked it all out already. Find out when they'll let him go.'

The doctor had been waiting expectantly near a corner bed, oblivious to the groans of the patient there. He sprang forward when Ghosh looked at him.

'Rapist or robber?' he asked gleefully. 'You should have seen him screaming when he was brought here. I knew at once he was a criminal. They're the biggest cowards.'

'When can he be released?'

'But it's not that simple,' the doctor said. 'We took some advanced tests and there is an indication that this man may be suffering from thalassaemia. Not thalassaemia major, of course, but the minor form due to which he's anaemic. That's why the leech bites and the blood loss caused such a severe reaction.'

'Oh!' Clearly, Bikram had not expected this. Ghosh looked troubled.

'With the transfusion, the haemoglobin's fine now but we need some more tests. The spleen needs to be looked into, so, an ultrasonography or two. I've written as much in the patient's sheet.' Here, the doctor cleared his throat with relish and tried to sound as delicate as possible. 'We're all here to help you, so don't worry about payment. In fact, Mr Churiwala would like to reassure you about that. He'll be here in half an hour's time.'

'I'm afraid I can't wait today,' said Bikram, 'but I have his number and will talk to him about it.' Privately, he cursed the crooked ASI for admitting him to Angel. Now Bikram would have to pay the hospital bill from his pocket rather than have Churiwala waive expenses and later claim a favour. Raja, listening to the conversation, looked at Bikram pleadingly as he turned to go.

'We'll talk later,' said Ghosh curtly and then added in a kinder tone, 'we'll work out a deal. You look after us and we'll look after you, but don't go yammering all this to any of your friends.'

Back in the car, they discussed the failed raid and wondered if some good might come out of it after all. It was nice to imagine a chastened Raja feeding them delicious tips about cross-border smuggling. Bikram glanced out the window and noted that the roads were getting wider, the billboards sleeker and the pavements almost free of cycle carts and beggars as they entered affluent neighbourhoods. All this reminded him of the unsavoury task at hand and increased his annoyance. Flat-topped, boxlike buildings gave way to lovely houses shaded by trees and high walls covered with ivy and luxuriant bougainvillea. There were no buses or auto rickshaws. Sleek cars purred noiselessly through polished gates that opened briefly to offer glimpses of smooth lawns and white wrought iron garden chairs. Mistry stopped in front of a large black gate. The pillar on the left side of the gate was lettered 17B and the marble plaque on the right said, simply, BOSE.

A durwan was peeping at them through a slit in the gate. Mistry blew a raucous horn and then ducked his head out of the window. 'Open up, you. We're from police headquarters.'

'He's not been told about our visit,' said Bikram. 'I wonder why. If we're here to exhibit ourselves and frighten the staff, as Toofan Kumar wants us to, it would have been a good idea for the owners to inform all of them about it.'

'What's the household like, Sir?' asked Ghosh.

'The gentleman's paralysed and the wife runs the show. She does all kinds of things; teaches at a school, sells paintings, organizes exhibitions. General order supplier, as we used to

say in our youth. Throws parties, too, though where she gets
the money for that, I don't know. Well known in the movie
circles, I'm told.'

Here, Ghosh cast a quick look at Bikram before looking
away innocently. There was little office gossip that did not
make its way to Ghosh, and Shona Chowdhury's romance with
the boss was a favourite topic these days.

He can be sly, thought Bikram. And he's too friendly with
that *Calcutta Times* reporter. Trading secrets for gossip in Park
Street bars on Sunday evenings, I guess. A vision of the party
last night and Shona in it, with him standing ineffectually
beside her, sent a sudden spurt of anger through him.

Aloud, he said to his security guard, 'Get down and open
the gate, won't you, instead of sitting back and leaving
everything to that useless driver.' The durwan then escorted
them to the house and handed them over to a maid who looked
warily at them as she led them into the drawing room. The air
conditioning was on and the doors were closed, but the curtains
had been drawn back. Through the windows they could see
a homely-looking garden with a patchy lawn bordered with
all kinds of shrubs.

A silken voice greeted the two policemen as they went in.
'Come in, Inspector, do come in, this is a surprise. I didn't
think Toofan would remember me and my silly complaints so
faithfully. Perhaps you'll be more comfortable on this sofa.
That one gets the full blast of the air conditioner. Robi and
I have been meaning to buy a new one for ages but we've
never really got round to it.'

Bikram felt himself expertly led away from a large and
expensive sofa in white satin to a narrower chair in dark
corduroy. The room was laid with a rich carpet that stopped
just short of the chairs to which they were led. The lady of the
house seated herself before him and arranged her sari delicately

over her toes. Her carefully tinted hair was swept back from
a wide forehead. A white handbag and a mobile phone stood
on a table beside her.

'I asked Toofan for help, I really don't know how to solve
this on my own . . .' Her voice trailed as she stared at Bikram,
then, as recognition dawned, it changed altogether. With
a little gasp she exclaimed, 'Wait a minute, I know you. You're
Bikram, Shona's friend.'

He said nothing.

'But of course, I saw you last night, at the party, Nikki
Kumar's! Can you imagine that? What a coincidence! How
nice of you to come! Really, Toofan should have told me! Tea
or coffee, or maybe some lemonade?'

'Thank you very much,' said Bikram as equably as he could.
'That's not necessary.'

'Oh, but it is, what would Shona say . . .'

Even as Bikram sought to soothe her excited trilling with
calm refusals he felt a tightening rage inside. You win, Toofan,
he said to himself, you brute. You've sent me here like any
ordinary thana constable just to show me my place.

Nisha Bose's voice trailed away and they now looked
at one another, aware of the delicate nature of the situation.
Then the ever-faithful Ghosh cleared his throat and broke
the spell.

They were served coffee in gold-bordered china cups and
delicate biscuits on matching plates. Bikram left the biscuits
alone but Ghosh reached out and unabashedly took two. Then
Nisha Bose waved the maid away and leaned back in her chair.
She turned her head to look out at the garden, presenting
a perfect profile to her guests. Her skin gleamed in the half-
light and her lips formed a perfect pout. Her long arms stretched
alluringly and the folds of her sari seemed to slip ever so little
over her tight chest. A sort of electric charge enveloped the

room and, all at once, cops and robbers seemed far away. Bikram was aware that the whole show was being put up for him. Then Nisha turned round and began to talk.

'Somebody's been pilfering money,' she began, 'and I suppose it must be one of the servants, but I can't quite pin down who. We have quite a number of them and most have been around for many years.'

'How much money?' asked Bikram.

'I don't know the exact sum because it's been dribbling out for some time. The maid used to come back from shopping and I would be busy and ask her to put the change on the dressing table or by the bed. Then I would forget about it and the next time I looked for it, it wouldn't be there, so I would suppose I had put it away. Fifty rupees, seventy, perhaps even a hundred.'

'How long ago was this?'

The lovely forehead creased itself into thought. 'One month, or I suppose two. I really can't be sure. Then, one day, I asked Buro—he's the man who looks after Robi, my husband—to withdraw five thousand rupees from the bank. I needed to pay the chap who comes in to help Robi with his physiotherapy. Buro put the money on top of the bureau in the bedroom and left. I was having a bath and when I came out, the phone rang and by the time I finished the call, Masterji, he's the tailor, came for some orders and finally Reeta, my masseuse, arrived. What with all this, I forgot about the cash and only remembered when the physiotherapist wanted his payment. That's when I found that the money was gone.'

'Did you question anyone?'

'Oh, I did. I asked Buro and Mithu and the woman who sweeps and cleans. Mithu said she had been too busy to notice and Buro swears he saw it on the bureau when he came in to give Robi his bath. Of course, the cleaning woman had gone away and we asked her the next day, but she didn't remember seeing it at all. She was terrified when we asked her about the money. She's quite old and we keep her on out of pity.'

'Do you think she did it?'

'That's what we all thought at the time. Robi wanted me to ask the police to search her house. Buro disagreed with him.' A slight smile played over Nisha Bose's face. 'I told Buro to leave it to me. I called her to the thakur ghar and made her stand in front of the gods and swear to tell the truth. She fell at my feet, crying and begging me to believe her. I decided to leave the matter as it was. Then, two days ago, something similar happened, only this time, it was much more money. Ten thousand rupees, in fact.'

'Where was the money kept?'

'Very safely, in Robi's drawer. It's always locked.'

'And the key?'

'On my dressing table, of course.' Nisha Bose turned a pair of limpid eyes on Bikram.

'From where anyone could have taken it?'

'Oh, but they wouldn't dare!'

'How can you be so sure? From what I gather, anyone, from Buro to Mithu to the daily maid, not to mention the masseuse and the physiotherapist and Masterji, could have sneaked in.'

'Because,' said Nisha Bose, elegantly spreading her hands and raising her eyebrows, 'they all love me and would probably give their lives for me. No one would dream of robbing us.'

The visit ended with Ghosh and Bikram being paraded through the spacious and beautiful rooms of the Bose residence. They went through a dining room to a pantry with built-in racks containing an assortment of table napkins, dish towels and other delicately embroidered pieces of cloth whose uses Ghosh could only wonder at. The kitchen shelves gleamed in marble and granite and a door covered with heavy mesh led out to the shade of a jackfruit tree. The maid, busy at an enormous steel sink washing the coffee cups, flattened herself against the wall and stood with her head down. From outside, the sound of water splashing on pots told them that the other maid was also hard at work. The time, thought Bikram, was chosen well, mid-morning, when all the staff were busy with various household chores and would not fail to miss the police. He wondered how many more faithful servants there were and how their mistress paid for them without any ostensibly remunerative job. He reminded himself to ask where they lived and how many came and went during the day and how many lived in at night.

Then they went up a polished wooden staircase to the 'upstairs rooms' as Nisha described them, where three rooms opened out from the landing. From the first one, they could hear the chatter of a television through a half-closed door. In the second, they could see some chairs and gym equipment. The door to the other room was shut. Nisha Bose hesitated. A troubled look appeared on her face which only heightened her beauty, now giving it an effect of innocence and helplessness.

'I must warn you, my husband may appear to be unpleasant; it's the effect of the medicines he takes. Also, do leave whenever you have to, he gets bored sitting around and can go on talking without noticing the time.' She said all this to Ghosh, addressing him for the first time and deliberately looking away from Bikram. She paused with her hand on the door handle. 'I've told him about the money and that I've asked Toofan Kumar to help out informally.' Then she squared her shoulders and went in.

Bikram stood back for a moment, looking at the door with interest. It was painted ivory, as all the others in the house were, but there was one small difference. All the other doors had round brass doorknobs of the old-fashioned variety, without any locking mechanism. This one had a round knob set in a rectangular frame, with a great sturdy bolt that could be locked from the outside. He wondered if Robi Bose was a prisoner of a malignant destiny in more ways than one.

Robi Bose was forty but seemed much older. He was leaning back in a folding chair. His feet, shod in rubber slippers, were pale and swollen. His face hung heavy and puffed under the onslaught of a range of medicines that had preserved the body but rent the mind. The right hand was clutching a television remote control while the left arm lay twisted across the chair arm. He was clad in a pair of Bermudas and a striped half-sleeved blue linen shirt. Beside him squatted a young man of twenty-two or so, clean shaven, hair cropped stylishly, wearing a pair of denims and a T-shirt with a motorcycle print. A faint fragrance of eau de cologne wafted from him. When the visitors entered, he rose hurriedly and positioned himself behind Robi's chair, hands folded demurely, head bowed low. Nisha Bose sashayed in and stood before her husband, looking down at him for a moment before speaking. 'They're here,' she said simply.

Robi Bose screwed up his eyes and stared at Bikram and Ghosh and the two stared back. For about ten seconds all four in the room, with the exception of the boy behind the chair, inspected one another. Then, in a low drawl, the words slurring occasionally, Robi said: 'Why aren't you in uniform? You're supposed to be on duty here.'

'This was an informal call, Mr Bose. We didn't want to frighten anyone.'

'But if you're policemen you have to. How can you find out who took the money otherwise?'

Beside Bikram, Ghosh shuffled uneasily and Bikram knew

what he was thinking. He himself looked at Robi with the gathering interest of a man who was waiting for a dreary movie to end, only to find that it plumbed unexpected depths.

'I *told* Buro to put in a case at the thana.' Robi stressed the word 'told' and tried to look around at the young man standing behind him. 'Didn't I, Buro? You just don't listen to me nowadays. We could have asked for police protection and have had a couple of armed guards posted here free of cost. All we needed to do was feed them some tea and the occasional scrap from the table.'

Nisha, silent all this while, now moved over to stand beside Robi and put a warning hand over his forehead. At her touch, Robi closed his eyes and leaned back. 'Ahh! How cool your hand is, Nisha.'

His wife looked down at him and said in a soft tone, 'Did you have your medicine?'

'Umm.'

'And the juice?'

'Rancid. I told Mithu she must have left the carton open but she only laughed and went away.'

'I'll get you some more. Don't worry.'

A faint flush spread over Nisha's face. As Nisha stood beside her husband, Bikram could sense in her weariness and beyond it, embarrassment. He wondered whether Nisha Bose was pitied and laughed at by all the wives whose husbands followed her with their eyes as she entered a room. Then he remembered another woman who also dragged men's eyes towards her and felt a kinship with Robi's plight.

From behind the chair, where her husband couldn't see him, Nisha pointed to the door and signalled the two policemen to follow her. Bikram, still unsure about his responses to her, felt this created an intimacy between them and against her husband, which he was not sure he liked.

As his wife turned towards the door, Robi opened his eyes and looked at Bikram. 'I know who took the money.'

'Would you like to tell us, Sir, or do you want us to find out for ourselves?'

A slow smile contorted Robi's face. 'You are clever *and* handsome. And not the usual corrupt variety. I'm impressed.'

'Robi!' Nisha Bose almost ran back from the door. 'How can you, he's Shona's friend. You met him and Shona last night at Nikki's, remember?'

'No, I don't! Who's Shona?'

'Oh, never mind. Leave it. Let them go.'

'But they're here for an investigation.'

'No, they are not. I told Toofan Kumar about all this and he said he'd send someone to look around but I didn't think it would be him, I mean, and . . . whatever, its finished now.'

Robi turned back to Bikram. 'She's too innocent for the real world. Someone's always got to protect her, see? She's scared of the consequences and that's why she won't let them tell you. But I know. It's Gopal. He's the durwan.'

'Stop it!' Nisha darted a quick look at Buro. 'How can you say such things without proof? Gopal's at the gate, how can he get into my bedroom so easily without being seen?'

'Oh, come on, my good wife, all kinds of men can get into this house without being seen. Have got in too, I'm sure. As for proof, that's for the inspector to get.'

'You're tired,' said Nisha. 'The party last night, and then this!' Her voice had changed from attack to the kind of soothing persuasion one uses with a petulant child. It had the desired effect on her husband. He said, 'It's my fault, I'm always thinking of myself, I forget how much you go through, all alone in this house without any children. Buro, where are you? I need to go to the bathroom.'

The young man sprang forward and bent over Robi. 'I'll get your walking stick, wait a minute.'

Nisha turned towards the door. 'I'll just see them off. Buro, give him his medicine, it is late already.'

When they were on their way, Ghosh asked, 'What do you think, Sir?'

'Think of what?'

'Oh, everything. The house and the lady and the husband.'

'And the crime?' Bikram asked in reply.

'The crime? Nah, who's interested in the crime? Very amateurish. It's probably Buro, with the maid, what's her name, Mithu. Did you see how fine and sleek he looks? I wonder what they'll do next. Drive up in a car for work, as they do in America, I'm told.'

'He has his mistress's backing, though,' said Bikram slowly. 'She didn't ask him to leave the room when we went in, though, in the drawing room, she waited for the maid to go away before she began. I imagine he's not just a servant. Probably a friend and confidant, in which case he wouldn't steal money.'

'You never know with this sort,' objected Ghosh. 'Around for years and then, bang bang one night and, in the morning, a dead body.'

'I hope there won't be a body here, Ghosh. You always make jokes about things which come true.'

But Ghosh was not so easily deflected. 'She's beautiful, though. I haven't seen such a beautiful woman in a long time. Like the goddess Lakshmi herself, as my mother would say. It's tough luck really, to be given everything in life—money and beauty and an adoring husband—only to be saddled with an invalid now. Though I must say, unwell or not, he didn't look at all dim-witted.'

But Bikram seemed to have lost all interest in the Bose household and was already flicking through a luxurious looking faux leather-bound diary marked APPOINTMENTS.

Ghosh, looking out of the window, the whiff of Nisha Bose's perfume in his nose and the savour of the cookies she had served still in his mouth, made a mental note to ask Bikram for a similar leather-bound diary as a New Year present.

Tara Bose sat on the edge of her bed and tried to look away from the table beside her. It was an ordinary bedside table, with a bottle of water and a melamine glass on a ceramic coaster along with a jar of cream. The charger was plugged in and the cell phone was being charged while the day's newspaper sat dishevelled underneath. Tara's hands were shaking.

Outside, it was hot, and the heat clung to the faded drapes on the windows and the few pictures on the walls. The fans whirred sadly, having given up all pretence of rendering any coolness. Tara's face was swollen for she had been upset, and her eyes were rimmed red for she had been weeping, and her hair hung limp and defeated over her shoulders. Then she took a deep breath and, opening the drawer of the table, took out an old leather bag. The bag was full of medicines. She shook them out on the bed and carefully selected four tablets. Though her hands were still shaking, there was a nimbleness to them, a newly-found agility as if they had been spurred on to some secret inner life at the sight of the items before her. She dropped the tablets into the glass, filled it with water and swallowed. Then hiccupping slightly, she opened the drawer again, extracted a bottle from the innermost depth, uncorked and drank noisily from the bottle itself.

The smell of brandy filled the room.

It took half an hour for the pleasure to rise. It took time now, and wasn't at all quick like earlier.

Tara felt the numbness creep into her shoulders, her thighs, the pit of her stomach, her legs. The room was far away already. She wondered on which side of the bed she was lying and she hoped she would not miss the floating sensation. It was good.

She was dropping out of consciousness already.

She would have to get some more tablets soon. Panic at running out of stock, at being left alone, defenceless, having to face a grim world each day without them, was always her last thought before the blessedness of oblivion.

# 5

D r S. Pyne, earnest and young, looking almost like a student with his tousled hair, 'I Love Bangkok' T-shirt and drawstring pyjamas, stretched out his hand towards the telephone and answered it grumpily. He knew he should expect these late-night calls, but still. Also, every time the phone rang at night, he'd be worried about his mother, ailing and fretful in the next room, being unnecessarily awakened. Dr Pyne loved order, dedication, hard work and his mother.

'Sudip? Chopra speaking. Go to 17B Bailey Road. That's off the Silver Mall in Ballygunge, down the lane, opposite a shop called Chutput Savouries, and look up a man of about forty who had a cerebral a few years ago. He seems to have died in the last hour or so. Probably a coronary case, so speed it up. He was alone except for his wife. Ask her if she needs anything.'

'Why me?' As Sudip Pyne struggled to wake up fully, his grumpiness became annoyance. 'There must have been a regular GP or neuro attending on him. I've never treated this chap before.'

'Oh yes, you have. He is, or was, Geo Sen's patient. Family friend too. I rang Sen up in London and he told me to get in touch with you. Or do you want Sen to speak to you personally? The way you young ones are, you might need phone calls from the President of India himself to get you going!'

Dr Pyne hesitated. He could, of course, refuse and ring off. But Dr Geo Sen was another matter. Pyne had been lucky enough to be noticed by one of the most eminent practitioners in the city and to be included on the fringe of the shadowy group that encircled him. Dr Pyne had a career wishlist which only Geo Sen could fulfil, so he heard himself tamely muttering that he'd be on his way. As he groped for the light switch in the bathroom, Dr Pyne hoped he could be back before 3 a.m. That was when his mother needed to use the bathroom, assisted by a sleep-sodden maid, with her only son glaring in the background.

The dead man was lying on his back on an enormous bed. His right arm was thrown across the bed. Sudip Pyne picked up this arm, felt for the pulse, put the lifeless arm down carefully and examined the face. There was a thin film of foam tinged reddish-orange around the nostrils and the mouth. The man's lips seemed black. Dr Pyne used his stethoscope on the man's chest perfunctorily and then bent down to look at the feet, following which he picked up the arm and scrutinized the fingers. As he had expected, they were blackish blue too. The doctor examined the arm again, then the other arm, then the rest of the body, paying special attention to the thighs and the area between the toes. Then he straightened up and looked around him.

On a marble-topped table beside the bed was a jumble of medicines. Sudip Pyne looked through them and found the usual combination of vitamin tablets, blood pressure medicine and anti-coagulant pills. There was also a half-empty bottle of water, which was chilled by the air-conditioning. Dr Pyne frowned and looked around for something he felt was missing, though he couldn't put his finger on it. Then he stole a look at the dead man's wife.

She was sitting on a chair and looking straight ahead, beyond the form on the bed, at the darkness outside the window. Her hair fell prettily around her shoulders and on to a cotton nightdress with a delicate print of fish swimming amongst fluted shells. There were no paroxysms of grief, no sobs and flailing, only this wonderful composure.

'Do you have your husband's medical prescription?'

'Prescription? I think there was one, with his reports and stuff . . .' Nisha looked around her helplessly. At the same time, a young man who had been lurking around outside the room noiselessly glided in. Nisha asked him, 'Buro, where is his medical file? The doctor wants to see his prescriptions.'

Buro opened a wooden cupboard, extracted a file and a sheet of paper, and handed them to the doctor. Dr Pyne glanced through the paper, then looked through the rest of the file and finally looked up. It had taken him a minute or two to do so, during which time two other ladies entered the room. They stood in a circle around him, and Sudip Pyne's uneasiness increased.

'Your husband took Valium and Tramadol tablets too, I see. I can't find those medicines on the table. Did he keep them elsewhere?'

The helplessness in the beautiful eyes increased. 'I don't know, I was so busy this week and this evening. Buro, do you know where the other medicines are?'

Buro went to the cupboard again, took out a leather pouch and handed it to the doctor. There were more vitamins, a strip of antacids, a headache balm and two skin rash creams, a bottle of Savlon and a wad of cotton wool, but no Tramadol or Valium.

Dr Pyne turned back to Nisha Bose. 'I suppose you don't know whether he took the Tramadol medicines this evening or not?'

She shook her head. For the first time now, the dead man's wife looked familiar. He had seen her before at the nursing home, near Geo Sen's chamber, being escorted in by the receptionist. He remembered the heads that turned to look at this woman who breathed life into the lugubrious surroundings of sickness and death.

This was an extraordinary situation! Should he risk what he was about to do or let the matter rest? Dr Pyne frowned and dug at his thumbnail with his forefinger—a habit when he was worried. Geo Sen wouldn't like it and there would be trouble enough later without incurring the wrath of his only potential mentor. The other doctors of his age would think him daft, and happily scheme to fill his post. His career might be in shambles. Dr Pyne looked around him once more, at the bereaved widow and her two friends, at the two servants waiting in the background, at the sleek opulent room, and decided. As a teenager he had furtively written verses celebrating the sweating millions and their fight against the fattened bourgeoisie, and the present situation seemed to bring out again all his latent class consciousness.

Clearing his throat he announced, 'I'm sorry, but I would like a further investigation. Your husband suffered from thrombosis and used blood thinners as well as the occasional sleeping tablets and painkillers. Any one of them could have made him drowsy and brought about his death. The fact that I can't find these medicines might mean he took them. He could have died as a result of another stroke, it is true. But, he could also have died of an extra dose of medicine that dulled his responses and made him sluggish and clumsy. It's probably nothing at all, but I'd like a further investigation.'

All the while he had been talking, the lady had looked at him with a steady gaze, now she stirred. 'What do you want, Doctor?' There was no shock or anger at what he had just said. Her voice was cold and perfectly in command.

'An autopsy.'

'Why?'

One of the friends rose from her chair and stood before the

doctor with her hands on her hips. 'Can't you see that it's a stroke? Robi's had one before and no one had expected him to live then. He's been bedridden for so long, he was just waiting to die.' Since the friend was wearing lipstick and had dabbed on some perfume before coming to comfort a widow at her husband's deathbed, Dr Pyne took an immediate dislike to her. The fact that she was wearing scarlet nail polish and that her hair was streaked blonde did nothing to improve her in the doctor's estimation.

'Let me deal with this, Nikki.' Nisha Bose, never taking her eyes off Dr Pyne, cut in smoothly. 'Why do you want all this?' Though the face was devoid of any emotion the tone was definitely frostier.

'Where are the Tramadol tablets? Where is the Valium? These are listed in the prescription, the usual pills any long-term patient would be expected to have. Don't you see, he could have deliberately drugged himself. This could be an unnatural death, a suicide or even, I don't know, a murder . . .'

If Dr Pyne had hoped for effect, he couldn't have been happier. The friends shouted in outrage, the servants shifted uneasily. Dr Pyne surveyed Nisha Bose narrowly and noted with relish that he had finally dented her armour. Her right hand flew to her throat and she looked stunned. 'What are you saying?'

'Because . . .' the doctor paused. He couldn't tell her that it was instinct, an unformulated unease with the way the man had died. And it was even more inconceivable that he should say to a new widow that the death of her invalid husband was very convenient. He decided to become curt and mysterious. 'I'm not sure whether he did actually have another stroke or whether he took something to end his life. The table seems to be full of a variety of medicines. You see, just as some people sometimes die before their time for no good reason, some continue to live long after their bodies are written off. I would like an investigation carried out on his organs, just to assure myself and you that there has been no accident.'

'An accident! Are you implying suicide? I don't believe it.' The blonde friend spoke harshly. 'You didn't know Robi!'

'It's true,' said the other friend. 'You didn't know him! You weren't his regular doctor, how can you be so certain that his condition hadn't deteriorated enough to cause a heart attack or another cerebral stroke?'

'Nisha.' The blonde friend bent over Nisha Bose, brought her mouth close to her ear and whispered something.

Nisha Bose looked at her friend once, then nodded and rose. 'All right, Doctor, I'll do what you say.'

Dr Pyne looked searchingly at her. 'You'll have to take the body to a hospital or inform the police.'

'I know. We'll take care of it.'

The friend who had whispered into Nisha Bose's ear came forward. 'I know someone at Calcutta Hospital. He'll manage something. You don't worry. Sorry to have woken you up at night. What are your fees?'

She was so eager to have him out of the way that Dr Pyne almost smiled. She must have underestimated both his courage and intelligence. He said, 'I can accompany you to the hospital myself and get the formalities done.'

'You don't have to. Mr Chopra will do the needful.'

Chopra, damn him! In his excitement Dr Pyne had forgotten the overbearing and arrogant Chopra, hospital administrator and friend to the rich and famous. What would Chopra say when he heard that Pyne had refused to give a death certificate and had insisted on a post-mortem? More importantly, what would he do once he found out?

But Dr Pyne was too far gone to think logically or to care anymore. He was flushed and angry, and his rancour made him obstinate, as it always did. He wanted a post-mortem and he would have it, even if he had to give up Chopra and Geo Sen and set up practice in some village of West Bengal.

'I have my car and I know my way to the Ballygunge thana. I will inform them on my way home.' Sudip Pyne then picked up his bag and swept majestically out of the room.

The night stretched out long and desolate for the duty officer at the Ballygunge police station. It was 1 a.m. and the flow of cars carrying party-goers and late-night revellers had ebbed. The duty officer yawned, dug his nose, scratched his crotch and looked at the clock. He was thinking of applying for a three-day leave and wondering how to justify it when the sound of the constable outside arguing at the door alerted him.

'Go back, it's too late, come back in the morning,' the constable said.

'What is this, a police station or a restaurant?' answered an agitated voice. 'Of course I know it's late. Do you think I'm here to have a good time?'

A young man with a thin moustache and large, slightly bulging eyes entered, carrying a black bag and a stethoscope flung around his shoulders. Sudip Pyne, parking his car outside the police station and prior to locking it had, after some hesitation, decided to appear as official as possible. He would have saved himself some trouble had he taken the constable's advice. The duty officer looked bored and was, indeed, completely unimpressed by the doctor's story when it was finished. Any marks of injury? Signs of burglary? Any signs of violence? Were the cupboards open? What were the servants doing?

Dr Pyne became increasingly restless. The duty officer began to regard Pyne with unrestrained curiosity and started a new line of questioning that increased the doctor's discomfort.

Who had called him in and how? The victim's wife, perhaps?
Did he know the victim personally? If the dead man had been
a patient with cerebral thrombosis and confined to his
wheelchair, why did the doctor suspect foul play?

'Oh god, I don't know! That's why I'm here, to find out.
Something has happened there, I can't put my finger on it,
but it's not a case of natural death. They hadn't expected
a fuss, they had thought I'd take a cursory look, issue a death
certificate and go back home. Why can't you start an inquiry?'

The duty officer looked pityingly at the doctor as he picked
his front teeth with a thumbnail. 'If I were to start inquiries
every time a man suspects a potential murder, I'd be sitting
under a mountain of unsolved First Information Reports.
Go back and tell them you're sorry, the more you think of it,
the more you realize that the man did die of a stroke. In
any case, they've probably got another doctor in by now
to certify otherwise.'

It was a long time since anyone had told Sudip Pyne to
stop being an idiot. He had a good nose for his job, his clinical
diagnoses were usually correct and the numbers outside his
chamber were swelling every day. Though his colleagues were
privately jealous and scoffed at his humourless attitude, they
dared not speak out openly because of Geo Sen's patronage. And
here he was, being ticked off by this surly lout of a policeman.
Bristling with rage, Dr Pyne returned to his car and sat at the
wheel for some time, thinking. He had apprehended trouble
from Chopra and even Geo Sen and had switched off his
cell phone; now he remembered his mother and turned it
on. Sudip Pyne sighed and scrolled his contacts for Chopra's
number, then he paused. Before Chopra came Chatterjee and
a number flashed into view. Sudip Pyne hesitated. He
remembered their last meeting. The circumstances had been
difficult but even the grudging doctor had been forced to
admit the other's sincerity. Since Dr Pyne himself was a man of

passion, he recognized and respected feeling and flair in another. If anyone in the police could give him a patient hearing and understand what he was trying to say, it would only be this man. Behind him, he heard the duty officer come out on to the veranda and exclaim, 'He's still here! Hey you, you'd better push off home.'

Without further deliberation Dr Pyne dialled and waited.

Bikram Chatterjee had gone to sleep an hour before midnight after a rather elaborate dinner of fish cutlets, crab curry and rice. Throughout the week Bikram maintained a Spartan kitchen, subsisting on bleak rotis and a mixed green mash while the cook, who also ate with him, writhed with envy at the smells of mutton curry that floated in from the kitchen next door. On Sunday mornings, the cook and Mistry, in a joint conspiracy, rushed to the bazaar and came back with all the things of which they had been dreaming all week. Since Bikram did not want to lose either Mistry or the cook, he relented and at dinner all three glutted themselves on fish and meat.

Bikram lounged half-heartedly around the house for a while. He then sat on the veranda and watched the vehicles run up and down, the traffic thinner on a Sunday, but as untidy as ever. He and Shona hadn't met this week and he was thinking of her. He hated an empty weekend because there was little police work to be done and nowhere to rush off to. On days like this, he would think of the future and the decision that had to be made. He continually put off the thought, primarily because it was too much effort to surrender the known for the unknown. By tacit arrangement, Shona never spoke of it either. By 11 p.m., Bikram had taken a cold shower, checked his email for messages, put his cell phone to charge and, with some relief at the passing of the weekend, gone to bed. The last thing he remembered before drifting off to sleep was the party at Nikki Kumar's and his discomfort there, now blurred and distant after nine days. When the phone rang Bikram knew by instinct that he would have to summon Mistry and go. He had not, however, expected Dr Pyne. The person at the other end of the line seemed excited but diffident. He was taken aback to find that Bikram recognized him almost at once and seemed not at all surprised at being rung up at 1.30 a.m.

Bikram listened patiently and then asked Dr Pyne where he was.

'In my car outside the thana. But the duty officer's checked on me once, oh god, he's here again, what am I to do now, he doesn't believe me at all.'

'Wait in the car. He'll call you in again presently.'

It took Bikram forty-five minutes to reach the police station. Mistry, who had expected a peaceful Sunday, had gone to bed drunk, and they spent half an hour trying to rouse him and make him fit for duty. At the Ballygunge thana, the duty officer, still smarting from the humiliating turn of events, had given the doctor a seat, shuffled papers irritably and flung a set of keys at the constable ordering him to open the borobabu's chamber quickly. Two minutes after Bikram entered, the officer-in-charge of the police station puffed in, an elderly man of about fifty-five, grey-haired and fat. The duty officer sighed resignedly and, rubbing his sleep-swollen eyes, prepared for a long haul.

The officer-in-charge, Chuni Sarkar, had often been in trouble. A well-known real-estate crook was close to him and there were whispers of underhand deals. Sex rackets and gambling dens sprouted and flourished mysteriously wherever he went. He was therefore anxious to please Bikram.

He saluted Bikram and listened intently to what Dr Pyne had to say, then cleared his throat. 'If you permit, Sir, I can accompany the doctor to the house and do the needful. You needn't trouble yourself.'

This suited Bikram. By rights, the case, if there was one, was still with the local police station and, therefore, under Chuni Sarkar's authority. He couldn't walk into the Bose house without involving other cops such as those from the homicide squad. They hadn't really established anything as yet.

'Let me know if you need help,' he said.

He watched as the officer and Dr Pyne walked to their respective cars, then yawned and got into his own. Perhaps there would be time for sleep after all.

The call came through on Bikram's cell phone almost immediately after they had swung into the main road on the way back home. 'Chuni speaking, Sir.'

'What is it?'

'I think the doctor might be right. There's vomit and froth on the dead body. Also, something's definitely fishy here. The doctor insists that they've changed the bedcover.'

'The what?'

'The bedcover, Sir. He says that when he first examined the patient, I mean the dead man, there were some brown stains on the bedclothes. He remembers because the cover was pale, a pattern of blue leaves on white, hold on a moment, Sir, what did you say . . . blue flowers on white, it's all the same isn't it, don't interrupt me unnecessarily, sorry Sir, what the doctor means is that the stains have now disappeared and the flowers are purple.'

'What does the family say?'

'They say that it's all wrong and the doctor is making up these details. Counter allegations, Sir. They pulled me aside and said that the doctor wanted a hefty fee on being called in so late and because they refused he's out to frame them.'

'Who's the "they"?'

'All kinds of people. It's difficult to assess who is family and

who's not. There's somebody who claims to be a close friend,
a lady with yellow hair, not Bengali, who is doing all the talking,
and a couple of others who seem to be family but are sitting
quietly in a corner and not saying anything.'

'Where's the doctor now?'

'Having a slanging match with someone called Chopra.
Seems to be an executive officer of a well-known hospital.
He called Pyne out as I was talking to you and they're arguing
in some inside room.'

Bikram thought for a moment and said, 'What's the
wife saying?'

'Not much, except that perhaps a post-mortem is not
really necessary.'

'How does she look, shocked or strong?'

'She's very calm, Sir. The man had been ill for some time
now, she might have been expecting his death. The room is
full of all kinds of medicines. Apparently, Robi Bose took almost
a dozen pills a day, including anxiety drugs, blood thinners,
beta blockers and what not, but the doctor says there are
many medicines listed on his prescription which are missing.
We searched the room and made the servant turn out some
cupboards but couldn't find them.'

'Did you suggest homicide?'

'No, but she's obviously had some ideas herself after she
found the doctor had returned with me.'

'All right then, here's what you do. Tell the photographer
and the sample people to wait for me. But first, get the doctor
out of there and get him to make the complaint before
the others make him change his mind. Send him back to
the PS immediately.'

Now that Sudip Pyne had made his point he re-entered the
police station glowing with triumph. This time, he actually

stamped after the duty officer and pretended to grumble about the time as he settled down in his chair. It was 3 a.m. but, for once, Dr Pyne didn't mind his mother being taken to the lavatory by the night ayah. This was exciting, this was excellent, he would show those blonde ladies and their ilk what he thought of them and their ways. Red lipstick at one in the morning! Sudip Pyne sniffed and began to reconstruct the night's happenings.

The duty officer began writing in a large unformed hand that straggled across the page. It took them fifteen minutes to sort out the night's happenings and condense them into an official document. Sudip Pyne read over what was written, nodded, and leaned back in satisfaction. The Boses' agony had just begun.

Back at the house, Bikram and Chuni Sarkar were coping with an enraged household. Nikki Kumar had rushed up to Bikram the minute he entered and wasted precious time babbling about old acquaintances and Shona Chowdhury. 'It's a blessing to have someone civilized to talk to. This man just won't understand that there's nothing wrong with Robi, I mean, he's dead, but that was natural, considering his health.' It took him a while to shake her off.

There was chaos at the dead man's house. The gates were unattended because the durwan was inside. The room opposite the bedroom had been converted into an impromptu waiting room where five men and women sat hunched on chairs. The officer-in-charge had summoned the most competent sub-inspector he knew from his area, who was now taking down the names, addresses and relationship with the deceased in a big diary with a brown cover. The corpse was being photographed by a fat man with a florid moustache and stinking socks. Another man was busy collecting vomit and froth samples. Robi Bose was dead and all around his non-being was the busy machinery of life, clicking pictures, clinking glass bottles and sniffing in corners.

Though the room was luxuriously furnished, it was still an invalid's room. There was a wheelchair, a walking stick and a jumble of medicines on a marble-topped table. The man who had been collecting samples now came over to the table and began to note the names of the tablets before dropping them into a plastic bag.

Nisha Bose was sitting quietly on a chaise longue. Her face was slightly puffy and she clutched a wet tissue in one hand but there was nothing else to indicate that she had become a widow in the last two hours. When she saw Bikram, however, her eyes widened in surprise. She was clearly unprepared for him. Bikram hesitated. Was he to approach her as a police officer or as a social acquaintance? His ingrained reticence inclined him towards the former, but there was death in the room and a certain decorum had to be maintained. Besides, a friendly attitude might make things easier. Thus he sat on the chair Chuni Sarkar had set for him before Nisha Bose and said, 'I am sorry for this intrusion but I hope you will understand my predicament.'

'And I hope you will understand mine.' She spoke in measured tones and her face was pale. 'What that doctor suggests, is it really necessary?'

'I think it is. You see, if someone has raised certain questions, it's usually better to complete the formalities required and get matters over with. That way you can be in the clear, especially later on, when you file for insurance claims and things like that.'

'But it makes all this so hateful, so sordid. I mean, to live one's last years like that and then to be tormented further by an autopsy and things like that. Oh, will his spirit ever be at peace . . .' She broke down and two large tears rolled slowly down her cheeks.

'I know exactly how you're feeling, and doubtless I would have felt so, under such circumstances. But it's always better to be sure rather than live one's life in a cloud of . . .' Bikram paused. 'A cloud of uncertainty,' he finished. Then he went on quickly, 'I promise to be as quick as possible about the . . . about it, in fact, I'll talk to the doctors and they will cooperate.'

Nisha Bose shook her head and murmured, 'If only I could have got Toofan Kumar on the phone, all this wouldn't have happened.'

Bikram turned his head away so that she could not see the sudden surge of anger. Toofan Kumar had been out of town for a day and had returned by the late-night flight, and had doubtless forgotten to switch on his phone once back home. He could only visualize the trouble that would have been caused had Toofan Kumar been informed.

To distract her, Bikram asked when her husband had last eaten. He seemed to have touched something there. She shot him a quick, furtive look and said, 'Around 10 or 10.30 p.m., I think. I'm not too sure, because I had some guests over. I went up to bed, around 12 a.m., I think, and found him lying on his back, sleeping. At first, I didn't look too closely, his head was turned away from me, so I brushed my teeth and changed and scrubbed my face, then went down once to see if they had cleared up downstairs. It was only when I went to bed that I, I realized he was cold, and, and . . .' There was a pause, then Nisha Bose continued breathlessly, 'I screamed and cried out for Buro. He took one look at Robi and said, he's dead. Mithu made me sit here, and then they made some telephone calls, I don't know to whom. I was feeling sick, sick! He had been alive only two hours before, and then this!'

Nisha looked past Bikram with unseeing eyes, as if she were living through it all again. Her forehead glistened with sweat and night cream. Her hands shook as she raised a tissue to her mouth.

'Where did he eat?'

'In his room.'

'Did he have anything to drink this evening?'

'A glass of Scotch, diluted with lots of water, so mild it tasted like a digestive. One glass only, because he had been begging for one for months. I didn't think it would do him any harm.'

'Who served him?'

'Buro, of course. He's the man who looks after Robi, I mean, looked after him. God, this is terrible!'

'Has Buro been here long?'

'Long enough, about five years now. He came right after the stroke.'

'How much can he be trusted?'

She drew in her breath as she looked at him, and there was something like alarm in her eyes. 'You're not suggesting that Buro had anything to do with it? That's impossible!'

'You've said that before, on my last visit here, and you say it again now. Why do you trust Buro so much?'

Nisha Bose looked searchingly at Bikram and their eyes held. Then she lowered hers demurely and said, 'It's illogical, I know, but, but, I believe in him. He would never do us any harm.'

'And the others? There is a maid you trust too. Do you think she could have made a . . . mistake tonight?'

Some of Nisha Bose's composure had returned. 'You've got an admirable memory, Mr Chatterjee. Yes, I trust Mithu, besides, even she was in the kitchen the whole evening. It's difficult to get her up here on normal days, so I don't think Mithu would have been here on a day like this.'

'But she might have, all the same,' Bikram persisted.

'Well, if it comes to that, anyone could have.' Nisha Bose shrugged her shoulders. A gleam came into her eyes. 'That means eight or nine people to interview, including my sister-in-law, Tara. Have you spoken to her yet? I think she's in the next room.'

'I think I will, thank you. One last thing. Who makes the beds at night in your house?'

She looked quickly at him again and looked away. 'Buro usually does, but he didn't, tonight. He was too busy.'

'But would your husband go to sleep on an unmade bed? He was very particular, from the little that I remember of him.'

'Normally he wouldn't, but tonight there was too much work and he came up because he was feeling tired, so he just lay down anyhow.'

'On the bedcover?'

'Yes, I mean no, oh lord, I don't remember. Why do you go on about that hateful bedcover like that doctor? When I came up he was lying on the sheet, with the cover down over his body, like it is now. That's all I know.'

Bikram rose. 'Would you permit me to take a quick look around the house?'

'By all means.'

'And this room?'

Nisha Bose swept her hands around her. 'It's all yours.'

'One other thing. Have you checked the almirahs and cupboards where you keep your valuables?'

There was the ghost of a smile on her lips. 'I have. Everything's safe. You needn't ask me to inventory my losses, apart from Robi.'

Before leaving the room Bikram paused before the bed. The dead man was lying peacefully, his mouth a little open, as if he'd died mid-snore, one arm flung out, his pyjamas

bunched up slightly around his ankles. Bikram turned to Chuni
Sarkar and asked in a low voice, 'Did you examine the body?'

'Yes, we did. No marks of injury, I checked.'

'Did you get the bedcover?'

'I looked around for the one Pyne claimed they had
substituted but found nothing. Perhaps he was wrong.'

'Have you got all the statements?'

'Yes Sir, and I've talked to the cousin also, she's in the next
room. Do you want to have a go at her?'

Bikram hesitated, then made up his mind. 'No, I'd rather
look around the house. You can let the friends and relatives
go, if they want, and get the body shifted to the morgue
once you've finished.'

He lingered in the room a little longer, taking in the
furniture, looking for things which would give him a personal
view of the dead man and his family. But it was an oddly
discomfiting room, without photographs or books or pictures.
The furnishings, though luxurious, were impersonal.

He opened the bathroom door and found a plastic bucket
in which there were a pair of trousers, a pair of shorts and an
expensive T-shirt in red and black. On a clothes peg hung
a woman's underclothes and another pair of trousers, also
a woman's, along with a white top, all flung haphazardly. He
looked at the washstand and found a tongue cleaner, a bottle
of liquid soap, but only one toothbrush. A bedpan stood in
a corner and bottles of disinfectant stood ranged on the window
sill. The bathroom was clean, but smelled of urine, probably
from the urine pot Robi used. Bikram closed the door and
wondered if he could open one of the wooden wardrobes
that stood ranged against the wall, but decided against it.
Nisha Bose still sat on the sofa and he knew he would feel
uncomfortable and self-conscious looking through personal
belongings before her.

On the landing were two more doors, one leading to a room where the friends and relatives had assembled. Bikram passed that one without so much as a second look and paused before the last one. He remembered it as being shut the last time. Feeling faintly guilty, he gingerly opened the door and stepped in. It was dark inside. He waited for his eyes to get accustomed to the darkness and then pressed a key on his cell phone. In the blue glimmer of the luminescent display screen he could just make out where the switches were. The room sprang to light and Bikram blinked. This was not one room but two. He was standing in a small anteroom, ten feet by ten, used as a dressing room. Three sides were lined with built-in wardrobes with full-length mirrors on each, the fourth had a large table with a smaller mirror mounted on it. The effect was disconcerting. Bikram stared at himself, reflected in various angles, an almost insane multiplicity of images. A door led out from beside the table and Bikram peeped inside. He switched on the lights—there were big old-fashioned switches—and nodded his head slowly. Yes, this was Nisha Bose's room. The bed was covered with an elegant bedspread, flowery satin curtains hung on the windows, fat lace cushions were scattered on a patterned durrie and a tallboy carried photographs of herself, CDs and books. In a vase drooped a bunch of withering sunflowers. Another door, locked, presumably led out to Robi's bedroom. Two other doors, fashioned in the old style with long glass panes, looked out on to a veranda. Several perfumes mixed together to give the room a special fragrance. Bikram was sure the room was kept locked when Nisha was not around. Bikram idly wondered how often the Bose couple shared a bed, and how much time Nisha spent in her boudoir. Feeling like a voyeur, Bikram stepped out of the room and closed it softly behind him.

He went down the steps lost in deep thought and made a

quick round of the rooms downstairs, the pantry, the kitchen and the outhouse, with an abstracted air. He stood in the garden and inhaled deeply. A bird hooted, and another, and soon a long trail of koels took off in a burst of chirrups, which meant that dawn was breaking and night was almost at an end. Bikram stood for a minute, drinking in the clean smells, then yawned and turned to go. He looked at his watch. It was 4 a.m.

He was about to go back inside when he hit his foot against something. The light was bad and once again he had to use the pale half-light of his cell phone. It was the dustbin. Actually, it was a large tin drum used at construction sites, now overflowing with empty cartons and refuse. Bikram bent over and caught the sharp smell of onion and coriander chutney. He could dimly make out chicken bones, paper napkins, string, leftover food and a piece of twisted foil. He gingerly picked up the foil. Something fell at his feet. Bikram groped around on the ground, then straightened up and looked at what he had found. In his palm rested five torn strips of medicine, the kind where the tablets have to be pushed out from the back. He took the strips into the kitchen and held one of them up to the light. B. No. 281 . . . 9P, Mfd 11 . . . Exp 11 . . . Schedule H Drug. It was so torn and mutilated that he could barely read the letters. Tramadol . . . Diazepam . . . He counted the empty squares. There were five strips of ten tablets each and all were empty.

# 6

The morning after Robi Bose's death, Bikram Chatterjee was shaving when Toofan Kumar called. Bikram sighed. He had been expecting the call but nevertheless had hoped it would never come.

'Good morning, Sir.'

'It never is good when you are around, Bikram. What's this about you ordering a post-mortem for Robi Bose? And why didn't you tell me that he was dead?'

'I thought it could wait till morning, Sir. I would have reported to you in any case.'

'How could you wait when practically the whole city was there! And why did you register a case? The man has been ill for years. It was just a bloody stroke.'

'The doctor they called in didn't seem so sure. He tried to convince the thana and then called me.'

'And convinced you to make unnecessary trouble! Don't you know that the Boses are one of the most honourable and distinguished families of the city?'

'Honourable and distinguished families face a higher risk of murder, Sir.'

'Will you stop being so dramatic? Murder! What are you trying to suggest?'

'That we wait for the report.'

'Nisha Bose is a personal friend, Bikram. How dare you suggest a PM without consulting me?'

'If she is well known to you and yet didn't telephone you when the trouble broke out, perhaps she too wants an investigation, Sir,' said Bikram with studied innocence.

There was a moment's silence as Toofan Kumar worked this one out. 'If you don't stop this investigation at once I'll have you transferred.'

'The body is at the hospital already, Sir,' answered Bikram but Toofan Kumar had rung off.

The king rageth, thought Bikram, and resumed his shaving. The phone rang again. Bikram put down the razor and connected without looking to see who was calling.

'Busy?'

Bikram had been expecting Shona's call, though they usually took care not to ring each other in the morning when both were gearing up for the day. Bikram took a deep breath to reorient himself.

'Sort of.'

'Can I help?'

'You've never asked me that before.'

'You might think I'm intruding. It's hard work with you as it is.'

'Then why today?'

They had been together for too long to circle and hedge.

'I suppose you've guessed why.'

'Don't listen to Nikki Kumar, Shona. She's no good.'

'She's a friend, Bikram, and important to me.'

'Some friend.' He did not bother to hide his contempt.

'We've been through this before, Bikram. Let's not begin this now, at nine in the morning.'

She sounded tired. Bikram could imagine her sitting on her unmade bed, chin resting on knee, head bent over the receiver, the day's appointments already tinkling on her cell phone.

'Did she tell you to call me?'

'Yes.'

'Why?'

'You know why.'

'She thought you could change my mind?'

'She thought you could do something.'

'Did you think I would listen to you?'

Silence, then softly, in almost a whisper, 'No.'

Was she crying? She often quivered on the verge of it. He wondered often what exactly it was that she found in him.

He said, 'How is your mother, Shona?'

'Okay.'

'How were Dolly's pre-tests?'

'Fine.'

Silence. A series of beeps announced a long line of calls in waiting. 'I have to go now, Shona. I'll talk to you later.'

She sighed. 'Bikram.'

'Yes?'

'Be careful.'

Then she rang off, firmly, as she always did.

The day had started unpromisingly and got gloomier as it went on. When Bikram reached office he found a stream of visitors waiting for a variety of reasons. Two or three people had been sent by his superiors, including Toofan Kumar, because they had lent money in various murky deals and now wanted the police to do some arm-twisting. There were also complaints from tenants about landlords, landlords about tenants, from fathers about young boys eyeing their daughters, and daughters about fathers assaulting their mothers. Most were there by some special reference from one or the other of Bikram's superiors and demanded special attention and courtesy. All through, Bikram's phone kept ringing as the journalists who hadn't been able to corner him early in the morning now kept up a steady interrogation. Was it true that the body bore signs of knife injuries? Had Robi Bose led a sinful life?

Did the wife kill him alone or with her lover? And why were the police harassing the widow instead of arresting the servant who was obviously the one who did it. But of course, it was probably suicide.

To everyone Bikram said equably that the body had been sent for a post-mortem and they could do nothing without the report, that there were no signs of injury and the police hadn't quite begun their investigation.

The phone rang again, this time, mercifully, the land line. A hoarse voice asked in broken English whether he was talking to DSP Vikram Chattopadhyay.

'Speaking,' said Bikram.

'I am Makhan Mandal, councillor, Ward 65, speaking.'

'Yes?' asked Bikram, puzzled. Another landlord–tenant case?

'Last night there was a mishap at the residence of Robi Bose in Ballygunge. Mr Bose died of a heart attack, I am told.'

Another one! What did he want?

'It seems that the officer-in-charge wrongly and rashly ordered a post-mortem.' Though the man was now speaking in Bengali he used the words 'wrongly' and 'rashly' in English.

'Many of his relatives have been ringing me up since morning, requesting me to look into the matter and call the post-mortem off. I would like you to do the same.'

'Do what?'

'Discipline your officer-in-charge. Stop the post-mortem. Return the body for cremation.'

'Why?'

'Because the . . . Mr Bose died a natural death. Any fool can see that. He had been very ill with heart trouble. Died of an attack.'

'The doctor doesn't think so.'

'Which doctor? He's just a junior fellow running after cheap publicity!'

'I'm sure he wouldn't want to anger so many important people for publicity.'

'Ah, so others have also been telling you to stop the PM. Has Toofan called you yet?'

Bikram could have bitten his tongue off. He should have anticipated Toofan Kumar's proximity to the politico. 'I don't think I can stop anything at this stage. It would look as if the police were trying to hush up things. Besides, the press has picked up the scent now.'

'But the police *should* hush it up. Why else would we put the officer-in-charge there?'

'I've survived for a long time without hushing things up, as you suggest. I don't see why this should be an exception.'

'If you want to be difficult, I will be nasty too. I suppose you're aware that, as the local councillor, I can certify that there was no foul play and a post-mortem is not required.'

This was true. Indian laws and rules are quirky and this was an unusually unreasonable proposition. And all that was required was a letter from the local politician to put Bikram in all sorts of legal tangles.

Bikram thought quickly. 'What'll I tell the press? I'll have to let them know that you ordered me to stop.'

'Are you threatening me, Mr DSP?'

'You're challenging me, Mandal babu, to go ahead with the post-mortem against all opposition.'

'Think about what I'm telling you. Someone from the family will meet you in half an hour with the letter.'

'I don't think it will be possible for me to receive that letter, Mr Mandal. I really don't think you should concern yourself with this case.' Taking a leaf out of Toofan Kumar's book, Bikram cut him off firmly. Then he rang a bell, asked the constable who answered to turn away all remaining visitors, and, summoning Mistry, went out to look for Ghosh.

Ghosh was on duty at the airport where a senior American bureaucrat was due to arrive from Delhi. A bunch of women from the women's wing of the Communist Party was preparing to burn an effigy of the US president. The women were jubilant. Traffic had piled up into a higgledy-piggledy mess and they were making a troop of policemen increasingly nervous. The usual flow of events was this: after some slogan-shouting, the women would pick up stones and begin pelting the cops. They would continue throwing stones till they had provoked a reaction, and then complain about human rights violations.

Ghosh stood at the head of the troop, a glum figure in a uniform a couple of sizes too tight for him. Beside him fidgeted Sheena Sen, a slightly built young woman officer on whom the khaki contrasted with a baby face and coloured hair.

'They're all so ugly,' said Sheena Sen chattily. 'Humph! Why don't they marry and bring up children and look after their in-laws like other normal girls?'

Why don't you, thought Ghosh. He disapproved of working women and hated women cops.

'Or study and get good jobs,' continued Sheena.

'They have,' grunted Ghosh.

'Really! You mean they're all working women?'

'They're in the business of politics,' he said caustically.

'Then they're definitely better paid than me,' tittered Sheena.

A wireless that had been crackling off and on sprang to life and emitted a series of screeches. Only a policeman could decipher what the man at the other end said: Charlie Mike's convoy was sliding away down the river road and was expected to arrive at the office destination shortly.

'Why Charlie Mike?' asked Sheena rather pointlessly. 'Why not Caspar Mutton or Calcutta Mumbai or Caring Mother for chief minister?'

'Hush,' said Ghosh as if worried that the chief minister would somehow hear her remark. 'It's the old British code. It is carved in stone.' Just then the activists grew bored and began looking around for some fun. They charged through the cordon and began by pulling at the sticks of the nearest constables.

Ghosh shouted, 'Here it comes. Watch out for the stones. Protect your noses. Forward!'

When Bikram arrived fifteen minutes later, the battle had subsided and Ghosh was wrapping his handkerchief around a reddish bulge on his arm, cursing all the while. The lines of women had been broken up and put into police vans where they were already shouting slogans. The roads had been given over to the angry traffic which began a bellowing of horns.

'How's it going?' shouted Bikram above the din.

'As it always does,' Ghosh shouted back. 'They'll be let off in an hour or two, still yowling away, but who's going to look after my arm?'

'All sound and fury, signifying nothing?' asked Bikram, remembering a textbook.

'What?'

'Nothing. What's the matter with your arm? Sprain?'

Ghosh tested his arm dubiously, then sighed. 'Nothing much that ice won't mend. But why are you here? I didn't see your name in the roster.'

'Can you get out of this now and spare me an hour?'

'I think so.'

'Then get in,' said Bikram, 'and I'll brief you on the way.'

'That's funny,' said Ghosh when Bikram had filled him in on Robi Bose's death and the circumstances surrounding it. 'First the theft, and then this! One of the servants, I suppose.'

'That's what I hoped too when I heard of it. But nothing is

missing, no one was hurt, none of the servants has fled and no one would have thought anything suspicious about the death had it not been for a pesky doctor who refused to sign "Death by cardiovascular failure" on the dotted line.'

'Family, then,' said Ghosh with an air of certainty. 'Wife, probably with the aid of a lover.'

'Possibly,' said Bikram. 'But investigation will be an uphill task, judging from the number of phone calls I've already received. In any case, we can't proceed till the autopsy report comes in.'

'Then we might as well wait till next summer,' said Ghosh cynically.

'I think they will find something in the post-mortem,' said Bikram thoughtfully. 'I suppose it was some kind of poison. After that it will get really bad.'

'Because of TK?'

Bikram smiled. Ghosh, beneath that potbelly and the crusty temperament, had a quick mind.

At 3 p.m., a meeting was held in the inspector general's room. Inspector General Prem Gupta was a quiet man in spectacles with a soft voice and a benign temperament. On weekdays, he arrived in office by 9.30 a.m. and immersed himself in work, diligently clearing files, meeting visitors and attending to police work. On Saturdays and Sundays, he supervised the flowers in his garden, logged on to various gardening websites, exchanged notes with other gardening enthusiasts and settled down with the gardening book of the week with as much ardour as he had reviewed the crime situation in office.

Prem liked Bikram. He disliked Toofan Kumar but took care not to show it so that service camaraderie and hierarchy were maintained. He trod a careful tightrope when all three came together for work and defused explosive situations with a nod and a word. They sat down in his room over cups of steaming coffee. This was the gentlemanly touch Prem used to lighten the depressing burden of policing.

'Good work on the child-lifting case,' he began. 'Have you got anything out of the man?'

'He's pretending insanity, Sir,' said Toofan. 'Sometimes he says he kidnapped five or six, all those reported missing from the Station area, and the next minute he clams up.'

'Do you think he could really be a bit off in his head?' Prem asked.

'Look at his modus operandi: tucking a nine-month-old under his lungi! How did he ever think he'd get away with it?'

'We've put an extra guard outside his cell,' said Toofan. 'Just in case he *is* a little insane. What we've also done is lock up another guy with the man. He'll pump the child-lifter for info and keep an eye on him as well. I'm hoping he'll lead us to the other gangs.' They discussed the child-lifting and how it could just provide them with a badly needed break.

'We need to put CCTVs in all our cells,' said Prem Gupta. 'Think of the enormous amount of money wasted each year without fulfilling this basic need.'

'No planning,' said Toofan deprecatingly. 'No funds and no planning. These IAS guys will finish us altogether.'

'Perhaps we need to be more active too, Toofan,' said Prem Gupta mildly. He then turned to Bikram. 'Bad luck over Babul. What went wrong?'

'Same as always, Sir. Someone tipped them off.'

'You lost a good informer, I hear, but you've got someone new called Raja, I believe.'

'I have. That's what's worrying me. Was he left behind on purpose to throw us off the scent or was Babul too frightened to care? I can't quite make out.'

'Is he still in hospital?'

'We're keeping him there till we figure out under which section to book him.'

'Never knew criminals were scared of leech bites,' said Toofan Kumar. 'Never knew leech bites could rob us of a prize catch. The whole thing was mishandled. Someone from the house shot at one of our men. Suppose they had shot back and someone had got killed? Imagine the newspapers next morning!' Toofan Kumar's voice implied that the raid had been deliberately sabotaged and events were being neatly manipulated to ruin his, Toofan's, reputation.

There was a moment's silence. Prem Gupta began his tightrope act. 'We have to look into this fake currency,' he said to deflect the conversation. 'Too much of it is flooding the market. At this rate it'll get out of hand. Any ideas, Toofan?'

Toofan Kumar ventured some suggestions. Then they discussed a few other desultory cases ranging from illicit liquor to gambling rackets in residential areas.

The morning's newspapers were lying face down on the table. Prem Gupta pushed them aside to put down his cup and then casually asked about the Robi Bose case. 'I see the television channels are very happy this morning.'

'Ask Bikram. He's the one who began it.' Toofan Kumar's fleshy face quivered in anger.

'It couldn't be helped, Sir. I had to do it.'

Bikram briefly related the night's happenings and Sudip Pyne's refusal to sign the death certificate. He also described the last occasion of his visit to the Bose residence and the theft of money.

'They could be connected, the theft and the sudden death,' said Prem Gupta reflectively.

'But the death wasn't sudden. I knew the man,' said Toofan. 'He had suffered a stroke five years ago and this was the second one, Sir. Something's wrong with the doctor. Bikram should have known how to deal with him.'

'Draft a letter to the director of the forensic science lab, Toofan. Tell them to hurry up with the report. Two weeks at the most. Tell him that the press is on to us and that we need to find out soon what happened.'

'Nothing has happened, Sir. Except publicity for some people,' said Toofan Kumar darkly.

Prem Gupta ignored this. 'I'll speak to the director also; he's a good friend of mine.'

'They've got hundreds of cases piled up. It'll take them years to clear the backlog, let alone do this one. We'll give it a try, nevertheless,' said Toofan, remembering all at once that it was Prem who wanted a verdict.

'I suppose that's it, then.'

Bikram rose and saluted. Toofan Kumar waited for him to leave. He had decided to have a private chat with Prem Gupta and tell him exactly what he thought of Bikram and his meddlesome ways. Toofan had long waited for a chance to tar Bikram and this was the perfect time.

Prem Gupta plied Toofan with some more coffee, excused himself and went into the bathroom. There, he made a call to Bikram. 'Hang around somewhere. I want to have a word with you after Toofan leaves.'

Bikram smiled, took the lift to the third floor, slipped into a colleague's room and waited.


'What do you make of it, Bikram?'

'Something is wrong there, Sir. I wouldn't have gone ahead if there wasn't.'

'I know. I have great respect for your judgement. Had it been someone else I would have heeded Toofan but, well, you know I trust you completely.'

'Thank you, Sir. I'll try not to let you down.'

'Do you think the doctor is overreacting?'

'No. I've worked with him once before. He's genuine. Also, he's very good at his work. Ambitious, but has a conscience. If he feels there was some hanky-panky, I'm inclined to believe him.'

'But the report may take years.' Prem Gupta hesitated. 'Perhaps you should start making some discreet inquiries.'

'I was hoping that's what you'd say.'

'Robi Bose.' Prem Gupta looked thoughtful. 'I've met him of course. At parties and so on. He has a very beautiful wife. Quite a tragedy for her.'

'Beautiful and shrewd, Sir. Perhaps she has been set free by this death.'

'You know her?' Prem Gupta looked at Bikram closely. One of the reasons he liked Bikram was that he was so full of surprises.

'My . . . one of my friends took me along to a party to which the Boses had also been invited.'

'Did you like them?'

'I was worried about them. The husband was so dependent on his wife, it was pathetic. And the wife, she is a wild one.'

'Well, let's see what happens. I'll try and speed up the post-mortem. Toofan will be writing the letter, of course.'

The telephone rang. Bikram got up to go and saluted again. Prem Gupta picked up the receiver and absent-mindedly followed Bikram's lean figure out of the door. Then he sighed again. This one was going to be difficult.

# 7

At headquarters the next day, the Robi Bose investigation was pushed on to the back-burner. A number of fake-currency cases had mushroomed and the racket was threatening to get out of hand. At the same time, Angel Nursing Home declared Raja to be fit and healthy and ready to leave for jail.

Two constables escorted Raja to the district court and were immediately swamped by a crowd of hungry court clerks. A fan ground wretchedly on the ceiling and the floor was littered with cigarette butts and crumpled bus tickets. Men and women in high-necked white shirts and black jackets busily strode up and down, holding files and pens while a medley of law-breakers, their friends, their relatives, police constables, canteen boys carrying cups of tea and a host of busy bodies filled the rooms in bazaar-like camaraderie. A sleepy judge scratched inside his collar, mopped his brow and listened half-heartedly, looking at the clock all the while. Raja shuffled his feet, commented on the heat and idly followed the progress of a lizard that cautiously shifted from one end of the wall to the other, till a clerk thrust a couple of papers at him and asked him to sign them. Bail had been arranged and he was free.

Two hours later, Raja entered the Tollygunge police station with a jaunty step. His body was cleansed and glowing with bottles of fresh blood and multivitamin tablets. The diet in the nursing home had been wholesome, with no booze or flesh to taint him. He felt healed and invigorated. Babul would think that he was trapped and no one would suspect that he had turned informer for the police. Nothing could go wrong anymore.

Ghosh was waiting at the thana for Raja. Siddique Ali's death and the abortive raid still rankled and he decided to lose no time in finding information. The officer-in-charge had been called to headquarters and Ghosh wanted to use his room for the questioning because the swivel chair was comfortable and the tea and snacks wholesome.

Raja entered the room and hesitated, wondering where to sit, then decided to gauge Ghosh's response by sitting on the floor. Ghosh frowned and waved him to a wooden bench in a corner. Since this indicated a change in status—from thief to informer—Raja got up with a smile and stood for a moment with folded hands, then dived for Ghosh's feet.

'That's enough,' said Ghosh crossly. 'Now don't waste my time. Tell me what you do.'

'Everything cross-border, Sir, everything you want. I do girls, fake currency, cattle, motorcycles, cell phones. You can trust me, Sir, I'll give you good tip-offs. Hundred per cent success, no hanky-panky with my info, Sir, for you and that other sir, the one who came to see me in hospital, if you could put me in touch with him. His phone number, perhaps . . .' Raja paused slyly.

'You talk to me first. If the information's good, I'll see about putting you across to him.'

'Oh, it's good, very good.' Raja looked about the room, then lowered his voice to a whisper. 'I hope no one can hear us, I mean, if any of the men outside rat to Babul I'll be dead.'

Just my luck to be saddled with the dramatic kind, thought Ghosh morosely. Then he remembered Siddique Ali and softened a bit.

A dishevelled boy of fourteen or so, carrying two cups of tea and a plate of samosas, entered and put down his tray on the table. Ghosh reached out hungrily for a samosa, pushing a cup of tea before Raja at the same time. Raja goggled as if he'd been offered a gourmet meal.

'Thank you Sir. This is most kind of you. If I may take a sip . . .' He slurped noisily at his cup and rubbed his hands to show Ghosh that he appreciated the gesture and loved the tea. Then he darted some more furtive looks around and lowered his voice again. 'What I'm telling you now is big time. We are part of an organization called the . . .' Here his voice dropped so much that Ghosh heard nothing. He could only see Raja's mouth form an exaggerated O.

'What? Stop mumbling! What did you say?'

Once again Raja formed a silent O, his voice inaudible, his face contorting wildly.

Ghosh had his second samosa, wiped his hands with his handkerchief, leaned back, belched and looked at Raja with a benign expression. 'You're quite a comedy circus, aren't you?'

Raja looked genuinely injured. 'I'm just trying to help you,' he began sullenly.

'Help, you son of a swine?' roared Ghosh. 'You think I have all day to sit and hear you drivel and slurp like a fool? Just wait till Babul gets to hear of this . . .'

'But you won't know where Babul is until I tell you, and I won't tell you if you shout at me like I'm some common thief,' said Raja. 'All right, all right, just joking,' he continued hastily for Ghosh was beginning to look like he would burst. And Raja realized he still hadn't managed to wangle out the number of the other police officer.

'It's called the Dhoor Syndicate. Yes, Dhoor,' he spelt it out in Bengali. 'It's an organization that helps ferry people and things across the border, from Bangladesh to India and reverse. I work at this end, the North Twenty-Four Parganas end, though I was thinking of switching over to the Sunderbans side. There's good money there too, not just tigers but birds and turtles, easy money, just ship the turtle stuff to Bangladesh and off it goes to Bangkok and Dubai as legal exports. And good fun too, the deer are so easy to catch, the meat is delicious, especially with a bottle of . . .'

'Get on with it,' thundered Ghosh. 'Stop babbling about tigers and turtles. Tell me about Babul.'

'I'm just coming to it.' Raja sounded truly hurt. 'Just trying to help you, in case you want to conduct some wildlife raids. Anyway, Babul brings people from over the border and sends them to Mumbai and Delhi as servants. These guys are so well trained they can lie low for months, sweeping and cleaning, and then, one day, they can clean the place out in one shot. The "servants" then disappear, only to resurface two months later in a completely different place. Babul does it so well, he even gets them to convert from their religion and take on Hindu names, do pranam to Krishna and Hanuman; teaches them a smattering of Hindi, as if they were from Bihar or UP. He acts as a fence for the stolen goods, and transfers the servants' money home across the border. I used to handle the financial side of the border transactions, then he sent me to do the networking in Mumbai, the shithead that he is. I told him that place didn't suit me but he wouldn't listen.'

Raja paused to catch his breath. Ghosh, who had been playing with a paperweight, now used a matchstick to dig into his ears. It appeared as if he was only half listening to Raja but his brain was furiously turning over. His first thought was that Siddique Ali had failed to tell him Babul had become a national player. Now, tripping him up would not be so easy.

'Anything special about him?'

'About Babul? Like what?

'Any particular likes and dislikes, habits, anything funny about him?'

'Funny? I don't know. He loves biryani and wears only white clothes, just like a sahib, you know, white shirts and white pants and those shirt-coats that have buttons down the front and two pockets.'

'Safari suits,' said Ghosh mechanically.

'Is that what they are called? He gets them stitched by some tailor on Circular Road. Expensive. I had to pick up a set once, eight hundred apiece. He wouldn't be caught wearing stuff like mine.' Raja looked down at his striped T-shirt and tight pants. He dusted at a whitish patch near his thighs and studied his fingers adorned with three rings: one red coral, one a grimy pearl and one horseshoe. Then he looked up. 'You obviously know about Babul's hand injury.'

Ghosh didn't, but was not prepared to reveal that to him. 'Wasn't it an accident with a grenade or something?' he said evasively, pretending to fiddle with some papers and look bored.

'That was early on in his life, when he was still making cheap guns and selling them near the coal mines,' said Raja. 'Took off his thumb and half his forefinger.'

'Left hand, wasn't it?'

'No, the right one. That's why he needs people to do his dirty work all the time.'

Raja leaned forward again and Ghosh got a blast of the mingled odours of tea and garlic. 'If you can catch him off his guard, hit him on that right hand. He's weak there, fumbles at things.'

At that moment Ghosh's cell phone rang. It was Bikram, summoning him to a quick chat in the evening over the Robi Bose death. 'Where are you now?'

'Tollygunge PS, with that leech guy, Raja.'

'Anything interesting there?'

'Some.'

'I would have liked to have a go at him too, but now, with

this other thing, and all those court forwards . . .' Bikram's cell phone beeped its call waiting and Ghosh rang off. He looked dispiritedly at Raja. 'Where will you go now?' he asked.

Raja smiled. As his face lit up he looked boyish and guileless. 'Home,' he said simply.

Ghosh reached into his uniform pocket and extracted a hundred-rupee note. 'Here, buy something for the family.' He looked away as he put the money before Raja, refusing to meet his eyes.

'Thank you, Sir, but it's okay, I've got some of my own . . .'

'Take it!'

Raja reached out and humbly put the note into his pocket.

'Give me a ring now and then and don't do anything foolish. Stay away from Babul and his cronies and remember to put in an appearance at the court as agreed.'

Ghosh rose and, as Raja made as if to fall at his feet again, skipped nimbly out of the way, surprising in a man of his girth.

'When can I meet the other sir?'

'Give me some good leads and I'll set up an interview.'

'I will, I surely will. Can I call you up tomorrow, maybe by the end of this week . . .'

He's going to manufacture information just to meet Bikram, thought Ghosh disgustedly as he creaked into his car.

The rest of the day passed in a whirl of activities. Bikram wrote a lengthy report on a complaint from some members of an apartment block. A residential apartment had been converted into two open kitchens to illegally make potato chips and assorted snacks. The neighbours had sent deputations to the local police station, the municipal councillor, a member of the legislative assembly, the health department, three newspapers and four television channels to protest the highhandedness. Since the man who owned the factory had unleashed an impressive shower of money on almost everyone concerned with the case, Bikram knew precisely in which dustbin his report would end up. The thought was liberating. It freed him from all linguistic restraint and fired his dormant literary talents. In bursts of imaginative fervour, between telephone calls and visitors and leave-requisition letters that had to be signed, he indulged himself. When he leaned back at last he found that he had almost scripted a lurid potboiler.

Ghosh was not so lucky. Dogged by bad luck, he ended up supervising the arrangements for the shooting of a reality show in a water-sports park on the fringes of the city. He spent an unhappy hour touring the stage, tripping on wires and being addressed as 'uncleji' by an impresario with earrings, a tattoo and a sweatshirt with a picture of a spider's web on it.

Sheena Sen spent the day investigating a sexual harassment case filed by a research assistant against her supervisor who had tired of her.

Chuni Sarkar, having finalized some personal and delicate financial deals with the head of a truck-drivers' union, sought to assuage his guilty conscience by hurling headlong into a mess of reports.

Raja went to a flat in Howrah, rented under an assumed name, spent fifteen minutes placating his wife, inquired after his mother's health and loped off to the Savoy Hotel for a quick glass of beer and a chance to catch up with local news.

At 6 p.m., Bikram's cell phone rang. It was Sudip Pyne. 'Any luck with the post-mortem report?' There was a suppressed excitement in his voice. Bikram wondered at the stupidity of the question, coming as it did from a doctor who was fully aware of the post-mortem procedure and what it involved.

'You know how it is,' he said as non-committally as he could.

'Have you talked to Geo Sen?'

'Not yet.'

'But you should,' said Dr Pyne. 'That man knows more about the secret lives of these high-society types than he does about medicine.'

'Did Robi Bose have a secret life?' asked Bikram.

'Obviously.' Dr Pyne sounded incredulous that he was being asked the question. He then rang off.

Bikram rose from his chair and walked a few paces, stretching, then looked moodily out of the window. Cars had already lined up, waiting for the officers to go home, and the clerks had fastened the strings on the cardboard files and exited, crowding the bus stops and the Metro railway platforms. The cobbler and the fruit-seller were packing their cases while the hawker was removing his shiny calendars of Shiva and Kali from where they were strung on the wall. Was this a good time to call Geo Sen, who might have a room full of patients in his waiting room? But he would be even busier later on, at a party or at the club, a glass of Scotch before him. He sighed and reached for the phone.

A silvery voice answered, 'Dr Sen's chamber, how can I help you?'

Bikram explained.

'Do you have an appointment?'

'No. But it's not for a consultation, I need to speak to him . . . on business.'

'Hold on a minute, please.'

Bikram found himself holding on for three minutes.

'Hellow.' A thin voice with a British accent came on the line, the impatient voice of a man used to giving orders. Bikram explained again.

'Robi Bose? But I was away when he died. You'd better ask whoever treated him, then.'

'But he was one of your regular patients. I'd like to know a little bit more about his medical condition.'

'But I told Toofan all I knew when I met him at the club yesterday!'

'I'm afraid this is part of an official inquiry. I suppose you discussed the matter casually with Mr Kumar at the club, but that's not enough.'

'And why not? Who are you anyway?'

Bikram gave his name and waited. He thought it would make an impression, as it usually did. He thought of Shona and the ways in which their worlds overlapped, sometimes, as it undoubtedly would do now. The tone changed from cold disdain to effervescent conviviality. 'Oh, but of course, Mr Chatterjee, I would be glad to help you. Forgive me, I didn't quite realize who you are, you know how it is, with all these patients. How is Shona? It was nice to see you that evening at the Kumars' party. And poor Robi of course! How about seven-thirty? We could meet at the club.'

Bikram politely declined and settled for a meeting at the doctor's chamber. Then he put down the receiver and assembled the Robi Bose team in his office. They were a sad-looking bunch as they entered. Ghosh looked visibly tired and Chuni Sarkar, who was always hot and sweaty, had patches of sweat under his armpits. The April sun had been merciless and the heat seemed to have seeped by way of their uniforms into their souls. They sat dispiritedly at the table and refused the tea offered. Bikram knew this listlessness well; it was the usual mood at the start of an investigation that promised nothing but trouble. It was easier to tackle a dozen demonstrations, accidents, forgery and cheating cases than a high-society death under suspicious circumstances. Gauging their mood, Bikram was quick and brief.

'Chuni, you've done the preliminaries for the F.I.R., but we have to take it from there. Ghosh and you had better take down the details of the servants and check up on them. Also the dailies who came and went,' said Bikram, remembering the plethora of masterjis and masseuses and sweepers described by Nisha on his first visit there. How odd that this death should have taken place so soon after that visit!

'Could there be a connection between the death and the money stolen?' asked Ghosh, accurately reading his mind as usual.

'There must be,' said Bikram.

'Then that will clear her,' said Ghosh. 'If she was planning to kill her husband she wouldn't ask for a band of policemen to walk around her house a few days before the deed.'

'But did she actually want it?' said Bikram. 'Remember, it was TK who jumped at the opportunity of doing her a favour.'

'Why would she take the risk of talking about it then, and that too before Kumar sahib?'

'Loose talk,' said Bikram, describing the endless prattle that flowed at parties.

Ghosh said, 'She might not have done it herself, you know? She could have had any one of the guests at the party fix Robi his weak drink.'

'Or,' said Chuni Sarkar, 'it could have been an accident. Perhaps one of the more adventurous guests was spiking his drink with something more potent than alcohol but spiked Robi Bose's instead.'

'Which means that we need the names and addresses of all those at the party and have to interrogate each one of them. It will be hell, considering the set. Put one of your well-mannered, good-looking men on the job, the kind who can inspire confidence,' said Bikram.

'It could be suicide,' ventured Chuni Sarkar.

'Without writing a note? Robi Bose wasn't the type of man who would leave without a dramatic farewell.'

'He couldn't really have died of cardiac arrest, could he?' asked Ghosh hopefully.

'It is a difficult case,' admitted Bikram. 'This is not an

ordinary middle-class neighbourhood, with neighbours bursting with information, and the problems of the family fairly public. The rich keep their secrets well.'

He stretched and looked at the large colonial-style clock on the wall, salvaged from a pile of old files and rat droppings in a back room. It always reminded him of the clocks of his childhood, whirring out the time in stately chimes, sandwiched between mounted deer heads, and photographs of Rabindranath Tagore and of grandfathers in dhotis and severe black coats. 'In any case we must be careful not to ruffle any feathers at this stage. Just brief questions, in the manner of routine inquiries. The case is at the thana level, the crime branch still hasn't been given the investigation officially, so there's no need to be too proactive. We'll leave the rest till after the post-mortem report comes through. But that party list must be followed up.'

Bikram decided to go home and change before his meeting with Dr Geo Sen. The day had been hot and steamy and his clothes stuck to him damply. The lift which serviced the block of flats housing police officers clanked ponderously to a stop with a shuddering groan. The heavy iron grill door had to be manoeuvred back and forth twice before it shut painfully and the contraption began its reluctant ascent with a whining sound. Bikram slouched and put his left heel on the wooden wall behind him to steady himself. Grumpily, he eyed bits of straw scattered around in the lift.

He was unhappy but couldn't put a finger on the reason for it. The day's work came back to him in fragments. He remembered the illegal maker of potato chips and the helpless deputations against him, and then the men and women he had met at Nikki Kumar's party, sleek and glitzy, riding high on fortunes built on adulterated cooking oil and low-grade cement, money-lending, dubious chit funds and sham finance companies.

The lift ground to a halt and Bikram entered his flat. He went to his bedroom and sat down on the bed while the cook brought him a glass of chilled water and asked if dinner was to be served. 'No, I'm going out now. Get me a glass of lime sherbet though.'

He stared at the room for a minute, unlike a bachelor's den in its neatness, the books well arranged, the reading lamp with its raw silk shade, the wooden cupboards polished to perfection, the photograph of his parents encased in a leather frame, the whole set-up put together and cared for with the fastidiousness of a family man.

He rose and opened one cupboard. What should he wear? Something subtle and expensive so that Dr Sen could not slot him as a typical state service officer trying to rise from the DSP level. Bikram dug into piles of shirts and T-shirts for a blue checked shirt of an expensive make that he had stored after dry-cleaning and hadn't worn for quite some time. Where on earth was it? He rooted through the piles till, suddenly, his hand encountered the crackly feel of paper. He drew his hand out. It clutched a yellowed newspaper with Union Public Service Commission Examinations emblazoned on it. New Delhi, April 1996.

Bikram went very still. For a few moments he stared at the paper blankly, registering nothing, till the years shimmered and the memories broke and he was once again in a room filled with books, piles of them, a copy of *Manorama Yearbook* open before him, others scattered around him, a pillow over his eyes, weeping because the results had been declared and he had again failed to qualify for the Indian Police Service and this was the second time it had happened. Outside, someone was knocking on the door. Bikram, open up, you fool, it's not the end of the world, open the door, what are you up to, but it was the end of the world for him as he sat shivering in pain and the utter desolation of being rejected. He had preserved this futile reminder of his last attempt, but why? And all at once Bikram remembered Toofan Kumar and realized that his dislike for the latter had, at its core, envy. For all his brash and loudmouth ways Toofan had passed the one examination that mattered. And Bikram, for all his elegant ways and convent education, was still only a bloody DSP! So what did it matter what he wore? Bikram slammed the cupboard door shut, strode past the cook and the lime sherbet, took the steps two at a time and was in his car in two minutes. 'Drive fast,' he said to Mistry.

Half an hour later, Bikram pulled up before a sleek high-rise and took the lift to the third-floor apartment which served as Geo Sen's chamber. A young and pleasant secretary smiled at Bikram and offered him coffee or cola, while Dr Sen was seeing his last patient. She was as well-fitted out as the room in which Bikram was made to sit. This was clearly a private antechamber for important guests. Outside, there was a less imposing waiting room for lesser men and women, with plastic chairs and obscure medical journals.

The doctor was a prosperous man of fifty, immaculately dressed, his checked shirt bearing the crest of a well-known brand. He stretched his hands in warm greeting as he came out of his room. He waved Bikram into a chair, took a seat beside him, insisted on serving coffee and finally leaned forward confidentially. 'Is there going to be trouble?'

'The manner of his death might be suspicious.'

'It was Sudip, I believe, who refused to give a death certificate. Excitable chap. But solid, I admit. One of my best juniors, though perhaps, in time, he'll learn to handle things better. Had I been here, I might have talked him out of it . . .'

'Had you been here, he would never have gone there, I'm sure. You would have been the one to examine the dead man and perhaps you would not have gone into all this. Perhaps you would have been careful to be careless, if you know what I mean.'

Bikram looked into the shrewd pair of eyes that were sizing him up. The doctor, without averting his gaze, said: 'It would be useless to pretend before you, Bikram. I think you know how it is with us. Ethics versus reality, and sometimes there are rich families whom it would be fatal to annoy. We all have our . . . um . . . business interests. In that sense, policemen and doctors are so alike.'

'Then we understand each other well, Dr Sen, and I would appreciate honesty from you. You have been a close friend of the family's and will know much about them. I'll be frank with you. This is still a preliminary investigation because the autopsy report has not come through. Once that happens, the press will jump on to it and all kinds of juicy stories will make the rounds. It would be good for those with close links with the family to tell us all they know so that the investigation can be got through quickly before too much of excitable investigative journalism hits the papers and all kinds of probes are made.'

Bikram looked stony but inwardly held his breath. It was a gamble, of course, to hint that he knew the doctor and Nisha Bose were more than good friends. Were his opponent to refuse to play the game, to tell him to leave, he would have no option but to do so. But this man was clever enough to distance himself from the wrong people at the right time; he might take the chance offered.

For a while Geo Sen said nothing. Damn it, thought Bikram, I've bungled it. 'All right,' said Geo Sen finally, 'I'll tell you something of what I know. Not everything but some of it. The problem they had was the house. Robi isn't really the sole owner of the house, you know. It is a joint property on which an uncle and his daughter also have claims. The uncle was always timid and couldn't keep pace with Robi's mother, a smart lady who gradually took over the whole household after her marriage, so the uncle took his family away to a small house in a middle-class neighbourhood. But he's still got a valid legal claim. Following his stroke, Robi used to fret that after his death the family might move in and try to stake their right. I told him this was impossible, they would never be able to bulldoze in like that, and anyway, Nisha has an equal claim, but he wouldn't listen. He would spend hours planning and plotting to buy the cousin a flat somewhere and make her relinquish her claim or make over her inheritance.'

'Did that worry him so much that it affected his health? Could he have had an attack for instance, by working himself up?'

'Well, he used to brood about this all the time. I think, in a way, it was a kind of a release for him. You see, he was in the prime of his life when he had the stroke and so, when he recovered enough to be able to lead a semblance of a normal life, he found he had nothing to do. And so he took up this cause as a way to pass the time, and gradually the cause overpowered him and consumed him, till he could do nothing but think of his death and Nisha's property claims. It was frightening to hear him go on and on about it, sometimes.'

'This cousin, were they on good terms?'

'Nisha was very good to her, and tried very hard. I think she used to feel guilty about the way Robi's mother had treated that half of the family and tried to make amends. The girl is unmarried, by the way, and Nisha used to ask her over so that she could meet people, you know, in case someone

got interested in her. Robi too was fond of her, in his
own way. They had been playmates as children and that
friendship endured.'

'Did they make any settlement, finally?'

'I don't know, you'll have to ask Nisha, though it will be
very awkward for me if you tell her I briefed you.'

'Is there anything else you'd like to tell me about the family?'

The doctor took a deep breath. 'Not really.'

Was it his imagination, or was the doctor looking nervous?
When Bikram passed on to the next question there was
a palpable slackening of tension in him.

'Any trouble with the servants?'

'As for that, you will have to ask Nisha. I can't really
be expected to know what she said to the dhobi and how
she talks to her cook.' The doctor leaned back and looked
at his watch.

Bikram pretended not to notice his manner. 'But there
is one servant who was very close to Robi Bose, a kind of Man
Friday, Buro, I think, was his name. Do you think he could
have had anything to do with the death?'

'You've done your homework well, I see. You know the name
too—Buro! I'm impressed.' The doctor shrugged his shoulders.
'It could have been him, of course. Servants are the usual
suspects. Tricky creatures, hanging around the house, learning
about everything. Has anything been stolen?'

'Not that night, no.'

Bikram waited for the obvious query, but none came. The
doctor looked at his watch again. So he knows about the
money being stolen before that, thought Bikram. Possibly he
may have advised Nisha Bose to take the help of the police. He
probably knows about my visit too. Which means he's still her
lover. He wondered idly where they met to make love. The
doctor must have a flat tucked away somewhere! The wife must

know, as all wives usually do. And the doctor must know loads more about Nisha Bose than he had let on.

'One last question. Did they have any children?'

'Of course not, you know that.'

'But you didn't advise them any treatment?'

'Of course I did. I even fixed them an appointment with a specialist years ago, that's how I got to know them so well.' He paused, and then said, 'It's been hard for her, very hard. No children, and then Robi's attack, and now this!'

Sensing there was nothing more to be got out of him, Bikram rose and took his leave.

'You can give me your phone number. I'll let you know if I remember anything else. Keep me posted on what's happening.'

They walked to the door together. 'Good to see you, Mr Chatterjee. It's good to see handsome and upright men like you in the force. I'll tell Toofan the next time I meet him how impressed I am with his men.'

He shook hands warmly, puckered his lips into a mischievous smile and waved gaily as the lift doors hummed close.

# 8

Robi Bose's death had hit the newspapers, travelled from front-page headlines to the Metropolitan section, led to speculations on police apathy and the breakdown of law and order, fuelled related articles on the changing role of domestic help in an era of globalization, and the need for police reform in twenty-first-century civil society, and finally dwindled to a few lines on the inside pages. During the first few days, Toofan Kumar had feverishly briefed the press on important leads, valuable clues and impending arrests. Because he was talkative and indiscreet the reporters loved him.

Every morning, Toofan Kumar reached for the morning paper and put it down some five minutes later, hysterical. He would then spend fifteen minutes hunting down Bikram, Ghosh and Chuni Sarkar and giving them a mouthful of the choicest. Ghosh grew sweatier and Chuni Sarkar drank an extra peg each night. Bikram became increasingly taciturn. He stood aloof during procession and demonstration duty, listened to complaints disinterestedly, abandoned raids and round-ups and took no notice of the fact that Mistry often came late to work.

The intervention of Prem Gupta, however, brought in the post-mortem report quickly enough. The report was as expected: Robi Bose, forty, male, suffering from cerebral thrombosis, dead, with diluted pupils, discoloured fingertips, no marks of ligature on the neck or injury elsewhere, but with congested lungs, stomach, liver and spleen. In short, Robi

Bose had died due to the effects of oral consumption of toxic substances. Though the complete report remained pending till the arrival of the full report on preserved viscera, there was no doubt that there was a large amount of painkillers and tranquillizers inside him, taken within a short time of alcohol consumption, that had caused nausea, vomiting, dizziness, drowsiness, coma and death. Whether he had consumed the stuff accidentally or with intent, and whether the intent was his own or someone else's was, of course, another matter.

The autopsy itself was a wholesale overturning of all the textbooks of pathology ever written. The morning of the autopsy, Bikram summoned one of his constables. 'Haldar, you are to accompany a corpse to the Katapukur morgue. I doubt if anyone from the family will turn up except the servants. No gossip, please.'

The constable's stomach rumbled. Morgue duty! Shit! Thank heavens he hadn't eaten!

'Here's money to buy some plastic cans for the entrails. Don't forget the salt. You might have to help make the salt solution for the organs yourself, so keep your mind on the job. This case is important.'

The constable shifted uneasily. How the hell was he to get the morgue attendants to work? Everyone knew that the doctor, supposedly in charge, did nothing except breeze in at the end, if at all, and sign the papers. What if the corpse-carriers—the doms as they are known in Bengali—refused?

Bikram looked at the constable's expression and smiled inwardly. Poor beggar, the guy still looked flummoxed. He put his hand into the bottom drawer of his table and drew out a parcel wrapped in a large government of West Bengal envelope that clinked mysteriously—liquor seized from gambling dens, saved for occasions such as this.

'Argue for a while before handing it out, and don't let them get at the whole thing before they finish the job.'

The constable smiled in relief. A whiff of whisky would bring the attendants running. He would give them a swig each, of course, or they would never begin cutting the corpse, and then distribute the rest once the viscera were safe in his possession. An enormous load was lifted off Haldar's mind. If the stuff was good, he might have a bit himself. Not on duty, of course, but conceal it in a PET bottle and savour it in the barracks at night. God knows he would need it too, just to get the smell of the morgue off him.

Haldar looked around him as Robi Bose was carried inside. Robi was lucky. The rest of the corpses—the ones from the slums and the suburbs, the unidentified ones from the construction sites and the railway tracks, with burnt faces and protruding tongues, ghastly eyes and swollen stomachs, dismembered limbs and lacerated chests, lay sprawled in cycle vans or open trucks.

'Not today, come tomorrow, can't do any more today, power cut, no generator.'

'Please, he's been dead for four days, I need to bury him and get back to work.' The young woman cried out in despair as the attendant pushed her away.

A thin man wearing a hanky knotted around his neck like a scarf sidled up to her. 'Psst! Five hundred bucks and I'll get it done.'

'I don't have so much.'

The woman was crying. Her sari was torn and she was wearing rubber sandals, the heels of which had been ground down to paper-like thinness. The sun was climbing higher in the sky and the smell was getting worse. A pack of dogs, waiting greedily, found a bloodstained shirt and began licking at it and fighting amongst themselves.

'Four hundred, then.'

The woman, still sobbing, shook her head. 'I have to pay the van driver and the cemetery and the boys who will accompany me. I don't have that much.'

'Sod off.' The thin man kicked at her husband's corpse, sprawled on a rickshaw, his knobby legs dangling stiffly from the side.

The woman, still sobbing, turned to Haldar and, seeing his uniform, said, 'Help me, make him see sense, I don't have that much money.'

Haldar felt his stomach lurch. 'Take a hundred and be done with it,' he said gruffly.

'And who are you to dictate my terms?' The thin man turned upon him insolently.

Haldar gently shook the bag he held till the bottles clinked. The man's face cleared. 'Oh ho,' he said softly. 'Whisky?'

Haldar nodded.

'Foreign?'

'Yes, but only if you get her husband done for a hundred rupees. And I can't give you all of it, just a plastic Pepsi bottle full, but it is solid stuff.' Haldar was a sensitive man and, in a moment, had willingly relinquished his share to help a widow with a four-day-old corpse.

The thin man nodded and the deal was sealed.

Meanwhile, Robi Bose was being dismembered inside. An unwilling doctor entered the room. The windows were shuttered, the room reeked to high heaven and rats skittered about on the floor. The doctor found Robi Bose sprawled on an aluminium tabletop with a naked bulb hanging over him. He slit him open and unceremoniously tipped out the lungs, the heart, the stomach, the intestines, the kidneys and the liver on to a trolley. Meanwhile, the morgue attendant, surreptitiously primed with the whisky sent by Bikram, took something resembling a small hammer and fiddled around Robi Bose's skull. Snap! The skull cracked open. The doctor bent forward peevishly and muttered something, then muttered some more, cast a quick look at Robi, or what was left of him, and then nodded his head. It was over. The morgue attendant took a huge needle and hastily trussed up the body again.

'Next,' said the doctor, with some effort, trying to achieve the impossible task of simultaneously holding his breath and speaking. Robi Bose was then unceremoniouly slid on to the floor. From there, he was pushed onward to the 'Out' gate. And thus life described a full circle: Robi Bose, member of country clubs, guest at Marriott's and Hilton's, user of Gucci and Armani, lay on the floor amidst the rats and the dogs, with only Haldar the constable waiting outside to deliver him home.

Bikram sat in his office two days later with Ghosh on one side and Chuni Sarkar on the other. All three looked unenthusiastically at the task ahead. These were difficult times. A gang of credit-card cheats was busy on the southern fringes of the city, posing as courier men and robbing unsuspecting housewives. Another gang, specializing in motorcycle thefts, was ravaging the business areas at midday. The municipal elections were half a year away which meant that politicians were busy inaugurating flyovers and community bathrooms, and much of the police force would be whizzing up and down with them. All they needed was a first-class juicy homicide.

'I suppose we'll have to work out a scheme now,' said Bikram gloomily.

No one said anything. Ghosh scrabbled at his belt and Chuni Sarkar's shoulders drooped. The clock chimed eleven in silvery tones.

Bikram reached out for the original complaint, filed on the

night of 9 April at 0320 Hours, and read it through again. Then he read through Chuni Sarkar's report on the preliminary investigation made on the night of the death, including the finding of the empty medicine strips in the rubbish bin. He pushed the file towards the other two and pushed his own chair back, looked up unhappily at the ceiling, and closed his eyes. There was a rustle of paper as Chuni Sarkar and Ghosh found things to do.

Finally, Ghosh cleared his throat. 'Since no suicide note was found there, he might have killed himself without writing one.'

'That would serve our purpose very well, I know, but there's the matter of the party,' said Bikram dourly. 'His wife insisted he had been in high spirits that evening, especially that evening.'

'Five or six guests, if I remember correctly,' said Chuni Sarkar.

'Did the servants say whether anything about the party was unusual?' asked Bikram.

'Not a hope, Sir! Apparently they have a party a week, and this was no different from any other.'

'Who cooked the food?'

'Some of the snacks had been done at home and some came from outside. The main meal had been done by the maid and that jack-of-all-trades servant they have, Buro.'

'And yet nothing was stolen,' said Ghosh. 'So, if the servants did it, why kill him unnecessarily, and that, too, a man who would have died any day.'

'But didn't,' said Bikram. 'He was proving amazingly resilient.'

'They are like that, too,' said Ghosh darkly. 'The ones who are confined to bed and are expected to burn out any day just keep going on and on.'

Chuni Sarkar said, 'There was a cousin there that night,

his paternal uncle's daughter, along with her father and mother. She had been to see him a few days before and they had had an argument. Property matters, I think.'

'What is she like?' asked Bikram. Members of that family could only mean trouble.

'Very unlike the dead man. Poor relations. They didn't have their own car and had borrowed one from a neighbour. The old man was getting very restless about the car and made a phone call to the neighbour apologizing for the delay in sending it back. Kept saying police case, police case, over and over again on the phone.'

Bikram dimly remembered a thin man and a frumpy middle-aged woman in one of the rooms, sitting with worried expressions. He had spent most of his time with Dr Pyne and Chopra in the dead man's bedroom and had left the visitors to Chuni Sarkar.

'Anyone else?'

'That terrible woman called Nikku something who kept threatening us. Once you came, she stopped bothering us of course but, before that, it seemed as if every IPS officer in Calcutta was her friend.'

Bikram winced slightly as he remembered how Nikki Kumar had swooped down on him when he entered the house that night. He also remembered how Chuni Sarkar had hovered around in great excitement at such a scoop. Bikram had shaken Nikki off with great rudeness but she had continued to trail him. She was no doubt responsible for the phone call he received the following day.

'I'll talk to her myself,' he added hastily, not wanting Chuni Sarkar to savour details of his personal life. 'Ghosh, you had better interrogate the cousin and her family too.'

'What about Sudip Pyne?' asked Chuni Sarkar.

'What about him?'

'Shouldn't we talk to him? Check to see if he had known the family earlier? Did he have some personal interest in the case? Or a personal grudge? This insistence on an autopsy could be Pyne getting back at them.'

'He wouldn't draw attention to his own crime if he had committed it,' said Ghosh.

'You never know,' said Chuni Sarkar obstinately. 'I find it difficult to believe in a conscientious doctor.'

'Just as most people find it difficult to believe in uncorrupted policemen,' Ghosh said pointedly.

'I think it's time to begin work before we're assigned another demonstration to break up,' interposed Bikram smoothly.

After they left, Bikram fiddled with the paperweight, studied his nails, drew a monster head on a memo pad and then reached for the phone. He had to wait for a while before being connected. A personal assistant with a quavering voice asked him to hold on and played Mozart while on hold. Then the assistant came back and asked him to hold for some more time before Toofan Kumar's gruff voice came on. 'Tell me.'

'The post-mortem reports have come through, Sir.' Bikram outlined what it said.

'This is such a big mess,' Toofan Kumar said, as if Bikram had personally carried out the poisoning.

'Sir.' For lack of a fitting reply, that was all Bikram could manage.

'Have you gone to the house or have you left that for me to do?' shouted Toofan.

'I am going now.'

'You've been there before, you knew the woman. She is a friend of that girl of yours, isn't she? How could you agree to this investigation?'

Bikram said nothing and waited. Toofan Kumar was one of the few who succeeded in disturbing his carefully cultivated composure. And every time he said 'your girl' he made Shona sound cheap. Bikram's head swam in rage.

'Chuni's the officer-in-charge at the thana, isn't he?'

'Yes.'

'Tell him to report in two hours.'

'Sir.'

'Make some arrests by the end of the day.'

'I'll try.'

'You'd better. I'm going to be facing the reporters in the evening and I need something to say to them. And be careful with Nisha Bose. I don't want to hear that you've been unnecessarily harassing her.'

It was late noon when he reached Robi Bose's house. The heat was unbearable and the air heavy with fumes from the maddening traffic. As they reached the porch, though, the noise dropped away and the air felt cleaner. The house seemed to be slumbering in the noon haze. Bikram paused near the steps and looked around him. He was standing under an old-fashioned porch whose slanting top, once probably done in wood, was now a sheet of white asbestos. He remembered the air conditioning inside which meant that there were double windows, the wooden ones outside and the new glass panes inside. A creeper climbed picturesquely over the drawing room window and waved tendrils of yellow flowers in the hot noon breeze.

Inside, it was cool, as cool as on the day of his first visit. Once again, Bikram was led into the drawing room but, this time, he was permitted to sit on the satin sofa. The impassive maid who opened the door waited for a moment, as if ready for questioning. Wait till Ghosh gets to you, thought Bikram. He asked for Nisha Bose.

Nisha glided into the room. She was wearing an embroidered

cotton salwar kameez. Her hair had been gathered in a loose ponytail and her face was scrubbed clean of make-up. A faint smell of flowers came from her. She had tried her best to look subdued, and to present a picture of calm acceptance, but it was obvious that death had no place in her existence. As Bikram rose, he wondered whether she was aware of the palpable feeling of relief that she was exuding.

As if she had read his mind, she said, 'I won't pretend to be the grieving widow, Mr Chatterjee, at least not before you.' And after a pause, 'But I didn't kill him. It would be too obvious, don't you think?' She had been given a copy of the autopsy in the morning.

'Why were you resisting the post-mortem then?'

'Resisting?' Her eyes widened in challenge. 'Put yourself in my place, Mr Chatterjee. My husband had been as good as dead once before, and now, there he was, as stiff and unmoving as the first time. Obviously I assumed he had had a stroke. The doctors had told me to be careful and be prepared for any mishap. When that chit of a boy came in and started acting funny, I thought he was making a mistake because he knew nothing about Robi's medical history. Besides, who wants to have policemen crawling about the house? You're different, but the rest are not. Nasty, bumbling, fat creatures, frightening servants and getting in the way, tramping around the house and spoiling the carpets. They would have asked for bribes, too, I'm sure. Oh, I know you hate me for saying all this but I just had to get it out!' She took a deep breath. 'There, it's finished. Buro told me about the post-mortem and how the morgue works. Oh, it's terrible, what you are doing to me!'

Her hands were working on the sofa, plucking at the piping, elegant manicured fingers which were now shaking under some intense emotion. Bikram cleared his throat and said, 'And the bedcover?'

'What about it?'

'The doctor claims that it had been changed.'

Nisha shrugged. 'I can stand here till the world ends, protesting my innocence, but you have made up your mind, anyway.'

Bikram figured nothing much would come out of further discussion and decided to leave the matter there. They had searched for the bedcover on the fateful night and hadn't found it anywhere. It was unlikely they would ever find it.

He changed the subject. 'How long had your husband been ill?'

'It would be five years this year.'

'What happened to him?'

She began in a monotone, in the manner of a rehearsed speech. 'His career had just reached its peak. He had changed three jobs and was working in a German firm that paid him excellently. We had been cautious with money till then but Robi told me not to scrimp any longer. Enjoy yourself, he said.'

'What kind of a job was it?'

'Sales, mainly,' said Nisha vaguely. 'He used to travel a lot. Sometimes he would come in the morning and take the evening flight out. But he always squeezed in time to see me and ask how I was.' As she spoke, her voice had lost some of its tonelessness. It was difficult for Nisha Bose to be lifeless for long. 'It was Diwali. He had cancelled a trip to be at home. We had eaten out for three nights running. You know how it is, meeting friends, joining up in bars, going on to someone's home. Robi had blood pressure problems and was on medication, but he always complained that the medicines made him use the loo too often and he felt he looked like an old man. He didn't tell me anything, but I think he skipped doses, or maybe he was too tipsy to remember, or maybe we were just on a high and felt invincible and that nothing could go wrong with us.' She paused, as if to remember, but the whole exercise was beginning to feel like it was for effect. She was looking at the window and presented her perfect profile to him.

'What happens to perfect couples?' Nisha turned around and looked Bikram in the eye. 'What do you do when you've spent years working for something and it all goes for a toss? You see your husband lying on the bathroom floor, for god knows how long, twitching a little now and then, while the garden outside is all lit up with diyas and candles. I thought he was dead. Fortunately, one of our friends is a doctor and he rushed him to the hospital. I still thought he was dead. But twenty-four hours passed and forty-eight and seventy-two, and then they said he would live but in a wheelchair.

'I've been a good wife ever since. At first, his friends would fill the house and it was like Diwali again. As soon as he was better he would pretend to do some work and the office would dutifully give him something to chew on. Then the friends dropped away and his office settled his compensation and everyone went back to their own lives . . . but ours changed forever.'

Bikram looked down at his cell phone. He had put it into silent mode and it had been vibrating every few minutes. He wished he had brought someone else along with him. He cleared his throat and asked about money. She said that with the compensation, as well as their investments, they were comfortable. She herself had gone into some small businesses—partnerships with one or two close friends that gave some returns. 'We have no children and lived for ourselves,' she finished. 'In a sense, that spoilt us more. We lived from day to day.'

She leaned forward to pick up an imaginary something from the carpet and her ponytail fell over her shoulder. Even underneath her dress, Bikram was made aware of her fair throat and full breasts.

He asked her about the house and, all at once, a subtle change came over the conversation. The impassioned unburdening of the heart gave way to a sudden restraint. 'I suppose it's Tara. What's she been saying?'

'I want your version.' Bikram hoped she wouldn't realize he had no idea about either Tara or her accusations.

'What Robi did was stupid. I told him to leave it to me but he went ahead . . .'

He listened intently to Nisha's account of the spat between her husband and her sister-in-law. He listened without comment when he asked about the servants and she reiterated their devotion to her. He was unaware that he had made as strong an impression on Nisha Bose as she had on him, because men either fidgeted, tongue-tied, in her presence or became garrulous and awkward; few listened keenly with deep grey eyes. Before he left, he asked about the stolen money.

She seemed anxious to play it down. 'It must have been a mistake. I probably left it lying around and then put it back absent-mindedly.'

'You forgot repeatedly, over a month or so?'

'It sounds absurd and I know you think it suspicious but I honestly forget such things. I just mentioned at a party that I must be getting old, I misplace money and Toofan jumped to help. I thought he would forget but then you came along and I was too embarrassed to say the whole thing was just party chit-chat and not to be taken seriously. You do understand, don't you? I mean, you've worked so long with Toofan, you know him.'

She had changed the subject by establishing a cosy understanding between them and excluded Toofan Kumar from this linkage. She had been at Nikki's party and had researched Bikram well, including his relations with his superiors.

'What do you think happened to your husband?'

'It was a mistake, what else?'

'Someone fed your husband a lethal dose of high-potency painkillers and sleeping pills by mistake?'

'Do you think it's one of the servants? If so, where would he get it?' She hesitated, knowing that whatever she said would go against her household. 'He may have taken it himself, I suppose.'

'But he seemed to enjoy partying, meeting people, forgetting his illness in the laughter and music of a full room, and he had enjoyed himself that evening. That's what you told my men.'

'That's right.'

'Was he suicidal or depressed?'

'Robi? My god! He was so scared of dying, he has made me check his blood pressure twice daily for two years!'

Bikram ran into Ghosh as he was leaving the house. Ghosh's arm was wrapped in a crepe bandage, his collar was limp with sweat and there were patches under his armpits. On seeing him Nisha resumed her icy manner. All three stood uncomfortably on the porch. Ghosh proposed that the servants be interrogated at the police station. Nisha replied in glacial tones that she couldn't spare all at the same time and the questioning had better take place in the house. Ghosh, looking angrier by the minute, demurred. Sensing a potentially explosive situation, Bikram decided to leave. Ghosh was a veteran at dealing with social sophisticates and would eventually get what he wanted.

He left with a sense of relief. The house and its mistress had a cloying femininity about them which was suffocating. In the car, Bikram settled his missed calls. The evening rush was on and the traffic lights seemed permanently red. Squat Ambassadors were stuck alongside purring Hondas and,

beside them belched his battered Sumo. Many of the cars had
stickers lettered on the front and back denoting the owners'
rank and importance and, by extension, the car's immunity
from traffic rules. Bikram counted five stickers announcing
members of the press, a sessions court judge, the office of the
accountant general, the ministry of defence and his own police.
Then he gave it up and closed his eyes. He must have been
dozing. When he awoke something was buzzing near his
chest. For a second he wondered if he was having a heart attack,
and then realized it was his cell phone on vibrate mode. All
this talk of heart attack and cerebral strokes had clearly seeped
into his subconscious.

'Bikram?'

It was Prem Gupta.

'Sir!'

'If you're not busy, nip down to the airport police station.
They've just nabbed a man who might be part of that fake-
currency gang. Take a look at him.'

It would be a welcome change to go back to the world of
regular crime. Bikram happily redirected Mistry towards the
other end of town.

The scene at the airport police station was melancholy as
only a police station can be. Ceiling fans ground away with
mournful squeaks above piles of abandoned files. A medley of
visitors and complainants moved between various tables and
negotiated different kinds of rudeness. There were law-abiding
citizens who had come to report thefts of purses and cell phones.
The regulars—either the officers' hangers-on, goons from the
local political parties or junior lawyers looking for bail cases to
pick up—looked aggressive and well settled, as if this were
a home away from home. Needless to say, it was hot and dusty.

Chairs screeched back and there was a flurry of khaki and
batons. Bikram picked his way daintily through salutes. The

police station had been considerably enlivened by the arrival of two pickpockets rescued from a mob bent on stoning them to death, a vagrant caught chasing heroin outside a residential building and a boy of about twenty who stood with tears streaming down his face. The boy was being bullied by an assistant sub-inspector who had slapped him six times already and had stopped to have his tea. On seeing Bikram, the sub-inspector hastily put down his cup and aimed two more blows at the slobbering boy.

'Now tell us again, why did you not stop when you saw the VIP pilot car and the convoy behind?'

The boy fell at his feet and grabbed the sub-inspector's shoes. 'Let me go, Sir, it was a mistake, I had a bet with my friend and it was only a joke . . .'

The officer-in-charge at the police station hurried out of his room, nearly tripping over the pickpocket who had been tied with ropes to the leg of a nearby table. He had a bustling, cheerful manner, like a kindly uncle welcoming guests to his home. 'I've got a room ready for you, Sir,' he lied.

He shouted to a constable who entered with another beggar tied with a rope. 'Hey there, get those guys out from the room at the back, move it, quick. DSP sahib will conduct an interrogation there.'

The constable looked around him helplessly and, finding an empty chair nearby, tied the beggar to the chair leg and scurried off.

Ten years of policing had desensitized Bikram too to a great extent, but a vestige of some squeamishness remained. He stopped before the lock-up where the heroin addict was sliding into cold turkey. His face was contorted in a terrible grimace as his body shook in great spasms, a gust of agony lived out in a private world where nothing else existed.

'What can we do, Sir, it gets worse day by day.' The

officer-in-charge looked disgustedly at the addict. 'We had to bring him in here. He was shooting up in front of the house of a high court judge and the judge saw him.'

'Have you made the necessary arrangements?' Bikram asked softly.

'Yes, it should be here by now, though once these guys figure out they can get stuff here for free, god knows how many more will come crowding in.'

The back room had by now been emptied of five constables grinding tobacco in their hands. They stood in a row, clicking and saluting. A squat dark man sat on a broken bench. He, too, had the standard rope around his middle, but looked calm and self-possessed. Bikram signalled the accompanying constables out of the room, sat on a crimson coloured plastic chair and looked around. He first untied the man, then located a pen and a piece of paper. He began.

'Name?'

'Montu Mondol.'

'Age?'

'Thirty-four.'

'Residence?'

'Borojaguli, district Nadia.'

'Family?'

'Father, mother, three sisters, and one brother studying in class eleven.'

'Married?'

Hesitation, then, 'Yes.'

'Children?'

'One son.'

'Goes to school?'

'He's studying in class two.'

'How long have you been in this business?'

Silence.

'You were caught with four bundles of five-hundred rupee notes. How do you explain all that cash?'

'I had borrowed the money for my mother-in-law who needs to undergo an operation.'

'Whom did you borrow it from?'

'A man in the adjoining village who lends out money.'

'What is this man's contact number and address?'

'I have forgotten.'

'Then how will you ever return him the money?'

Silence.

'Do you know that two of the bundles had false notes?'

'No.'

'In which hospital is your mother-in-law admitted?'

'A nursing home.'

'Name?'

'Moonlight Nursing Home, near Kidderpore.'

'Who is her doctor?'

'She hasn't been admitted yet.'

'Where is she right now?'

'At home.'

'Then why did you rent a room in the Ekbalpore area?'

Silence. At this point, the officer-in-charge bustled in, a bottle of Coke in hand.

'Can you get us another one?' Bikram asked.

'Yes, Sir.' The officer-in-charge looked puzzled but took care not to ask any questions. Bikram was known for his quicksilver moods. 'Is there anything else you want, Sir?'

'Thanks, everything is in order.'

The officer-in-charge tried hard not to take a peek at the sheet of paper before Bikram but his eyes strayed there nevertheless. He indicated the accused with his head. 'Very stubborn, this one. Took a shot at him in the morning but he's difficult.' The second Coke arrived in the meantime, borne by a constable.

'Thank you,' said Bikram to the officer-in-charge coldly. The man took the hint and scuttled out of the room.

'Have this.' The man took the bottle and sat with it, the dark colour of the Coke blending with his dark trousers and black T-shirt. But his hands were trembling.

Bikram drank from his bottle and put it down on the floor. 'You must be thirsty, drink,' he said.

The man sat still, the bottle in his hands.

Bikram stifled a yawn. He marvelled at the situation. Montu Mondol, at thirty-four, had lived a fuller life than he had. Certainly, he had a son to bear the Mondol name. If he, Bikram, were to die, whom would Ghosh go to with the flowers and the incense? Bikram looked at the rough cement floor and felt a sudden and illogical desire to rush out of the room and meet Shona. Are you ready to marry me on the first available date? He knew what Shona would say, and how she would look while saying it. Would their son look like him or like Shona? He shook these thoughts off and began again. 'Which class did you say your son was in?'

'Class two.'

'How does he address you?'

Silence.

'Does he call you Baba, or Abbu, or Papa or what?'

Montu Mondol was too surprised at this line of interrogation to maintain his sullen speechlessness. The bottle quivered in his hands and he looked up at Bikram. 'He calls me Bapi.'

'Does he know that his father is a smuggler? How do you think he would feel if he were to see you now, with that rope across your waist, sitting at my feet? Is this the Bapi who takes him out during pujas and buys him toys? Is this the man who buys him new clothes and comes back from the city with gifts?'

For just one minute the gambit did not seem to be working. Then, the man gurgled. Bikram, intently drawing two stick figures climbing up hills, slackened and breathed easy. Pleased

with himself, he drew a brilliant sun over the hills and signed
off with a relish, then looked up at the man who had put the
bottle down and had buried his face in his hands. Bikram got
up, went across to the bench, picked up the drink and gently
touched the man on the shoulder.

He left the police station forty-five minutes later with his
mission partially accomplished. This time, the sheet of paper
in his hand was full of names and addresses. Montu Mondol
had revealed some information, sketchy at best. He had two
wives, one in India, the other in Bangladesh. Wife number
two had a cousin who had introduced him to the fake-currency
racket as a courier. Bundles of fake Indian money were made
into neat packets in Bangladesh and stashed under a pile of
clothes in a kitbag. Montu carried the bag from Bangladesh
into India, crossing the border quietly at strategic places
where it was unmanned, slipping through paddy fields and
bamboo groves. In Calcutta, he handed the bag over to other
men, meeting them in seedy hotels where he received payment
for his work. Where did they make it? He didn't know,
but heard it came from Thailand and beyond. Who headed
this business? Montu didn't know, because he had never
met anyone else, save for his brother-in-law and another
man, Sheikh Hassan, also known as Apple Hassan, the guy
to whom he gave the packet here in Calcutta. He had
a flourishing trade in garment manufacturing. It was said that
he had bars and restaurants also and was lately diversifying
into producing movies.

And yes, the group for which he worked was known as the
Dhoor Syndicate. Anything else? Well, lately, there had been
a packet or two from Calcutta to Bangladesh which had carried
medicines, for the brother-in-law's family. He had been given
orders not to open the packet but to deliver it straight away,
but once, over a bumpy stretch of road, the packet had clinked

a bit, and Montu had known there was a bottle in it. Apple Hassan had a sari business here and traded with some Marwari traders of central Calcutta in Dhakai and Tangail saris. Montu knew, because he had asked for a sari once for his first wife, to gift her for the pujas, but Apple Hassan had refused to lower the price even a little.

As Bikram rose to leave, he smiled at Montu. 'I don't know why you're keeping information from me. It is actually quite silly. We could have struck a deal, you know. I would have booked you under some of the easier sections of the penal code, you would have got bail but on condition that you feed us information now and then. Now, what I'll do is frame heavier, non-bailable charges against you and keep you out of circulation for a long while. Really bad for your business, as far as I can tell.'

Montu sat biting his nails.

'And you haven't told me who you really are—carrier, fixer, contact, eliminator, money launderer or a bit of everything.' Montu never opened his mouth to speak.

'Well, take your time. If you want to speak to me, just tell the officer-in-charge.'

They never could be rushed, these people. Everyone needs time to mull things over and these men would do so in the privacy of the lock-up.

It was dark outside. Glowing billboards lighted the stream of evening traffic. Bikram decided to end the day with the Robi Bose case. He wondered, idly, whom he should take along. Ghosh was following up on a case and Chuni Sarkar was depressing company, so he decided on Sheena Sen. He didn't like Sheena Sen much, she was far too talkative, but there were very few lady officers to choose from. At least Sheena, unlike the others, did not try to flirt with him!

Bikram's intention today was to interrogate the cousin who

had been at the Boses' on the night of the death. He expected tears and drama, and Sheena would come handy in controlling any such situation. From experience he knew that a woman suspect should never be interrogated unless there was a policewoman present, just as he had learnt that no suspect should be clubbed on the lower back, especially near the kidneys. These weren't matters of delicacy or discretion but simple lessons of survival.

These Boses lived in a squalid two-storeyed house in the older part of the city. Bikram and Sheena went up a dark staircase and were shown into a drawing room. There was a sofa that seated two, two single chairs and a divan. Smells of cooking filled the room and mingled with the smell of burning incense. A pressure cooker whistled. Sheena Sen perched herself on the divan, looking rather pleased with herself at having been included in the investigation. There was rustling and shushing in the next room. Bikram saw, all at once, in this room, a reflection of the life he had once lived. He could almost see his father standing in the middle of the room, surrounded by books, preaching the benefits of plain living and high thinking.

Bimal Bose came in. Bikram stood up, extending a common courtesy. Bimal seemed taken aback. His face reflected the fear most people have of the law, and the fear manifested itself in bluster. 'I know why you're here,' Bimal Bose began without preliminaries. 'Nisha told me about the post-mortem report. There must be a mistake.'

Bikram said nothing.

'Try and understand. He was ill and we all knew he wasn't going to last long. It was obviously a heart attack. They must have mixed up cases and got it all wrong. Doctors nowadays!'

'Suppose they had been careful and the report was correct?' asked Bikram mildly.

'Impossible! Don't you ever read the newspapers? Rats nibble on corpses at the morgue, bodies get mixed up and policemen take bribes to fudge reports . . .' Bimal Bose stopped himself, but not in time. 'Well, anyway, I don't believe it.'

A timid woman entered the room and stood near the door. 'You mustn't mind him. He gets upset easily,' she ventured tentatively. And, addressing Bimal, said, 'The police have their duty to perform.'

'Don't talk about things you don't understand,' he snapped.

'We'd like to speak to her too,' Bikram smoothly interjected. 'My colleague will ask her a few things, just to get a better picture.' He added, seeing the scowl on Bimal Bose's face, that the questioning could be done at the house rather than at the thana.

Sheena Sen, eager to prove herself, immediately took over. Her manner became brusque and businesslike and was now so much in contrast to her playful appearance that Bimal Bose was taken aback.

When they had left Bikram began in what he hoped was a suitably detective-like manner. The last domestic tragedy he had investigated had been more than a year ago. It actually felt odd to talk to someone with no known history of crime.

'When was the last time you saw your nephew?'

'Only the other day.'

'When was that?'

'Oh, about fifteen days ago, or it could have been a month.'

'Did he come here or did you go to his house?'

'He wouldn't come here! How could he, being in a wheelchair? I went to see him, obviously.'

'Did he never go out of the house?'

'Never.'

Bikram thought about Robi Bose at Nikki Kumar's party and wondered what Bimal Bose would say if he informed him of this fact.

'What was he like when you saw him the last time?'

'His usual self, patient and resilient. He was laughing and joking all along even though Buro was late in attending to him. How he loved that rascal! I often told him that Buro was too slack but he would never agree. If you ask me, it was Buro who killed him.'

'Assuming he was murdered,' said Bikram. 'According to what you just said about the reports being mixed up, he might just have had another stroke.'

'That's for you to find out,' said Bimal Bose gruffly.

'Did he ever talk about having enemies? Or of grudges against him?'

'Never. He was loved by all. He had been endearing right from childhood. Just like his mother, well behaved and beautifully brought up. When he went to America to study he would always return with presents for all of us. Table mats and scented soap, and a lovely travelling clock once.'

'And his wife, she looked after him well?'

'Of course she did. Even after he had his stroke Nisha was the perfect wife. Got him the best doctors and all the expensive medicines. They even imported some from abroad. Nisha was always worried about him. She told me once that expenses were mounting and she would have to think of getting a job in order to make ends meet. I told her never to do that. We would sit together and think of something, I said. God will help us. She burst into tears and said that God had probably deserted her. You are all that we have now, she said. Poor thing! So lonely and frightened in that big house!'

They fell silent for a moment. Bikram pictured Nisha Bose, tears rolling picturesquely down her cheeks, unseeing eyes staring out at the garden outside, pouring her heart out to Bimal Bose. There must have been a reason for the act she put on but would it have any bearing on the death of her husband? He detested sentimentality and felt weary at the thought of having to sift through masses of tangled emotions to solve a homicide.

'Buro, Robi Bose's attendant, told us that your daughter had a quarrel with Robi Bose the last time she was with him. The attendant said that your daughter shouted at and abused his master and at one point she even threatened him.'

'That is impossible. Buro would never say such a thing. Your men have heard it all wrong.'

'And what if I say Buro reported all this to me?'

'Then I would say that you have misunderstood him,' said Bimal Bose smoothly.

'When can we see your daughter?' Bikram asked him.

Bimal Bose's face darkened.

'Why do you need to see her?'

'Because she happens to have been the last visitor Robi Bose had before he died. I think we made it quite plain that we want to meet all the members of the family together.'

'Your men spoke to her the night Robi died. I see no reason to harass her again.'

The word harass had an odd effect on Bikram. Over time he had grown used to having routine police procedure dubbed as harassment and would probably have not reacted at all. But it had been a long day, he had been assigned another raid tomorrow and his cell phone was ringing maddeningly every few minutes. He got up to leave. 'Ask your daughter to report to the police station for questioning at twelve o'clock tomorrow,' he said. 'You may accompany her if you wish but we'd like to question her alone.'

'It's Friday. She has to report for her tutorial,' said Bimal

Bose hurriedly. 'They pay her according to each lesson. She can't afford to miss it this week.'

Bikram found Sheena's number on his phone and called her. 'Where are you?'

'In a room on the rooftop,' she said. 'It's the daughter's room. I've nearly finished.'

Bimal Bose was now pleading. 'It's not very far. She'll be here in ten minutes. I'm calling her now. It's better you meet her here. Please . . .' His voice climbed to a shrill bleat.

Bikram went up the stairs two steps at a time. He paused as he entered the daughter's room. He always felt squeamish about the task, as if he were a voyeur. Why had Sheena been led into an unmarried girl's bedroom? A glance inside told him why. It was different from the rest of the house. It was the room of a girl who was delicate and sensitive and who had done her best to create a world beyond the bleakness of the rest of the house. It was small, about twelve feet by ten feet. Into this space the girl had poured in as much of her personality as inherited, rickety, ancestral furniture and up-to-fifty-per-cent seasonal discounts would allow. The walls were lined with an assortment of framed prints. There was Monet's *Water Lilies* alongside Renoir's self-portrait. There were calendar reproductions of Chunar Fort and old Banaras. There were postcards of hibiscus and geraniums stuck with glue on the door leading to the bathroom. There was an old birthday card placed on the television. A money plant in a brilliant blue vase stood on the study table. Elsewhere, there were a small bed, a teakwood bedside table with drawers, a large old wooden cupboard with graceful fluting on the edges. One of the windows in the corner stood closed, the edges masqueraded as a bookshelf lined with books stacked in narrow shaky columns. Beside the bed and along the walls stood two large windows out of which could be seen a higgledy-piggledy smudge of rooftops and clothes lines and cable TV wires and dusty potted plants. It was probably the most presentable room in the house, and Bimal Bose's wife, mindful of guests, even if they were policemen and policewomen, had led them here.

Sheena Sen was sitting on an old rattan chair. Bimal Bose's wife sat on the bed, a faded woman plucking unhappily at the bedspread. Her hunted eyes strayed over Bikram's shoulder to the door behind.

'What do you think happened?' he asked.

Her eyes darted to the door again. Heavy breathing and the smell of coconut hair oil announced Bimal Bose behind him.

'I don't know,' she said. 'Robi was a good boy. I can't imagine anything like this happening in our family. Perhaps it was suicide. Like the death of their aunt, so many years ago.'

'Roma's death has nothing to do with this. That was forty years ago. What's got into you?' Bimal Bose was back to his customary bluster.

'I'm sorry. . . I didn't realize . . . I shouldn't have brought it up.'

Bimal Bose turned to Bikram. 'Roma was my sister. Married off early but her husband died a year later of typhoid. Her in-laws made her life miserable so she returned to us. No children. Hanged herself one morning.'

'In which room?' asked Bikram on a sudden inspiration.

'The same one in which Robi died,' broke in Bimal Bose's wife before he could stop her. 'I always told Nisha that was an unlucky room but she would laugh. Said she could change everyone and anything, even ill luck.'

'Now that Robi is dead, what happens to the house?' asked Bikram.

Bimal Bose's face became wary. 'I don't know,' he said shortly.

'But you must have some idea,' pursued Bikram. 'After all, your nephew had been ill for quite some time. It had been touch and go for five years, hadn't it?'

'We're still in mourning. The funeral rites are yet to be finished. We aren't very well off but we know our duties. We haven't thought about property matters yet.'

The hostility in the room was overpowering and Bikram could feel great waves of it pouring over him and Sheena Sen. 'Twelve o'clock tomorrow,' said Bikram, ignoring another round of protests from Bimal Bose. Then he turned to leave. There was nothing more to be had from this pair.

'What did she say?' he asked Sheena Sen when they were back in the car again. A clot of maidservants had formed around the car, pretending to discuss shopping lists but keeping their eyes on Mistry and Lalbahadur.

'There was some kind of negotiation going on between Robi and Bimal Bose. Robi was buying a flat for them somewhere, in exchange for sole control over the ancestral house. The daughter, Tara, was resisting the settlement and said that they would be cheated if they went ahead. The old lady claims not to know anything more than that.'

'What did she have to say about the death?'

'She too feels it was some kind of accident, if he died of drug overdose. Says that Robi was getting better and wouldn't have killed himself. The boys in our family are strong-minded and have a will to live, she said, they wouldn't do stupid things like suicide.'

'Did she say anything about the servants?'

'Not much, she doesn't seem to know how many there are, or what they do. I don't think she went to Robi Bose's house too often. She said it was her daughter who went there sometimes and kept him company. I felt very sorry for her, you know. She kept saying how pretty her daughter was and how it was a shame that she hadn't been married off, and now that she was involved in a police case, the girl would probably stay unmarried all her life. Kept pleading with us to keep her name out of the papers. I couldn't see any picture of the girl, but the room looked nice enough, didn't it?'

Sheena Sen had resumed her perky manner which Bikram invariably found annoying. 'If you don't mind, I'd like to get off at my house,' said Bikram stonily. 'Mistry will drop you off wherever you want to go.'

# 9

Eleven a.m., and Tollygunge police station was at its worst. A typist bashed away at a battered machine in a corner and a burly man shouted out duty rosters to groups of sleepy young constables who had just joined the force and were being relentlessly pushed from one picket to another. Other constables came and went, carrying their lunches and drinking water in dirty plastic bottles. The tea boy had begun his rounds and the day's criminals, who would be sent to the court for proceedings, were being led out from stinking lock-ups. Both criminals and police guards paused to leer at Tara who, in her carefully chosen clothes, looked utterly out of place. Her father was beside her, fussing, as ever, fear coming through, once again, as bravado. Tara looked around for Bikram and her heart began to beat. It had been this way ever since the party at Nikki Kumar's when she had first seen him. Thoughts of Bikram had taken hold of her and ruled her mind.

This particular morning, mixed feelings filled Tara. She eagerly looked forward to seeing Bikram but the thought of the interrogation filled her with unease. Since Nikki Kumar's party, Tara had been engulfed by a range of emotions. She was filled with an intense jealousy of Nisha and Robi. Then the cousins had had another meeting which, too, ended in disaster, and then, Robi had died, filling Tara with both a sense of vindication and guilt. Here she was today, at a police station, presumably to be interrogated, and all because of some stupid things she had said to Robi at one of their last meetings. And while Tara was fearful of what might happen at the police station, she was also wary of her other, unexamined, feelings. Perhaps these feelings caused her to dress carefully and look at herself in the mirror many times before they left.

'Mr Bikram Chatterjee asked us to come here,' Tara's father began. 'Please tell him we are here, my daughter doesn't want to be late for work.'

The duty officer ignored her father and looked Tara up and down before he replied. 'Who are you?'

'My name is Bimal Bose. Mr Chatterjee came to my house yesterday but couldn't meet my daughter, that's why we are here today.'

'At what time did he ask you to come?'

'At around twelve o'clock.'

'And what time is it now?'

'Well, we are a bit early, but well, we didn't want to be late . . .' Tara's father trailed off uncomfortably.

'Sit on that bench, and don't disturb me.'

Then the duty officer vanished into the room in which the additional officer-in-charge conducted his business. The additional officer was having a difficult conversation with a colleague over the phone. 'That's your area, not mine. Oh hell, I can't be saddled with all the bloody cases . . . one moment . . . what is it?' he asked the duty officer irritably.

'A young girl and her father want to talk to Chatterjee sir.'

'Who asked them to want such things?'

'DSP Bikram Chatterjee, Sir, at least that's what they say.'

'So send them to him! Why bother me?'

'He asked them to come here.'

'That is all I need!' The additional officer-in-charge mumbled something else into the phone and hung up before erupting in disbelief. 'He was here last evening and now you say he's going to be here again today.'

He frowned darkly at the duty officer. 'Any fresh General Diaries this morning?'

'Nothing much till now.'

'That's better. Send everyone away quietly; don't record anything as long as he's here in the thana, understand?' The DSP was known to be difficult about F.I.R.s. A complaint taken down in his presence could not be left to moulder away but had to be followed up with frenetic zeal. The duty officer understood. Grumbling to himself, the officer dialled Bikram's number and hoped bleakly that Bikram was at a briefing and had forgotten. For once, Bikram had. He had just got into office and was going through a mountain of correspondence when the phone rang. Oh hell, he thought, when the additional officer-in-charge wanted to know what was to be done with the two Boses. 'Put them in the room in which I was yesterday, I'm coming.' It took him half an hour to reach his destination. Tara and her father sat on hard wooden benches, waiting, as people went in and out. The atmosphere was saturated with an unspoken anxiety, the sort one encounters in doctors' chambers.

Tara knew at once that Bikram had arrived. Chairs scraped and heels clicked as a tall, clean-limbed man, wearing a pair of sunglasses and speaking into a cell phone, went into an inner room while another man trotted behind him. Tara's eyes devoured Bikram unashamedly; for she was sure he wouldn't know her or care if he did. In uniform, he looked heartbreakingly handsome. She closed her eyes and imprinted him on her mind.

They were called in almost at once. Tara rose with a lurching sensation in her stomach and her eyes almost filled with tears. To think that this man, of all others, was calling her in for an interrogation! Feeling gauche and stupid, she stumbled into the room after her father and sat down, her head lowered all the while that Bikram was talking on the phone. He had motioned them in and was scribbling something on a memo pad. Then he put down the phone and said, 'I'm sorry to have kept you waiting.'

Pulling out a very crumpled piece of paper he looked at it, then at Tara, then said to Tara's father, 'I suppose this is your daughter, whom we missed seeing last evening. I would like to ask her some questions about Robi Bose.'

'You have to hurry up,' said Bimal Bose sullenly. 'She'll be late for work.'

'Ah yes, Wisdom Press.' He consulted his notes again. 'What kind of work do you do there?'

'She's almost in charge of the whole office,' began her father. 'She goes through the books, does the . . .'

'I do the editing,' Tara interrupted. 'I put the whole thing into shape.' Her voice was low and controlled.

'Do you like your work?'

He was looking at her directly now and Tara found herself gripping her fingers. With something of an effort she said, 'Yes.'

'Which college are you from? What subjects did you study?'

Tara replied in a calm voice.

'So the things you studied in college help you in your work?'

'I suppose so.'

A short uncomfortable silence ensued. Bikram wondered if he should take a chance and speak to the girl alone. Bimal Bose was bristling with anger at being dragged to a police station like a common thief. Tara sat in a state of numb despair. Somewhere, a tiny part of her had hoped that Bikram would recognize her from earlier but that hope had been wholly extinguished.

'I know it must be painful for you, but could you please tell us about the last time you saw your cousin? I think you know by now that you were one of the last people to see him alive.'

'He was fine when I saw him.'

'At what time was that?'

'Around 10 p.m., I think.'

'You were in his room, I believe.'

'Yes, he asked me to come up with him.'

'And where were you before that?'

'Downstairs, with the other guests.'

'Do you often get invited to their house?'

'Yes.'

'For parties only, or at other times too?'

'Why should she go only for parties?' Bimal Bose could no longer contain himself. 'We were close to him, his dearest relations. She went all the time.'

'Why?'

'To give a sick man company, of course.'

'And what did he tell you this time?' Bikram did not bother to acknowledge Bimal Bose's interjections.

'Nothing much,' said Tara. 'He, he just said that he was very tired and that he didn't feel like eating much. A tray had been brought up for him. He asked me to move his medicine table close to him. Then he asked me to make him a glass of Horlicks.'

'Is that all he said?'

She hesitated for a fraction of a second. 'Yes, that's all he said.'

'Had he been drinking?'

'A little, yes.'

'I suppose he was not allowed to, because of his illness.'

'He shouldn't have, but he did all the same. But very carefully, and only if he was excited. And after a drink he'd say things like, I don't care what happens and a little alcohol can't kill me. But that day, he also said that whatever would be, would be, because everything was destiny.'

'Then what did he do?'

'He went to the bathroom, Buro helped him, and then came back and lay down.'

'Had the bed been made?'

Tara paused. 'I don't remember.'

She looked at him, and found herself looking straight into a pair of deep grey eyes. She held his gaze defiantly and, unconsciously, straightened her back and pulled her tummy in.

'Think, please,' he said. The eyes begged her to help him.

'It's all so hazy now, and I didn't pay much attention to the bed. But I think,' she wrinkled her brow in concentration, 'I think he kind of sat down heavily on the bed and then lay down. No, the bed hadn't been made. I think Buro pulled down the bedcover halfway and then draped it on him. The room was very cold because of the air conditioning. Buro was in a hurry to go back down.'

'And so, while Buro took him to the bathroom, you were alone in the room for a while?'

'A short while, yes.'

'Did anyone else come in?'

'No.'

'And the food, his dinner, was it lying covered or was the tray open?'

'It had a plastic cover.'

'And did you make his Horlicks with water or with milk?'

'Hot water. It was there in a flask by his bed.'

'And it was on the same table as the medicines? How long had the water being lying there unattended? Did anyone see you mix the Horlicks?'

There was silence again.

'Will you answer me, please?'

Tara looked at him again and, this time, the eyes that looked back at her seemed to be hooded and distant.

'I didn't mix anything with it, if that's what you're trying to say, least of all sleeping pills and painkillers.'

'And who told you that Robi Bose had died from an overdose of medicine? I haven't mentioned it.'

'I did, of course.' Tara's father let go again. 'Nisha told me about the report and warned me that the police would be swooping down on us because my daughter had been with Robi last. Don't you understand, Robi must have taken an accidental overdose? Are you suggesting my daughter had anything to do with all this?'

'You know, Mr Bose, your daughter's well past thirty and can speak for herself,' said Bikram in a casual tone. 'If you keep interrupting I will have to ask you to sit outside.'

'And leave her in your clutches?' Spit sprayed from Bimal Bose's mouth in anger and a vein on his forehead pulsed.

'Baba, I'd like to talk to the . . . to him alone.' Tara's voice was shaking as badly as her hands, but she steadied herself as well as she could. There was a ringing in her ears and her voice seemed to come from a great distance away.

'You, what?'

Without saying a word, Bikram rose and went to the door. 'Come along please, Mr Bose. The sooner we finish, the better, I think, for all of us.'

It was the still calm of Bikram's voice that perhaps convinced Tara's father. Bimal Bose scraped back his chair noisily, cast a murderous look at his daughter, and shuffled to the door.

'I don't know what my father has told you, but I think you ought to know certain things.' Tara lifted her chin fiercely. 'Robi had had a bad time that evening. Nisha had called in about five people, two couples, really, who were very close to her, and another friend. Did she tell you this?'

Bikram nodded.

'But she didn't tell you that she was everybody's woman and had had a string of affairs, and that two of the invitees had been her boyfriends. Did she tell you that?'

'No, but I gathered as much from other sources,' hazarded Bikram.

'Robi and I had a fight some days before over some property matters. We made up, and went out to a party together, but after that I had vowed never to speak to him or see him again. That evening, however, he rang me up in office and begged me to visit him once. I refused, of course, but Robi pleaded so hard that I relented. I told him I was not going to sign any papers but he said that wasn't why he wanted me over. He said he was lonely and feeling out of sorts.' Tara paused. 'In a way, I often feel like that so I, well, I understood him. I said yes. I got in around 8 p.m., and Nisha seemed very surprised to see me. For once, Robi hadn't taken her permission for something.' Tara smiled bitterly. 'In fact, now that I think back, she was actually very displeased to see me. Her face clouded over, and she went up, before I could, to shout at him, I think. When Robi came down at a quarter past eight or so, I could tell they had been having a row. But strangely enough, Robi did not try to get rid of me. He was extra sweet, in fact, and kept flattering me and saying nice things and then looking back at Nisha as if to say, see, I can have my way too. In a way, my presence was there to prove a point—that he was still the lord and master of the house.'

'And then?'

Tara shrugged her shoulders. 'And then nothing! The guests came in and I sat around for a bit. Robi kept plying me with snacks, and since I figured that I probably wasn't being invited to stay for dinner, and since I had told Ma that I would not eat at home, Robi and I gorged on the snacks. But he soon began to get very tired, I could sense that, and the other guests kept on looking at the clock, as if they wanted us out of the way. At about 9.45 p.m. or so, Nisha said the driver could drop me before going off duty. That was when Robi wanted to go up.' Tara stopped. 'Buro helped him. I went up too, because I was feeling a bit humiliated at the way Nisha had treated me that evening, like I was a drag or something, and I wanted to tell Robi not to keep calling me like this when his wife didn't want it.'

'And did you say that?'

Tara shook her head.

'Why not?'

'Buro was there, and Robi lay down, and I didn't want to say anything before Buro. He's Nisha's spy. Then Robi asked me to mix the Horlicks for him and move the table close, and I did, and then, he looked so pale and droopy that I didn't want to start another scene. I was tired, myself. So I left.'

'Did you see Buro giving him his medicine?'

'No, I didn't wait that long. I just turned around and came down and let myself out of the house. The driver had the car ready and I left. That's the whole story.'

'I asked your father the other day, but he wouldn't give me a direct answer. Was there any trouble over property between the two families?'

'I don't know why my father wouldn't tell you, since practically the whole world knows. Robi and I hated each other over that house. It's a beautiful piece of property and will probably fetch a lot of money. And Nisha's after that money. Robi worked around my father and tried to make me agree to sign off our claim on that house by offering to buy us a shabby two-bedroom worker's flat.'

'So with no deal struck, your father is still a part owner. Would you like to make your claim felt?'

'We might.'

'Have you discussed it with Nisha Bose?'

'I will, when I have the time.'

'Does your father feel the same way as you do?'

'He doesn't, but I've made it quite plain that if he comes to an agreement with Nisha without my consent, I will move out and have nothing more to do with him. He says he doesn't care, but I know he does. He's scared of neighbourhood scandal. Besides, whom will he rage at and bully?'

Bikram, doodling all this while, was listening intently. His apparent reverie was interrupted by his ringing cell phone. It was an impersonal sort of a ring and Tara found herself wishing that he had personalized it somehow. She immediately felt ashamed: her infatuation was getting out of hand.

'Hello . . . yes . . . no, I'm not in office . . . half an hour, I think, is there anything special . . . right, I'll be there.'

Then the grey eyes were on her again. 'Did they have any children?'

Tara shook her head. 'She didn't have the time, I suppose.'

'And did you . . . like Robi Bose?' The question was a murmur but Tara understood its subtext.

'No, I did not,' she said composedly, 'but I didn't spike his drinks either. Robi was being punished enough by her and all the others in her enamelled set. It must have been terrible to hear her laughing and enjoying herself while he sat upstairs with his useless body and a bedpan.'

'And so, would you say he was especially depressed that night?'

'I've been thinking about that too,' said Tara slowly, 'and I feel that there was a definite change in him that evening. He had always been resentful and fussy, but that night, he was unusually quiet.'

'And no obvious enemy of his comes to mind, at all?'

'I see what you're getting at. But aren't we jumping to

conclusions? I mean, was he murdered at all?' Tara's voice was quiet and measured. 'He was always very excitable, and the strain of having to keep up with Nisha might have got to him.'

Bikram stood up and said briskly, 'I will keep that in mind. Thank you very much for coming all the way and for your cooperation.'

Tara hesitated and then said softly, 'If I think of anything else I'll let you know. May I have your telephone number?'

Bikram scribbled on the memo pad, tore out a page, and handed it to her. He said, 'If you can't get me, there's a Mr Ghosh handling the investigation along with me, here's his number, you can give him a call too.'

Tara reached out and put the chit in her bag without looking at it, then turned and walked out of the room. Her father rushed at her but Tara walked on, ignoring him. Outside the thana, cars stopped, doors slammed, bus conductors shouted and horns blared, but Tara barely noticed the noise and bustle.

The first thing Bikram did on returning home was ring up a lawyer—a former schoolfriend—and spend ten minutes with him.

'Had the dead man made a will?' he asked after Bikram had explained the circumstances of the case to him.

'Would it matter if he had?'

'He might have got fed up with his wife and left his share of the house to his uncle and cousin and that might make it look really bad for the cousin. She spent a lot of time with him too. Got him to sign away his end of it and then bumped him off.'

'And if he hadn't?' asked Bikram.

'Then the wife, what did you say her name was?'

'Nisha Bose.'

'Nisha Bose and Bimal Bose are equal inheritors, one as the widow and the other because of his ancestral right. That will mean a lot of squabbling and bitterness once they start dividing up the property.'

'Can Bimal Bose and his daughter take half-possession of the house?'

'They can, leaving an equal share for the wife. The other option would be to sell off the old bungalow to a third party and divide the money equally, perhaps get two flats once the high-rise comes up. Ballygunge, did you say? That's a lovely area, near my club. Keep me informed and maybe I'll collect an apartment out of Robi Bose's misery!'

Inheritance is a tricky thing, mused Bikram that night. After the tears and the formal courtesies of death, come the often troublesome profit and loss of life, all excellently jointed in the matter of succession. Too often had he seen prim sons, daughters, brothers and wives turn ugly the moment the body was sent to its maker.

In his room with the television on, lights off, sound muted, Bikram leaned back on his bed and gazed at the ceiling unhappily. He wondered if he was going wrong somewhere. Was the cousin, Tara, correct in assessing that Robi Bose had simply dosed himself to death and that they were making a mountain out of a molehill? Pretty girl, he thought. His thoughts soon began to wander and, in a minute, he had fallen asleep.

# 10

The next day was Mistry's day off. Even as Bikram was being driven to office by Dorjee, the replacement driver, Mistry lounged around in his official two-roomed driver's quarters in a blue-checked lungi till 10 a.m. His CD player blared soulful Bhojpuri songs while his nephew brewed strong, sugary tea and placed it on a rack beside the bed before slipping out of the room to catch the Metro to his college. Mistry had married late but preferred to leave his wife and children in his village in Bihar. His residence in Calcutta was a useful, informal hotel for the lucky few from his village who could gain access to it. Mistry was choosy and waved away the taxi and truck drivers, the chauffeurs and the courier company peons. He preferred students—boys who came from his village to acquire a degree in some nameless college or those apprenticed to shops in the older portions of the town. He charged them five hundred rupees per month and gave them a roster of household jobs, including cooking, washing clothes, sweeping the rooms and a quick head-and-shoulder massage at night if he happened to be let off early.

The hours stretched lazily ahead as he considered his options. He would abandon himself to Bijlirani and her charms, of course, in the afternoon, after lunch at his favourite biryani place. He would visit the temple in the evening and secure the god's blessings for continued prosperity in exchange for a hundred-rupee note. But first, there was business to be dealt with—the routine weekly trip to a narrow lane deep in the heart of the city, where the roads got smaller and tighter, like the core of a cabbage, and the people looked shabby and sweaty but held, nevertheless, most of the keys to the vast floating underbelly of the chaotic metropolis. Mistry finished his tea and went for a bath, humming the Bhojpuri song under his breath.

He alighted near his destination an hour later and paid off the cab driver, after cautioning him about the dangers of overtaking from the left when the car ahead had its indicator lights on. Occasionally, he took a bus but, this morning, he felt like some luxury. Besides, Bijlirani had mentioned the new outfit on which she had splurged and it would not do to be hot and smelly when he reached her. Mistry covered his nose with a handkerchief sprayed with a foreign perfume he had wangled out of a smuggled-goods shop in the dock areas of Calcutta, and picked his way through the clogged roads. He turned down one lane selling brilliantly coloured saris, then another selling beads and sequins to be sewed on to dresses, and finally vanished through the doorway of a house that seemed bent under the burden of innumerable sign-boards.

Shiv Ram Prasad Tewari was resting when Mistry arrived. He was a short, fat man with a pockmarked face, a drooping moustache and flaming red hair. Mistry frowned. 'Why did you colour your hair? White suited you better. This makes you look like a thug.'

'Oh, it was just one of those things. The henna will grow out in time.' Shiv Ram Prasad spoke airily enough but looked troubled.

'Shave off your hair and pretend your uncle's dead.'

'Impossible! I'll have to live on fruits.'

Shiv Ram Prasad Tewari lifted one buttock, let out a low rolling fart, then punched a cordless bell. A boy with long hair tied into a ponytail appeared. 'Usual stuff, right?' Shiv Ram Prasad Tewari looked at Mistry who grunted in assent.

The boy reappeared with a bottle of beer and two glasses. Mistry asked, 'Where did you pick this one up from?'

'His dad deposited him here, to learn how to work hard and all that. From Siliguri. Mother's from the hills but father's a Bihari settled there.'

'That ponytail is all wrong, like your red hair. Have all of you been watching too many cheap films?'

'What can we do? We don't have beautiful heroines to drive around like you and your sa'ab do! You get to see the real thing, we can only make-believe.'

Shiv Ram Prasad Tewari raised his glass to his lips and drank noisily, but his eyes were glued to Mistry's face, anticipating a reaction. Mistry, loyal, said nothing.

'How's work going?'

'Same as ever, there's nothing new.'

'Your sa'ab couldn't get Babul, I hear.'

'Uh huh.'

'Is it very important to get him?'

Mistry shrugged his shoulders.

'Babul's getting worse day by day, I know.' Shiv Ram Prasad sighed. 'Getting out of hand, in fact. I've warned him but he feels confident enough to strike out on his own. Let's see, if it gets too bad, I'll let you know.'

'What does he deal in nowadays?' asked Mistry casually.

Shiv Ram Prasad looked at him with a twinkle in his eye. 'As if you didn't know!'

Mistry frowned. 'I really don't. I just have a feeling he's moved on from liquor and gambling.'

Shiv Ram Prasad looked evasive.

'You know, don't you?' Mistry had refilled his glass and decided to take the first step forward.

'I might.'

'So out with it.'

'All right, but I want something in return.'

'Like what?'

'Get your sa'ab to put some people who are troubling me out of the way. Put them behind bars for some time.'

'All right, I'll put in a word. Mind you, I can't promise anything, but I'll try.'

'Oh you can do anything if you want to, Mistry bhai.'

Mistry tried to look modest.

'So what about Babul?'

Shiv Ram Prasad Tewari scratched his back and looked thoughtful for a moment.

'I'm not sure, but I think it's drugs. Cross-border, of course.'

'What kind? Heroin and all that?'

Shiv Ram Prasad Tewari shook his head. 'Pills for the rich folk. Tied up with fake money, of course. Money from across the border to Calcutta, and tablets and stuff from here to there. Fifty per cent of the stuff circulates here of course. But there's so much of it that I think he must have made a good contact here, someone who's really manufacturing the stuff in good quantities and quickly. I do not like it either. He is getting too big. Also, he's slipping under my radar too often.'

'You can always let me know if you want him out of the way,' said Mistry softly.

Shiv Ram Prasad Tewari smiled. 'That's what you came for today, didn't you? You are really fond of your sa'ab. But he's a good guy, so I can understand why.' Tewari drained his glass, then ambled across to a steel desk, took out a bunch of keys from his pocket, fitted one into the bottom drawer, opened it and took out a large brown envelope. He fished out a bundle of notes, then waddled back to the sofa and put the bundle down before Mistry.

'I hope you're not passing off some of those fake notes to me,' said Mistry warily.

'We've been together for years, Mistry bhai. How can you even think of something like that!'

'Times are changing, my friend.'

'You can check it out if you want to,' said Tewari in an offended tone.

'No, of course not. Just joking.' Mistry slipped the packet into the pocket of his trousers and rose. 'I really wish you would dye your hair black. You're conspicuous like this, and Babul might decide to have you put out of the way.'

Shiv Ram Prasad Tewari pointed to the rings on his finger. 'I have a long way to go yet. That rat will go before I do.'

'Let me know if anything new turns up.'

Mistry belched, took out his handkerchief and pressing it to his nose again, exited, leaving a heady trail of perfume behind him.

He took a different route on the way out, passing shops with cool interiors and gaudily dressed mannequins offering lacy crimson nightdresses and sequinned saris. The shops spilled out on to the pavements where bamboo staves created a canopy of more saris and nighties. The shopkeepers picked their noses or shouted into their cell phones as they came out for a quick smoke or a cup of tea. Mistry ducked under a jumble of electric wires hanging dangerously from the electric poles from which they had been illegally tapped and surreptitiously linked to the pavement shops. He stood near a paan shop, mopping his brow and debating whether to buy Bijlirani a present when he started in surprise. A familiar face was hurrying down the very road from which he had come. It was Buro, from Nisha Bose's house.

Mistry hesitated, taken aback, then drew breath and plunged into the swarming crowds before him. This was an area he knew well, a broth of vice that simmered and sputtered behind the gaily decorated shops and their colourful ware. Flushed with beer and the excitement of a potential catch, Mistry panted on. Mistry's curiosity reached fever pitch—Buro was taking the same lanes he'd just walked. Finally Buro stopped, looked around him and vanished inside a doorway. Mistry stopped. The building was the one in which he had been only minutes before. Abandoning discretion, Mistry climbed recklessly up the stairs, using his handkerchief as a partial cover. Buro walked slowly ahead of him, halted before a door, looked around one final time and darted through a doorway. Mistry gaped, shocked. Buro had entered Shiv Ram Prasad Tewari's office.

# 11

Nine thirty a.m. was still too early for police headquarters to begin functioning. As usual, Bikram was the first to arrive and went up the three storeys in the ancient lift that creaked and groaned. He passed by the control room, the wireless set inside spasmodically issuing instructions to an empty chair, past the stenographers' room, with its muddle of wooden chairs and desks and computer wires, past the visitors' room with its picture of Mahatma Gandhi staring sadly down at the mess, and into his den. The air conditioner had been switched on and a constable with a red flannel cloth in his hand was enjoying himself before it. When Bikram swung the door open, he jumped to attention and stood as if graven in stone. The morning post was on his table, along with a heap of free gift vouchers, invitations, two telephone bills and three anonymous letters written in a melancholy scrawl on yellow postcards. Bikram tossed the file he was carrying on to the sofa, selected a violently coloured envelope promising a warm cultural evening at a musical soirée, put it into the astonished constable's hands and propelled him out of the room. He said, 'Give your wife a break, take her out to this programme and tell me how it was. And change the duster you're using.'

He snapped the door shut after the constable, leaned back in his chair, and closed his eyes. He remained like this for five minutes while the clock ticked on ponderously. Then the door flew open and Ghosh stamped in. 'I've finished with the cell phone and thought you might like to take a look at it,' he said. 'I keep forgetting to hand it over. The laptop, I didn't touch. I'm too old for it.'

'What about the pills? Did you trace the dealer?'

Bikram's eyes were still closed and he had laced his fingers over them. Ghosh looked at Bikram with paternal fondness and noticed the furrows beside his nose. He thought of Shona with some irritation. What was she waiting for? Couldn't she see that what Bikram needed was a home and children and some properly cooked meals? What was all this nonsense about courtship and weekend trysts? Bikram looked up suddenly and their eyes met. For a brief second, both men understood and acknowledged the unspoken bond between them. Ghosh then fiddled with the file he had with him and fished a paper out of it. 'A list of as many names and addresses of contacts as I could get is here,' he began. 'The servants were so uncommunicative that you would think it was one of their own families I was trying to trace. Too much solidarity there, I couldn't break down any one of them.'

Bikram reached for the paper and glanced through the addresses. He knew, more than anyone else, the amount of hard work it had taken Ghosh to compile that list. Ghosh had also put Nikki Kumar in right at the end, almost as an afterthought. Bikram put the list away and turned to the laptop. He plugged in the charger and turned it on, then handed Ghosh the foolscap sheet he had been working on the night before. 'The best way out, of course, is the suicide theory,' he said. 'A sick man, depressed, an array of medicines within easy reach, a party at which his wife was enjoying herself, and rather indelicately too; the anger, the helplessness and the final push over the edge. What do you think?'

Ghosh said nothing for a moment and then scratched his head. 'But what about the pilfered money? It could have been one of the servants too. Perhaps he was caught by Robi Bose, and before Robi could tell everyone about him, the servant decided to do away with his employer. Given Bose's condition, it wouldn't be difficult to fake a murder.'

'Why "he"?' mulled Bikram. 'The house had maids too.'

'Okay. Then the maid and the servant together,' said Ghosh. 'But how are we ever going to prove all this? How are we ever going to connect the theft to the murder?' Ghosh asked mournfully. 'Then again,' he continued, bent on mining all the ghastly possibilities of the case, 'it could also be the cousin, the girl who was being pressurized to sign away her claim to their house, and she was the last one with him.'

Bikram frowned and picked up the paper with the cell phone numbers. Robi Bose seemed to have spent a lot of time on the phone. He'd called doctors, physiotherapists, acquaintances, men and women who worked for firms, had well-known businesses, Chinese and Continental restaurants, diagnostic labs, the Flower Power Boutique, Tara and Bimal Bose and a lawyer six times in the days before his death. On the day of his death, Robi had made six calls, all morning and noon, one to the lawyer, the other four to a Mr Nandi, Amal, Bunty and Nikki Kumar. After Nikki Kumar, the last call had gone out to Tara in the evening, presumably to ask her over. Had Robi's wife kept that evening's party a secret from him? Why? The man adored her, she would have no trouble doing what she wanted, and yet, Robi Bose had his moments of irascibility. The house, too, looked a little too luxurious for an invalid with a wife who had no reliable source of income. And as hard as Nisha tried to seem an enigma, Bikram understood exactly what she was—a hardened gold-digger.

He turned his attention to the laptop that Ghosh had recovered. The desktop background was a photograph of Nisha Bose on holiday, wearing a sleeveless top and a pair of capris, a cliff looming in the background and palm trees behind her, waves dashing in and curling around her feet. Bikram clicked through the icons desultorily. Under games, he found solitaire and a bad version of snooker, with no indication that the user had much use for them. The contacts folder was empty, and the folders containing photographs had a couple more of Nisha Bose on holiday, wearing the capris and the top. The phone rang as he clicked the Word Documents folder.

It was Prem Gupta. 'In office early, Bikram, as usual?'

'Well yes Sir, a little time to myself.'

'I know, I do it myself. Any leads on the fake currency? Toofan forwarded me a report but how far does this chap you've got, Montu, right—well—how much does that give us?'

The laptop screen flashed a black-and-white picture of Alice in Wonderland, talking to the caterpillar on a mushroom with a hookah. Even as he was answering Prem Gupta's questions, one part of Bikram's brain registered surprise. Where did it come from? Downloaded from the Internet, no doubt, but why?

'He's way down in the hierarchy, Sir, I don't think he knows much. I'll have a go at him again but I don't see much hope there'.

'I suppose you've checked out the addresses he's given?'

'Apple Hassan floats all over the city, Sir, but I think he operates from somewhere in central Calcutta, from one of those hopeless lodges for across-the-border visitors. I've asked the local police station to give me some details but they are taking their time.'

Another photograph on the laptop, this time of a familiar plant with beautiful star-shaped leaves. A caption underneath it said, 'Get It Man, My Mouth's Watering'.

'Well, keep going. The director general seems very keen on the fake currency case. Maybe you should check out something that happened in Howrah last night. A trader dealing in garments was returning home around 11 p.m. when two men on a motorcycle came up to him, stabbed him twice and made off with his bag. Nothing much happened to the man, but the funny thing is that some local guys in a chemist shop picked him up and alerted the police, then sent him to the general hospital, but the man himself wasn't too keen on lodging a complaint. You never know, something interesting may turn up there.'

'I'll go over just now.'

'The officer-in-charge is on leave, I think. Daughter's exams, and I don't much like the next-in-charge.'

Bikram hung up. The constable on duty in the visitors' room came in with two visitor's slips, bearing unknown names and addresses, carrying references of obscure people Bikram had met once or twice and forgotten. It was 10.45 a.m. and the office was warming up. Bikram shut down the laptop, put it carefully inside its case—of good quality leather and expensive—leaned back in his chair and stared at the ceiling. After thirty seconds or so, he rang up Sheena Sen.

'Hello.' He could hear traffic in the background which meant that she was not in office yet.

'Can you find out if Robi Bose used the Internet frequently after his illness, and if he did, for what? Do they have friends abroad with whom he corresponded, or some old office acquaintances he was in touch with? Did anyone else use his laptop?'

He rang the bell for the first visitor. The phone rang again. This time it was Toofan Kumar. 'What's new about this currency guy?'

'I've asked the local thana for some help, Sir.'

'Haan, so you should have told me. I would have asked the deputy commissioner to organize a raid! The amount of time you guys take. What about the Robi Bose thing? The newspapers want a bite and I can't keep feeding them lines about ongoing inquiries.'

'I'm working on the call details, Sir, and have interviewed the family as well as the servants.'

'So arrest one of them! Something is better than nothing. At least it will look good in print.'

Toofan Kumar was in full spate and it was useless arguing with him. 'I've sent someone to meet you this morning, a lady who has been cheated of money. Her name is Lily Lahiri. She's a good friend of mine, so listen to her carefully and start working on that straightaway. And don't forget to follow up on the airport thana guy, the currency fellow. I want an updated report by next week.'

While they were talking, a lady of about fifty-two, wearing a crisp cotton sari, had been ushered in. Her eyes were outlined in well-smudged kohl, her sunglasses were perched fashionably on her head, there were diamonds in her ears and she carried a crocodile leather handbag which she placed on Bikram's table. She had been carefully made up to project a very specific look. Lily Lahiri, no doubt. 'I'm in a lot of trouble, Mr Chatterjee. I've been to the police station and filed a case, but they are so-oh inefficient, that's why I called Toofan and he directed me to you. Only you can help me.' Her voice was hoarse, with a slow drawl to it that perfectly fitted her attire. 'Toofan must have told you all about it.'

'Not much, I'm afraid. What is the problem?'

Lily Lahiri placed her elbows on the table, leaned forward slightly, and began her story in a low, husky tone. As always, Bikram marvelled at sunglasses which sit so delicately on the head without slipping an inch.

She lived alone in a house in a well-known residential neighbourhood on the eastern fringes of the city. She was a single woman with a daughter studying abroad. She was well off, but had lived extravagantly and had negotiated with a property dealer to sell a flat in the older part of the city, fetching good money with the rise in real estate prices. The terms of payment had been complicated but she had trusted the dealer, a friend of a friend. The first round of payment had been made, then the second, after which the dealer had reneged, leaving about fifty per cent of the total amount unpaid. The friend who had recommended him didn't know much about him anymore, it transpired, and, indeed, was surprised that she had negotiated with him at all. She had rung the dealer up umpteen times but he had hummed and hawed, citing deaths in the family and illnesses and then, finally, had issued a cheque which bounced at the bank. Would Bikram arrest him immediately and help her get her money back?

'Did you get the first part of the payment by cheque or in cash?'

'Cheques, mainly, with some cash. Recently I bought a new washing machine and was dismayed to find that some of the notes he had given me were fake. Can you imagine my embarrassment, Mr Chatterjee, when the shop rang to say that three one-thousand rupee notes were dud? How awkward I felt! The shopkeeper was rude and wanted me to make fresh payments. What cheats! That's when I told him I would take the matter to my friends in the police. It isn't my fault, is it?'

The perfume Lily was wearing bothered Bikram, whose nose was sensitive to strong odours. He sneezed twice and wondered how to ease her out of the room. The only way, of course, was to make a show of great activity. Bikram rang the police station to which she had been and spent a few minutes talking to the officer-in-charge there, who repeated the facts he already knew. As expected, the phone call calmed Lily. Though Bikram had said nothing, she was assured that a majority of the personnel of the Calcutta Police were treating her problem on a priority basis and would solve it soon.

'I have heard so much about you, Mr Chatterjee; I knew you would be the one to help me. I meet Shona here and there, and it would be so nice if you two could come over for a bite at my flat some time. Such a well-matched couple, I say.' She was still gushing as Bikram escorted her to the door. It was 11.30 a.m., and time to visit the businessman who had been stabbed in Howrah.

The man broke down in three minutes. The clothes shop was, as suspected, a front for other businesses. The man had just exchanged a large consignment of fake notes for real ones and was on his way back home when the attackers had swooped down and made off with the money. Now he had been robbed, was in debt, and was the subject of a police investigation. The man began sobbing in great whoops. And in between sobs, set up a lament about what he was to do now, with his parents and wife, his two sons and unmarried sister having no idea of the exact nature of his business.

'You should have thought about all of them when you began,' said Bikram crossly. The other patients were struggling to listen in.

'But I did, Sir. I dropped out of school in class eight, spent my time ferrying saris on my cycle, selling them at a discount in the houses of the peons and sweepers of the Railway Quarters. How much money could I ever have made that way? There were days when we ate only muri.'

'From whom did you get the money?' asked Bikram unkindly, refusing to be drawn into family crises and the finer points of slow starvation.

'We call him Lala, that's all; I don't know anything else about him.'

'Who's the "we"?' pounced Bikram.

The man's eyes became hooded. 'Pain, pain, I can't breathe . . .' he fluttered.

'Whoever you're protecting is probably the one who got you robbed, so unless you give me his name, I can't do anything.'

But the man refused Bikram's bait. He lay back and moaned once or twice, then closed his eyes. An attendant in a blue sari strolled up. 'Give me hundred bucks and I'll get the name out of him when I'm changing his drip,' she whispered.

'Hey, hey, get out now.' The uniformed constable tapped his cane on the ground and looked fiercely at the woman. She winked at Bikram and, laughing, turned away. 'All right, for you, I'll do it for free. Just drop by again and I'll have the name ready.'

Bikram raised his eyebrows, shrugged, and started for the door.

When he came back to the office, Mistry demanded an audience. It was almost one and Bikram was hungry, but the constable at the door wouldn't serve lunch.

'Sir, Mistry would like to talk to you for a moment.'

'Where's my lunch? Tell him to wait till I finish eating.'

'Sir, the lunch is almost ready, we've just run out of green chillies, I've sent Dorjee down to get some . . . shall I ask Mistry da to come in?'

Should he bow to this silent pressure and eat later, or should he force his way for once? He decided to become Toofan Kumar for a change. 'I don't need the chillies, just get me my lunch. Tell Mistry to wait.'

The defeated constable withdrew. The lunch came in on a yellow melamine plate, looking pinched and meagre—two chapattis and a mash of vegetable curry, the wedge of lime looking lonely without the chilli, and a plate of peeled apple for dessert. Bikram ate slowly, fastidiously tearing the chapatti and wrapping it around the vegetable, mopping the gravy with smaller bits, the absent chilli marring the meal. And so it was with him in love, work and leisure—a slow savouring of whatever he had, a painstaking attention to detail and the nuances of every case, and the love of order and familiarity. When he finished, he washed his hands with a small bar of perfumed soap he kept in his bathroom, rinsed his mouth, sprayed breath freshener, almost involuntarily looked at himself in the mirror, patted his hair and felt ready to meet the world again. The world began with Mistry.

When Mistry had finished his breathless delivery, Bikram felt no great elation. There had always been something suspicious about Buro, but now that there seemed to be a definite lead to him, he felt strangely upset.

'What is Shiv Ram Prasad Tewari's line of business?' A superfluous question intended to cover his feelings, since he had a fair idea.

Mistry giggled nervously. 'The usual, Sir, money collection and no questions asked, local land deals, supplying building materials, stuff like that.'

'I take it you've been pals for years,' said Bikram morosely. A good tip coming from his driver didn't look so good after all, in light of the fact that Mistry shouldn't have been there in the first place.

'Same village, Sir, his father and mine are brothers, all cousins from the same family, such ties cannot be forgotten . . .'

'Mistry,' said Bikram gently. 'For my sake, be careful. You know how fussy I am about silly things. Don't overdo it.'

'I am always careful, Sir,' said Mistry devotedly. 'Swear by God, Sir, we would never bring you any shame.'

'Give me the address and don't go there again this month, or at least until we decide what to do with Buro.'

After he had dismissed Mistry, and between three more telephone calls, during which the peon brought in two fat files, which Bikram's unseeing eyes used as a place board for a sheet of paper, he wrote 'Montu, Babul, Raja, Dhoor, Apple', encircled the words, put a large ONE; then wrote 'Robi, Nisha, Buro, Maid, Poor Cousin', encircled those words with a large TWO, and stood staring down at the names with a heavy heart. In a margin he wrote, Fake Currency, Suicide, Murder and Border. Then he wrote 'Buro' and underlined it thrice, signing in Tewari underneath. Then he looked at the mesh of interrogations, the running up and down, tailing, false leads, difficulty in procuring evidence, witnesses, warrants, convictions that the scribbling involved, and the mess that the mesh indicated and felt his heart sinking. On an inspiration he drew a stick figure with a large moustache and a car with five beacons on it and labelled it TK. Then he stared mournfully at his handiwork and looked out of the window.

Cars—beacons on top, in front, poles from which the flags with their stars fluttered and shone majestically—were roaring in and out of the driveway. Bikram's eyes narrowed. An idea stirred in his mind, he could feel it welling up from within him, some detail, horribly important, which he had registered and then missed. It would be back with him in a moment.

His cell phone rang, the screen blinked. Bikram swore. Briefing at 2.30 p.m., said the screen. Bikram looked at the clock. It was 2.10 p.m. He swore again, rang for the peon, and noticed for the first time that one of the files was for the briefing on the security for the football match, picked it up, unconsciously checked for his revolver and made for the lift. By the time the car moved forward, he had forgotten the fleeting thought.

The meeting was well attended though Bikram suspected that even the officer conducting it was half-asleep. The voice that droned was boring background music. Even Sheena Sen nodded twice and tried to cover it up by fiddling with her handkerchief. Ghosh was sweating as if air conditioning had not been invented, and his face was shiny with perspiration and the strain of controlling his wheezy coughs. The tea was served late and was raw, and the room had been oversprayed with freshener. Bikram realized with dismay that his uniform would be reeking of jasmine for the rest of the day.

When the ordeal of the meeting ended, the ordeal of the football match began. Bikram walked up and down the dilapidated galleries, shuffled around the run-down dressing room, watched the watchers—a melancholy lot, either from the suburbs, or unemployed, or plain riffraff toting violently coloured flags printed on crumpled coarse linen—and waited for a chance to corner Ghosh. He found him standing near the iron entrance gate and walked over to meet him.

'Any leads on that Babul thing? I had one more fake currency guy this morning, after you left.' Briefly, Bikram told him about the stabbed trader at the hospital.

'I'll have a go at the leech guy again, Sir, to see if he can lead us to Babul. He spoke of some cross border syndicate of which Babul was a member, I forget the name.'

'Dhoor?'

'Yes, Sir, I knew it was some worthless sounding thing, Dhoor.'

'I've picked up some information about Dhoor also, from the airport police station. I should have a go at this leech guy myself. Can you fix up a meeting some time?'

'Tomorrow?'

'Yes, why not, tomorrow. Same place, you can bring him there, and then, if you don't mind, I'll talk with him alone. But for heaven's sake, remind me about it well ahead in the morning, not like today, when you didn't say a word about this bloody match.'

'You didn't give me time, what with everything . . .'

'I guess. But I do have something interesting about the Robi Bose case. Mistry, as usual, pokes his nose and finds something funny.'

When Bikram's narrative was done, Ghosh's face looked as if he had just returned from a friend's funeral. 'Nice,' he said, with the air of someone who has discovered a strand of hair in his pilaf. Then he scratched his head and said, 'I always knew it was the servant.' There was silence. The match had begun and a roar rose from the audience, accompanied by a deafening chorus of catcalls, squeakers and drums. Ghosh chewed his lower lip, grunted, scratched his ear, and finally said, 'But I think I know someone who might be able to help us.'

Bikram waited. Part of the reason why Ghosh was invaluable was that when Bikram's mind was blocked, Ghosh's policing instincts stood up and simply clamoured to be let out. 'He's dying to meet you anyway, must have heard about you,' as they all do, he almost added in parenthesis, 'so when you finally get him tomorrow, Sir, you must play him well. If anyone's grateful for all you've done for him and will do a good tailing job and will not squeal, I guarantee it's him, for there's a kind of loyalty about that rascal that is genuine. Raja, the leech guy. He will lead us to Buro's game.'

# 12

'Are you feeling all right?' Shona asked. It was 7.30 a.m. and she hoped Bikram would be back from his routine jog at Eden Gardens. She could just picture him running on the crumbling track that snaked this way and that through the park with its plastic kangaroo waste bins and its unkempt lawns. Shona had long given up coaxing Bikram into a membership at a discreet air-conditioned gym or an exclusive weekend health club. With characteristic mulishness Bikram thought of such places as the epitome of the class divide and preferred to jog doggedly to the sound of clinking cups and the smell of frying chickpea curry that wafted over the boundary wall from the roadside eateries where the drivers of long-distance buses waited.

'Are you all right?' she asked him again.

'I'm all right,' he said, but the starchiness in his tone was unmistakable.

'No, you're not,' she said.

Bikram, who was still at Eden Gardens, had slowed down from a jog to a half-trot; now he quickened his pace again.

'Why this persistence? I tell you I'm fine.' Then, to change the subject, he said, 'No shoots today?'

'No, I've cancelled them. I thought, well, tomorrow's May Day, you might be free, we could go somewhere.'

The truth was that Shona was not well, had a sore throat and a stuffy nose and felt the flu coming on. At such times her confidence and ebullience deserted her, her profession grated and something in her cried out for a pair of grey eyes and a tall figure. There was a restfulness about him that could set her back on course like nothing else.

'Tomorrow? Impossible! I do have a job, you know!'

'I forget! Only you work, the rest of us gad around trees or sign silly slips of paper and lead frivolous lives best forgotten.' After she had said it, she at once felt foolish, childish, and cursed herself for falling into his trap. To earn Bikram's respect, one had to meet thrust with parry, answer his remoteness with amusement. But for how long, a voice in her screamed. Then she sneezed, and with the sneeze came a cough, and Shona, who was proud and dreaded compassion, most of all from Bikram, said she would talk later and disconnected.

He gave her five minutes to recover and then rang back. This time, his voice was pleading and hers harsh. 'Have you asked Dr Niyogi to check up on you? It's a long weekend, and he might be out, you'd better get him on the phone quickly.'

'I will.'

'I'm sorry, Shona, I was being unnecessarily rude, I don't know what's come over me.'

'It's that Nisha Bose thing, isn't it? I see it in the papers; your Toofan Kumar must be driving you quite mad.'

'That and other stuff also. I don't mind work, but somehow, this time, it's all so wearisome, nothing's falling into place, and I'm losing my temper all the time. I can't cope anymore.'

'Yes, you can. Your work is your refuge, Bikram. You know it and so do I, and it's the central purpose of your life. Without the Nisha Bose thing, it would have been all idleness and that would never do for you.'

'That's not entirely true.'

'Where's the lie?'

'My work is central to my life, but doesn't give me a purpose. Someone else gives me that.'

'But that someone else does not require plotting,

organization and methodology and so, I suppose, is not half as absorbing.'

Bikram could picture the laughter in her eyes as she said this, and suddenly, the green slatted bench on which he was sitting seemed to dissolve into nothingness and, along with it, Toofan Kumar and Nisha Bose and Montu Mondol and the football match and his office with its brown files and red tape. He said, 'I know a discreet little garden house in south Calcutta which overlooks the river and has an excellent cook. Can you drive me up there tonight, Shona?'

The only spot of business that Bikram had set up for that Sunday was a meeting with Raja prearranged by Ghosh. It was 4 p.m. and a thunderstorm was brewing. The afternoon was unnaturally still and black clouds were bunching up over the southern skies. Sweat dropped off the nose with annoying regularity, and clothes stuck damply to one's back.

Bikram parked his car near a dingy one-roomed restaurant called Scoop overlooking the barges and walked leisurely along the Circular Railway track. The smells of smoke and horse dung mingled and he slipped in through a tiny side gate and strolled on to a patch of grass over which towered the steel pylons of the second Hooghly Bridge. At the end of the patch stood a stately arch, with 'Erected to the Honour of James Prinsep by his Citizens' lettered on it in black. Bikram took a deep breath and looked up. An owlet, its eyes shining, peered down at him from the top of the Ionic columns. Bird and man surveyed one another curiously. Then a familiar puffing sound behind him announced Ghosh.

Raja was so surprised by Ghosh's announcement that the DSP sahib might want to meet him that he had spent a sleepless night. Afraid that he might overdo something, he had abstained, from whisky as well as from his girl of the week, and spent all morning at the barber's. Accordingly, when Bikram arrived, he saw a dapper young man with an air of innocence about him, wearing Levi's jeans and a crushed cotton shirt with the top button undone and a pair of glares tucked stylishly into his pocket. Both looked at one another approvingly, for though they did not know it then, they were in many ways alike and this was to be the start of a long friendship. Ghosh, with his usual grasp of situations, had gone away.

Bikram and Raja leaned against the iron fence that separated the railway track from the Prinsep monument. Cars and buses roared beyond, a bell chimed sleepily somewhere and a cell phone rang insistently in the pocket of one of a pair of lovers sitting on the grass.

'So, Raja, you were afraid that day at Angel Nursing Home. You're looking in perfect health now.'

Raja grinned. 'With luck, Sir, I met you, and that other sir there, gruff though he is, with a heart of gold. You, of course, I had heard of from everyone.'

'Really! And what does everyone say?'

'That you're different!'

'I wonder how?'

'I think I know how. You're a dangerous enemy but a good friend, and though policing and sympathy do not always go together, in you I think I can find both.' Raja, with his great gift of the gab, warmed to his subject. 'I will give you good tip-offs, Sir, you can always count on me. After all, you did save my life.'

'Don't be dramatic, Raja. I didn't snatch you from the jaws of death.'

But Raja, who had made up his mind to worship Bikram, would not be drawn away so easily and spent two minutes gushing about the raid. Bikram, itching to look at his watch, waited for the right moment to begin the real interview.

'Tell me about the border. What's happening now?'

'Currency notes, Sir, in bulk. Made in South-East Asia, and coming in via Bangladesh. You should see those notes, Sir, they are so good, a genius must have made them. And the network's expanding. Babul's a big player in the business but bigger ones are born each day and if Babul's not careful, he'll get left behind soon.'

'Anything else?'

'Cows, as usual, smuggled out from our side. And drugs, Sir, especially medicinal ones.'

'Cough syrup and things like that?'

'Cough syrup's old-fashioned.' Raja grinned, almost as if to chide Bikram for being so hopelessly out of date. 'A kind of powder's hot stuff now. They use it in cow and dog medicine but, I'm told, if you spike a drink with it, the girl won't remember a thing.' Raja winked. 'The next morning, you're up and away before she realizes what's happened.'

'Date rape,' muttered Bikram.

'Sir?'

'Just remembering the name. How does it come in?'

'All kinds of ways. Packed in the handlebars of cycles was the last I heard of it. And it goes out from here too, powder and readymade tablets, good market for it all over. Some things never go out of fashion,' finished Raja with relish.

A steamer hooted urgently on the river. The sky was almost black now, and a wind had sprung up. Bikram hated dust storms. They choked his throat and made him cough. And one thought constantly nagged his mind: should he take a chance with this man? He thought for a while and, in an inspired moment, decided to confide in Raja.

'Here's a small task for you.'

Bikram described Buro and how Mistry had seen him one morning at Shiv Ram Prasad Tewari's residence. Would Raja tail him and see what he was up to?

Raja's face lit up in eagerness and his eyes glowed with

happiness. When Bikram had finished he stood up and looked at him solemnly. 'In a week's time, Sir, I will get you all the information you need to finish this man off and send him to jail forever.'

'Very good! I wish you luck. How much do you need for expenses?'

Raja suddenly looked stern.

'Do you think I could ever take money from you, Sir, who has saved . . .'

'But you'll have to follow him, hang out in shops, drink tea . . .'

In the end, Raja was prevailed upon to take a thousand rupees as token wages.

They exchanged telephone numbers. A sharp wind blew and Bikram looked up at the sky anxiously. Then, just as suddenly as he had summoned Raja for this long-awaited meeting, he ended it.

'Be careful Buro doesn't notice you,' he said over his shoulder as he began to walk towards the gate.

'Notice me, Sir, Border Raja?'

'He might be Border Buro for all you know,' said Bikram as he hurried to his car.

Bikram was not driving his official Tata Sumo but a private unmarked vehicle, a steel grey Maruti Suzuki Swift, small and sleek, that he kept for his other life. The car was full of the debris left behind by a man who loves to drive: mineral water bottles, cushions, flashlights, chargers for his cell phones, an extra pair of sneakers and a spare pair of rubber sandals and, at the back, a policeman's helmet, a shield and a constable's stick. There were a couple of CDs too, with 'Shona' scrawled on them in black marker pen, and inside the dashboard was a pouch containing clips, sunscreen lotion and hair bands. Barely had Bikram adjusted the seat belt than the first call arrived. 'Sorry, Sir, it's me, Raja, sorry for bothering you so soon.'

'Tell me.'

'You didn't, I mean, you didn't ask me anything about my past life, my family, my childhood and things like that.'

'Your past is your own, unless you choose to share it with me.'

'But I do! You went away so soon today, perhaps another meeting, I mean, you could get to know me better, I mean, I could be betraying you.'

'I trust you,' said Bikram and rang off. Then, taking care to save Raja's number—the man was the indefatigable sort who would ring many times a day—he jammed his foot down on the accelerator and roared off. Everyone in the office spoke of Bikram's driving. Once behind the wheel, an alter ego took over and Bikram gave himself up to speed. Most of the traffic sergeants on duty knew him and looked the other way when he jumped the lights, shaking their heads sadly and remarking that something terrible would happen one day. Twice, on the highway outside the city, Bikram's car had turned turtle and he had survived. Shona refused to let him drive and took the wheel herself when they went out. So the steel grey car shot past an astounded Raja and it was only a minute before Bikram reached the west gate of Raj Bhavan and had to pull up unwillingly for an ambulance to pass by.

The storm would break any minute. Leaves and empty packets were being lifted off the ground and swirled around. Outside the massive iron gates, on the deserted pavement, sat a beggar with a red weal on his face, shielding a flame. Around him were scattered bits of cardboard and pieces of foil, and a bundle of rags. The flame sputtered and refused to light but it finally relented and the beggar leaned over for his slice of nirvana. Then the lights changed and Bikram moved on.

Bikram accelerated away from the light but the euphoria was missing and he felt uneasy. The image of the beggar kept dancing before his eyes and with it came a profound uneasiness and a sense of irritation. What was it that he was missing? He frowned: a room and a computer, and a caterpillar smoking a hookah. Then, suddenly, the cursor clicked and he could see Robi Bose's computer with a picture of a cannabis leaf downloaded from the Internet, and he could almost hear the boisterous partying downstairs and a puzzled Tara wondering what was going on as Nisha Bose stared astounded at this sudden interruption to her rave party. A young girl in a salwar kameez, jaywalking happily on the road near the China Bazaar, almost lost her life as the grey Swift bore down on her and whizzed past, a handsome man with one hand on the wheel and shouting into a cell phone held in the other.

# 13

O n May Day, Toofan Kumar threw a party. It was part therapy and part image-mending exercise for Toofan. The weather was hot and muggy already and the winter vegetables at New Market had grown limp and expensive. His wife objected, 'What'll I feed them, Tuff? The fools in the kitchen can't think beyond cholay and paneer. And bell pepper and zucchini are so expensive. Couldn't you have done this in Jan. or Feb.?' But the months of January and February had been a whirl of parties and picnics, weddings and engagements, not to forget, book launches and art exhibitions. And yes, of course, Robi Bose had been alive and Toofan Kumar's reputation undented. Besides, May Day was an important holiday in Calcutta's calendar, and Toofan Kumar was anxious to reinforce the impression of being in on an important facet of Calcutta's social life. There would be a Bengali bureaucrat or two who, though retired, would be flattered at being remembered and could secure Toofan enviable transfers. Perhaps a reporter too, who might be prevailed upon, with generous quantities of Scotch, to write kindly of him. There would be some friends from the club, others from his golfing set and still others who owned various businesses and were rich. The booze would be good and Mrs Kumar's dinner wholesome— results, after all, of expensive seven-day Lebanese and Mongolian cooking classes.

In the days before the party, Toofan Kumar was restless and discontented. Partly because the Robi Bose case was getting on his nerves but more so because, after all the planning, the party still seemed ill timed. Because nothing of note was happening in the city, the newspapers kept filling inside columns with updates on the Robi Bose case. And since the case dominated mindspace, the socialites he'd invited were bound to discuss it, and Toofan Kumar feared his evening would turn into an open debate on police inefficiency. From the club, he made two frantic telephone calls, one to the electrical wing of the Public Works Department to inquire if they were sending an electrician to his residence and the other to his residence to find out if they had. The Kumars had sought to make their box-like police department flat more attractive by rigging up expensive air conditioners in every room and the wires, incapable of supporting such mighty ambitions, frequently tripped. When the additional commissioner in charge of crime and murder rang up about the Robi Bose case, Toofan Kumar listened absent-mindedly and fidgeted impatiently. Yes, yes, the newspapers were getting out of hand. Certainly, there would be developments soon. Yes, a narco analysis if necessary. Oh, bugger Bikram and his crew!

On the morning of the party, Toofan Kumar went to the club to swim and play golf and to stay discreetly out of his wife's way. Mrs Kumar was at her injured best and, between shouting at the maid and the cook, had asked him to have fun and stay out for lunch, and tea if possible. As he heaved himself into his car, Toofan Kumar suddenly remembered an evening many score evenings before, when a young and bashful Mrs Kumar had cooked and prepared all day for a dinner for the superintendent of police and how, clad coyly in a sari, she had served her first guest with trembling hands.

At 5 p.m., Toofan Kumar raced back home and inspected the arrangements. The house was stuffy with the smell of pakoras and kebabs, and Thakur, Toofan Kumar's bodyguard, henchman and jack-of-all trades, rushed to open windows and air the drawing room. The staff soon began scurrying about with terrified expressions on their faces for Toofan, unmellowed by whisky, began rasping out orders and recriminations every burdensome minute. They ranged around the servant's room with tense foreboding and wondered whether it would be safe to slip out for a cup of tea.

The first guest to arrive at the standard party time of 9 p.m. was Mr De. Mrs Kumar muttered a frosty hello, seated him on an uncomfortable straight-backed chair, then vanished into the kitchen. But Mr De was too excited at being invited to mind. Months of sycophancy had paid off. He was beaming all over as he chose his drink and settled down for a long evening. Make new contacts, he thought happily, collect visiting cards, and all will go well at the shop. If only one could take photographs!

The doorbell rang. There were loud greetings from the door and Mrs Kumar trotted out her warmest hellos. Two fat men waddled in, followed by two fat ladies, both in wrap around skirts and sleeveless tops in which their bosoms bobbed energetically. The bell rang again and again. More men and women crowded into the room and greeted one another. The room swam with salwar kameezes, slacks, skirts, cocktail dresses and at least one exotic dress. I got it tailored in Darjeeling, said the wearer proudly, so comfortable!

By 10.15 p.m., the room was full. Chairs had been pulled out and little groups had formed. Cliff Richard's voice wafted sensuously over the gathering and mixed with the smells of kebab and cigarette smoke. Almost inevitably, the subject of Robi Bose came up.

'How do you protect yourself from your servants?' asked someone loudly. 'You feed them, rear their families, create fixed-deposit accounts for them, but they're never happy. Turn your back once and they'll stab you.'

'He wasn't stabbed, Malti, just drugged. And whoever killed Robi did him a favour. Not much of an existence, really, staying abed when the most fantastic parties went on in his own living room.'

'Obviously! I was being metaphorical when I said stabbed. And he was *never* left out of parties. Nisha took him along everywhere and was most patient with him. More than I would ever be with *my* hubby.'

'There's a poor cousin in it too, right? She used to keep Robi company now and then. Perhaps she did it.' An earnest young girl, her bobbed hair a throwback to the 1920s, put aside her fork and drained her beer.

Parry Prakash began, 'You mean someone from Nisha's circle of admirers helped bump him off? I wouldn't put it past the woman. It's amazing how people would do anything for her.'

'Parry, what are you saying!' Mrs Parry Prakash had been following her husband's tipsy misadventures and decided to interpose before further damage could be done. 'We're talking about Nisha, Parry, how could you even think of things like that?'

'Oh Mr Kumar, who do you think it was?' cooed Dolly Dewan. In her Darjeeling dress and with her face plastered with make-up, she looked rather incongruous. Dolly was fluttering towards Toofan Kumar because she had her eyes on a dashing young officer whom Toofan was mentoring.

'Well,' began Toofan Kumar ponderously, 'it's all very complicated. The young cousin, as Sheeba said, did have an argument with Robi over that house of theirs. There was trouble over succession and all that, so she could be the one. But they have a lot of servants and we're not forgetting that, in spite of the fact of death, nothing valuable was stolen.'

Parry Prakash decided to take another shot. 'In any case, you can make the servants the killers. You cops can beat them up and extract all kinds of confessions.'

'And solve the case! Convenient for all concerned save the maid's family.' Malti Mehta, who occasionally dabbled in an organization that looked after aged and out-of-work prostitutes, said this with some malice and enjoyed seeing Mrs Kumar's discomfiture out of the corner of her eye.

'It's not as simple as that.' The ex-secretary, industrial reconstruction, government of West Bengal, now adviser to the Asian Development Bank, was sufficiently mellowed by Toofan Kumar's Chivas Regal to clear his throat and come to the policeman's defence. 'Servants' rights are always welcome until your own house is burgled, Madam Mehta! Then you'll come crying to our good man here and clamour for justice and the immediate arrest of everyone who works for you, regardless of alibi and intent. Toofan is a good officer and has an excellent track record, I'm sure the culprits will be booked soon.'

A thrill of joy shot through Toofan Kumar as he gazed slavishly at the ex-secretary and congratulated himself on having invited him. Who knew, this man might even be able to put in a word for that UN assignment.

'I still think it's the cousin,' said Sheeba of the bobbed hair obstinately. 'Why else would a young girl in her senses spend so much time with an invalid? Must have made him sign a will or something. A shot of cyanide when no one was looking.'

'From where would she have got the cyanide?' asked Parry Prakash. 'A shopping mall or the local chemist?'

'Easy. She's got a boyfriend who gets it for her. A medical rep carrying a black bag with whom she makes out in the evening at the Academy of Fine Arts. Or Victoria Memorial. That's where they go for their pleasures, don't they?'

'I don't think she goes to Victoria Memorial, oh no. She looks very different.' Mr De, who had contributed very little to proceedings beyond rushing to get people drinks and offering snacks, startled everyone. Though a frequent invitee to these parties, he was much like a junior player on the substitute's bench, cheering and waving, but never allowed on the playing field. They all looked at him.

'You know her?' Malti Mehta added in an undertone, 'You would!'

Mr De was nodding and beaming all around. 'We saw her. At Nikki Kumar's party! Nisha Bose brought her along and introduced her to some of us. One of the few girls wearing a sari. She spent a lot of time in the library talking to Mr Dawson.'

'I know!' said Dolly Dewan. 'I too saw her. She was standing near Shona Chowdhury and that handsome policeman, that guy, oh what's his name, Rahul or Vikram or something. Her boyfriend. Shona Chowdhury's, I mean.'

'Bikram Chatterjee.' The young police officer, presently the apple of Dolly's eye, who felt that he should join the conversation but didn't quite know how, cleared his throat. An opening at last! 'Deputy superintendent of police, Bikram Chatterjee. Very efficient and dependable. He came down to my area once to look into some arms smuggling case. I was really impressed.'

'So was I,' Dolly Dewan put in breathlessly.

'I thought he looked quite arrogant,' said bobbed hair disapprovingly. Shona Chowdhury had once snubbed her at an embassy party and she was not inclined to speak favourably about anything connected with Shona.

'Arré Toofan, what have you done?' said Parry Prakash mischievously. 'Such a delicious cop lurking around in your department and you don't invite him here for the ladies to enjoy.'

'I, too, have heard of him,' said the ex-secretary unexpectedly. 'Good reputation. Good work. Builds a fine rapport with the people around him.'

Toofan Kumar, who had felt the turn in conversation to be unendurable but dared not openly disagree with the ex-secretary, muttered something and got up to fix a drink. Just then, Thakur sidled in with the telephone which he delivered to his master with an elaborate salute. Talk of the bloody devil, thought Toofan angrily, as he excused himself and went in to the bedroom.

On May Day morning, Bikram and Shona discussed the case, and where it stood, in the garden house overlooking the river.

'What do you think happened, Shona? Have you heard any gossip about these people?'

Shona shook her head. 'I know what you know, which is what the others know too. I don't think I've heard anything else, certainly nothing about raves with drugs and things like that. Nisha Bose is too chic for all that.'

The room was half-darkened, the curtains were drawn and the air conditioner hummed happily on the wall. She was sitting on a rocking chair with her feet stretched out before her and propped up on the edge of the bed. Bikram could smell her lemon verbena perfume and while one half of him was drowsy and contented, the thought of Robi Bose kept the other half hatefully hyper-alert.

'I'll make some inquiries tomorrow,' she said. 'It will be difficult, because everyone knows about you and me, but I'll try. In the meanwhile,' went on Shona, 'why don't you try Mr Dawson? At the very least you can talk things over with him. His experience as a police officer might be able to help you, certainly much more than I ever can.' And Bikram, not wishing to waste their stolen moments on Nisha Bose, agreed.

That evening, Bikram and Shona met Mr Dawson in an elegant room hidden amongst the fluted cornices of one of the old British houses in Calcutta's business district. The address was an exclusive meeting place for businessmen and bureaucrats and Mr Dawson, filled with pleasure at being able to meet

Bikram after a long time, rose energetically to meet them. Had Tara been there, she would have recognized the old man at Nikki Kumar's party who had offered her soup and spoken so politely to her.

'Bikram and Shona, again! What a perfect couple, each growing more handsome and graceful as the days pass. It is time for the wedding bells to ring.'

Mr Dawson had never questioned them on their relationship, for his fondness for Bikram had overridden all considerations of middle-class morality, but lately, his courtesy had turned impatient.

'He says he doesn't have the time,' said Shona mischievously.

They sat down in a corner of the lounge which, Bikram noticed, was empty. Mr Dawson had picked the perfect place for their meeting.

'How are things in office? Prem and I played golf last week, and I understand Toofan's giving you trouble.'

'It's my fault; I haven't been able to deliver for a long time now. How can I expect the love and respect of my seniors if I don't show results?'

'Dear, dear. This calls for some emergency measures.'

Mr Dawson turned round and flicked his fingers at a waiter. 'Some of that excellent wine you served last time, please.' Then he smiled, reached across, and patted Bikram on the shoulder. 'I know what you've come for. Shona called soon after you, unofficially, to brief me. I too have been thinking.'

The waiter arrived with the wine.

'In a way it's easier for me because I know Nikki well, and have a little more insight into her life. You don't know about their chanting group, I suppose?'

Bikram shook his head.

'I didn't either, till Nikki told me. Took me quite some time to get it all out of her, but in the end my methods prevailed. Also, she needed to get some money across to her scallywag of a son who's known distantly to my daughter in the US. I told her my daughter could pay him the money for the time being and Nikki could return it later. Ragini works in the World Bank, you know, and is doing well.'

The waiter reappeared with two plates of cheese, crackers and olives. Mr Dawson looked disgusted. 'What we need is some good old-fashioned kebabs and tandoori prawns. Can you get that for us, please?'

He continued. 'There is, of course, a group within a group. The chanting group meets every seven days at Nisha Bose's residence and spends time doing Tibetan and yogic chants. They have a boy from Sikkim who comes in to teach them, and other instructors from Bihar and Orissa, as well as someone from Goa.

'What she did not tell me, I got to know from someone else. Who he is, Bikram, does not concern us right now. What I got to know is that the inner group meets twice a week at Nisha Bose's house for quite a different sort of nirvana. They begin, apparently, with the lights low and the music soft, but by 1 a.m., the music is turned up high and the drawing room is in shambles.'

A plateful of prawns, their pink tails sticking out decorously, arrived. Shona took one and bit hungrily.

'Nisha's a strange woman, is she not?' Bikram looked up to find Mr Dawson looking at him curiously.

'Yes,' he said. 'She seemed too polished, too . . . how shall I put it . . . too finished, for all that.'

'And there, perhaps, you made an error in judgement. Not every beautiful woman is a Cleopatra. She had been faithful, at any rate, to Robi, and the two, though childless, had an outwardly hassle-free marriage. I say outwardly because there might have been tensions within of which we know nothing. It is always difficult to believe that a marriage is perfect if one party is plain compared to the other; though, if both man and wife are evenly matched in beauty and brains, it's difficult to predict the state of that marriage either.'

Really, thought Bikram, his comments are really loaded today. Could he have had a beer before we arrived? Shona's ears had turned pink and she fiddled with the napkin on her lap.

Mr Dawson hit his stride. 'After Robi Bose's illness, Nisha found herself in the peculiar position of being unattached and yet attached. She had a few flings here and there, but Robi was always a strain on her. Besides, I think, he became a worrier, went on and on about his health and was an embarrassment in public. Finally, you'll have to think about the one aspect of their lives we haven't discussed yet. Money! Where did the money come from—with Robi's job gone—the money for the parties and the clothes and the servants and the trips abroad? Yes, Bikram, Nisha Bose travelled frequently even after Robi's illness.'

Bikram's grey eyes had almost become transparent as he contemplated the rim of his glass. He remembered the polished silver on the sideboard, the table linen in the enormous pantry and the bin outside overflowing with party refuse. He also remembered the empty packets of Tramadol tablets.

'So you see, Bikram, this crime, if it is one, goes a long way back.'

Bikram looked up to find Mr Dawson smiling gently at him. 'And the evidence is something I can never put together, and the charge sheet, if ever there is one, cannot contain so much speculation. I'll just have to dump this one and wait for the press to forget it,' said Bikram bitterly.

'You could pass it off on the cousin,' said Mr Dawson. 'Wasn't she the one seen with him last? Toofan would be delighted. Do you think she did it?'

Bikram shrugged his shoulders. 'Going by the letter of the Investigation Manual and all we were taught as probationers, she could have, but, I don't know, somehow, I always felt she was out of it all.'

'So you, too, thought there was something murky going on there, even before you stumbled upon the drug angle?'

'It was just an instinctive feeling I had.'

They rose for an early dinner. Over a sumptuous spread of minestrone soup, penne arrabiata, linguini with pesto sauce and apple crumble, Mr Dawson also informed Bikram that Robi Bose's cousin had been present at Nikki Kumar's party, seemed a pleasant and interesting girl and had, in fact, been introduced to Bikram before she blushingly withdrew. 'I didn't see her leave, but she seemed to be very much like a fish out of water there. You could find out also why she had been invited to Nikki Kumar's house at all.'

Shona, over a second helping of apple crumble, remarked how frightening it was that a retired police officer seemed to know everything about everybody, much more than an officer still in service did.

The Swift drove into Bikram's police housing parking lot with a squeal of tyres and Shona stepped out. In the car, they had talked of Mr Dawson and what he had told them over dinner and then Bikram had sighed and shaken his head. 'No point in thinking of all that now.'

In the lift, they met Inspector Rafat Khan and family from flat 6B, who nodded briefly and sniffed disapprovingly. The cook made a great show of banging the door of the pantry shut, to communicate a tactical retreat, and they linked arms and walked into the bedroom.

Bikram's mobile phone rang. It was the Control Room.

'Bad phone,' said Shona snatching the instrument from Bikram and flinging it away. 'Come here!'

Later, Bikram made a crucial mistake—he called Toofan Kumar.
Having mulled over the case on his way back, he had formed
a theory but, instead of letting things remain till the next
morning, he found himself listening to Toofan Kumar's
telephone attendant's voice that evening. Bikram had
unconsciously made the call thinking, perhaps, that he should
get the unpleasantness over before the work week started. Also,
Shona was beside him. He could face anything with her nearby.

'What is it?' snarled Toofan Kumar.

'It's about the Robi Bose case, Sir. There are reports of
occasional rave parties being thrown at the deceased's house.
We might have to explore a drug angle in this case.'

'A *what* angle?'

'Drugs. Recreational drugs. There may have been rave
parties going on in that house and someone from the family
may have been involved.'

'I want a quiet life, Bikram, but you just won't allow me to
have one, will you? Nisha Bose and drugs? Do you realize
what you're suggesting? Who puts these things into your head?'

Bikram could feel a familiar pounding at the back of his
head, a feeling he frequently encountered when talking to
his boss. 'I'm sorry but I am just reporting what I learnt
during my investigations. The truth, in fact, which is
usually unpalatable.'

'What is most unpalatable is your manner of speaking!'
roared Toofan Kumar. 'I don't care what you have investigated.
The servants did it and if you were a good officer you would
know how to fit facts to conclusions and not the other way
round. And may I remind you that there was a first-class quarrel
with some female cousin over property a few days before
he died, so if it isn't the servants it's probably Tara Bose. Learn
to use your brains.'

Curious, thought Bikram. He knows the girl's name, most

unusual for him. He must have been discussing the case with someone else recently. Was he at a club or a party? He said, 'If it's a matter of gain, Sir, then who stands to gain the most? Nisha Bose. She gets the house, freedom and a chance to live life anew. If it's a question of gain, I'd put my bet on Nisha Bose.'

'You were rotting in some goddamned place near the Sunderbans before you came to Calcutta, weren't you?' asked Toofan Kumar in the tone of a man holding himself back with the greatest restraint. 'How would you like to take a walk there again? I'll have a word with the inspector general tomorrow about your transfer orders.'

Something snapped inside Bikram. All he could think of was the image of Toofan Kumar that popped into his mind— Toofan brutalizing and frightening witnesses, fitting convenient conclusions to facts so that the men and women he favoured could be spared; a travesty of all they had been taught at training school. Shona put out a steadying hand.

He said, 'I'm sorry, Sir. Tomorrow, I'll see to it that we're not troubled any longer by this distressing thing. We'll cite lack of evidence and close the case. That would be convenient for all.' He hung up before Toofan Kumar could make a comeback.

# 14

T he group that met in Prem Gupta's room the next
morning was sombre. The coffee went cold and the
biscuits remained untouched. Toofan Kumar scowled,
Ghosh sulked, Chuni Sarkar looked worried and even the ever-
perky Sheena Sen looked nervously around her. Bikram had
obviously not slept the night before. There were furrows along
the sides of his nose and his face was haggard. His eyes burnt
with a peculiar restlessness and his fingers played incessantly
with themselves.

Then Prem Gupta cleared his throat and began, 'What we
need to do here today, gentlemen, is to go back and give
our full attention to the death of Robi Bose. That is easier said
than done, because, through long years of experience, I know
how exasperating a case becomes when you keep having to
break off in the middle to attend training programmes on
police participation in community welfare—here he nodded
at Toofan Kumar—register two hundred other cases and look
into daily law-and-order situations, as my good friend Chuni
Sarkar does—here he graciously inclined his head at Chuni—
attend to VIP duty and the whims of the local politician—he
looked at Ghosh—or be deflected into other cases.' Prem Gupta
dared not look at Bikram. He then coughed and shuffled
through some papers. 'The case was registered as a murder
under Section 302 at 3 a.m. on 9 April, Monday. The
complainant was a Dr Sudip Pyne, the doctor sent to the
Bose residence to attend to the dead man. The doctor refused
to issue a death certificate, suspecting an unnatural death, even

though the man had suffered a cerebral thrombosis and was an invalid. The body was later taken to a government hospital, Robi declared dead on arrival, and sent for post-mortem examination. The report endorsed the 'unnatural death' theory and said that an overdose of painkillers and tranquillizers had resulted in cardiac arrest. The case diary further mentions that a party had taken place at the Bose residence that day, that Robi Bose had been fidgety and disturbed, both on the fateful day and the previous day, that he had eaten his dinner alone in his room along with a glass of Horlicks, and that when his wife came up to bed, finally, she found him dead on the bed. The officers discovered empty medicine packets hidden in the rubbish dump in the garden and the doctor complained that a bedcover had been switched. A cousin of the dead man's was one of the last outsiders to see him alive. Possible suspects include this cousin, the attendants and other staff, his wife as well as any of the other guests who could have easily nipped up to his room. Assuming it was murder.'

'Assuming it was,' said Toofan sourly. 'Sometimes some men assume too much. All this song and dance because of a junior doctor who didn't like to be roused out of bed at 1 a.m.'

'Chuni, what do you think?'

Chuni Sarkar had been dreading this moment. He excelled at fence-sitting and now he would have to take sides, one way or the other. He adjusted the collar of his shirt awkwardly and swallowed hard. 'The death was so sudden, Sir, it could be anything. The circumstantial evidence points to a sudden stroke, but then, money was being stolen there a little while before. I'm wondering whether that could have had anything to do with it.'

'Ghosh?'

Ghosh jumped. He had been secretly stealing glances at Bikram and wondering what Toofan Kumar had said that had upset him so. 'We haven't been able to fix on anything definite, Sir, because there's been no time to go thoroughly into the case. But I would stick to the assumption that a murder has been committed and say it's Final Report True and that it was murder.'

'Bikram?' The gentleness in Prem Gupta's voice was unmistakable. Toofan Kumar frowned.

Bikram was not going to put up a fight. He looked up briefly at Prem Gupta and then looked away. Then, in a tone of complete indifference, he said, 'You can say the doctor was pig-headed and I was wrong. You can say that it was all wildly off the mark and dismiss the case.'

'I can do what I like, and so I will,' Prem Gupta said with an edge to his voice. 'But I asked for your opinion.'

There was another uncomfortable silence, till Bikram said wearily, 'I feel sick of the whole thing. I had met the man a few days before his death at a . . . gathering, and he had looked perfectly all right to me. Full of life, in spite of his afflictions. Then, just days later, he dies, and I find empty foils of tablets stuffed under chicken bones and onion rings in a rubbish heap in the garden. I'd like to know how he swallowed them and why, whether someone had spiked his Horlicks with them, and whether that person or those people are walking around scot-free and laughing at us. I'm a realist, and there have been plenty of unsolved homicides in my career, but somehow this one is getting on my nerves. As Ghosh said, there's something about that house and its inhabitants that gives me the shivers.'

Prem Gupta looked at his watch. 'It is second May today, and, therefore, close to a month since the death of the unfortunate man. The municipal elections will be held in August and we'll all be busy by July. Thank heavens we haven't made any hasty arrests. I give all of you another month before

I begin to officially lose interest in the case. Circumstantial evidence points to something sinister in this death, but, as Toofan feels, that could also be our bias, set off by a hyper-excited doctor. But then again, this Pyne is the sort of man who will dig his heels in and not give up. I can tell you, Toofan, that even if we were to declare the murder to be a mistake and ask for the case to be dismissed, the good doctor will refuse to be beaten. And please don't forget the press. They will be baying for our blood, and the fact that both Bikram and Toofan have partied with the Bose family will be dug out and examined with great care. Either way, we're stuck, and have to make the most of it.'

Prem Gupta looked at his audience who were now all looking uneasy, except Bikram, whose brow was knitted in a tremendous frown. Prem Gupta waited for a moment and said, 'Well now, I think it's time for a truce. All of you have been working very hard, yes, even you, Sheena, though I haven't asked you your opinion yet, I know you've been helping all along. I'll order some more coffee, and this time it mustn't go cold.' The coffee was a bad idea. Bikram's annoyance had somehow vitiated the atmosphere and Chuni Sarkar and Ghosh remained quiet. Prem Gupta, who disliked scenes, turned to Toofan Kumar and discussed other departmental work with him. Bikram left his coffee untasted and sat brooding on his chair.

It was a relief when the meeting broke up. Prem Gupta tactfully asked Toofan Kumar to stay back, and worked hard at calming him down by judicious references to his past successes and his possible future ones. He asked about his attempts at bagging the United Nations assignment and promised to put in a word when in Delhi the next time. After Toofan Kumar had left, Prem Gupta tried to get Bikram on his cell phone, hoping to spend another ten minutes with him. This was impossible because Bikram's cell phone was switched off and he was not to be found in his office.

'That's funny,' said Prem Gupta to himself. 'I didn't know he was so unreasonable.' Puzzled and pained, he went about his business trying to put the morning's impromptu meeting out of his mind.

## 15

Bikram had given Raja a photo of Buro taken on the night of Robi's death. Mistry had surreptitiously taken Raja to the Bose residence and dropped him at the corner, so he could follow Buro's movements. Raja, at first, overpowered by the detective impulse, religiously watched the house from 6 a.m. to 8 p.m. This was quite an effort for him, because Raja was a creature of the night, and felt quite unwell in the incandescence of day. He carried chips and nuts in one pocket and packets of cigarettes and spiced chewing tobacco in another. For five days, he relieved himself in the bushes, slapped mosquitoes off his neck, listened to dial-in programmes on his cell phone radio and cleaned and dug his nose and ears. But Buro seemed to shun the outside world. Once a day, he walked to the grocery shop at the end of the road and came back with a bag of vegetables and soda bottles. Raja, tailing him from a distance, also had to buy things from the shop and, on the third day, felt that the shopkeeper looked at him significantly. Accordingly, on day six and seven, Raja took it easy and reappeared for duty on day eight. He spent a whole day on the pavement. At about 4 p.m., Buro drew up on a motorcycle at the Bose residence with a small bag strapped on to the passenger seat.

'How was your trip, Buro?' shouted the watchman cheerfully. 'We missed you these two days!'

'Fine! I don't think I need to go out again for some time.'

Raja stared, dismayed. Could it be, then, that Buro suspected? In spite of his playful ways, Raja was a professional

criminal and knew his job. He gave up his post immediately
and reported to Bikram. 'Trouble, Sir. I think the rat knows
I'm tailing him. He wouldn't stir out of the house all the while
I was there and drove off for a two-day trip the minute I wasn't.
Came back carrying a black bag.'

'Did they have any guests or parties on the days you were
on guard?'

'Not a thing. All they did was buy vegetables.'

'Did you see anyone who looked like masseuse or a tailor?'

'I saw a pretty young girl come in on foot on the third
day I was there, and she could have been the masseuse, but
I didn't see any tailor. The lady goes out a lot, that she
does. Drives out on her own. Cars come to the house in the
afternoon. Big, expensive cars with tinted windows. All stylish
people, looks like.'

You've been a great help, thought Bikram gloomily,
especially in tipping off Buro and Nisha Bose. But he thanked
Raja in honeyed tones and told him to lie low till fresh orders.
A relieved Raja loped off to the Savoy Hotel for a drink or two.

Tara hadn't quite realized how tired she was until she faced the
long climb up the stairs to her house. The roar of the evening
ride back still echoed in her ears. Without pausing to talk
to anyone, she went in for her bath. Towelling her hair,
she surveyed herself in the mirror. A narrow face, a little
lined, framed by straight dark hair with a pair of enormous
eyes looked back steadily. That evening, like many evenings
before, embarrassing, almost, in the regularity of monotony
and loneliness, Tara gulped down her evening mash of vegetable
curry and a shrivelled onion-and-chilli omelette before fleeing
to the seclusion of her room. She sat on the bed and eyed
the table, then flung open the drawer and extracted a leather
bag whose contents she tipped out on to the bed. Tara looked

at the tablets and capsules scattered before her. Her hands had begun to tremble already and the bottles of brandy wrapped in newspaper at the back of the drawer seemed to be beckoning compellingly. She hesitated. Then, on an impulse, she slammed the drawer shut, picked up her purse, dug out a piece of paper, dialled the number written on it and waited. Would he pick it up?

He did.

Tara almost choked when she heard his voice and tears sprang unbidden to her eyes. 'Is that Bikram Chatterjee speaking?' The connection was faulty, for the sound was echoing and, to Tara, her voice seemed hoarse and strange over the telephone.

'It is.'

'I'm Tara, Robi Bose's cousin.' Always a crisis of identity, she thought grimly. Even though the bastard's dead.

'Yes.' His voice sounded cool and distant.

'I have something to say, to . . . to confess . . . no, inform. About the Boses.'

There was silence and then the voice came back, stronger and certainly warmer. 'This connection is not very good, Tara. Would you like to come to my office tomorrow and discuss the matter? Unless, of course, it is something you would prefer to talk over the phone, and I can ring you back.'

'It's something very personal and it cannot be said in the office. In any case, I don't think I can trust myself till tomorrow.'

'Then this is what I suggest. I'll be at your place in half an hour. And thanks for calling. I know what an enormous effort it takes to ring up the police if you've got something to say. You're very brave.'

On his way to the lift, Bikram rang up Ghosh. 'The cousin's cracked.'

'Dead?'

'No, for god's sake! We don't need another corpse. She's

got something to tell me. I can tell you it's going to be good. I've asked Sheena Sen to be in the house, too, but . . .'

'But talk to her alone,' Ghosh completed Bikram's sentence. 'And give them the Bikram touch. Metaphorically speaking, that is,' he added.

'Your humour is reaching new limits nowadays,' said Bikram. 'Goodbye.'

Tara was waiting for him on the balcony. Bikram saw her as soon as he turned off the car engine. Without waiting to see him alight, she disappeared from view and reappeared as Bikram was struggling with a rusted iron padlock on the ancient gate. Bikram took a good look at her then, as she fussed with the latch and let them in. Though she was not plain, it was difficult to say whether she was attractive or not. Certainly her eyes, deep pools of black, gave her a curious Madonna-like quality. At present, those eyes were filled with distrust.

Tara took them up the stairs quietly. Bikram could hear a television blaring and a woman coughing in an inside room.

'Your father?'

'Does not know as yet.'

She motioned Sheena Sen down to the sagging sofa in the drawing room.

'I'd like to talk to Mr Chatterjee alone, in my room. If you could please sit here.'

Bikram looked at Tara with surprise and interest. Gone was the diffident young lady sitting coyly in the Tollygunge police station with her father ranting beside her.

Tara climbed up to her room on the roof, pulled out a rattan chair for Bikram and sat on the bed. She could hardly believe the events of the last half-hour or so. Was it really she who had phoned and made him come here, he, whom she had dreamed and hallucinated about on the very bed before which he now sat? Then she took a deep breath and began.

'For a start, I am addicted to prescription medicines. I've been hooked for the last year or so. If what I have to say here today is not worth anything because it's an addict's testimony then you'd better let me know.'

Bikram said nothing.

'Well?'

'Tara, swallowing a few alprazolams and codeine tablets does not classify you as an addict. There are worse things than that.'

'But . . .'

'For that matter, I take valium myself once or twice a week to help me sleep.' Bikram who, Shona complained, needed nothing more than a flat surface to fall effortlessly into a sound sleep, hoped he was making the right noises.

'Then you will perhaps understand the terrible compulsion of having one's life ruled by the absolute necessity of having . . . how did you know?'

Bikram pointed to the bedside table drawer. In her excitement, it had been left partly open by Tara, displaying its contents. 'They had rave parties, didn't they?' asked Bikram gently.

Tara nodded dumbly.

'Were there drugs involved?'

'I think so. I'm not sure. I wasn't ever asked to those parties, but I suspected.'

'Did Robi Bose know?'

'He was sharp enough never to discuss it with me. People thought he had lost his senses along with his physical well-being, but he was remarkably quick. He would have gone on for years, had it not been for Nisha.'

'Why Nisha?'

'Because she began this dangerous business. When Robi had his stroke Nisha had a kind of nervous breakdown. Her doctor friends prescribed her a whole array of mood lifters and tranquillizers. At first she stuck to the prescription, but she soon succumbed to the thrill of it. That's where I came in. The chemist in our locality gives us medicines without prescriptions. Nisha's fashionable neighbourhood chemist wouldn't do that. She used me to get herself a steady supply of painkillers and tranquillizers, and got me hooked in the process.'

'And did Robi too have access to all those medicines?'

'He did. I almost think Nisha hoped Robi would overdose himself on them accidentally and make things easier for her. She'd made that house a chemist's shop with all those medicines, or rather, a house of the dead. Never any laughter there, or joy. Only plotting and complaining, phony friends and wickedness. That house is fashioned in the image of its mistress and she is all-consuming, all-devouring. She finished Robi.'

'Do you think she murdered him?'

'Yes, I do. She was tired of waiting. She and the servants fed him all those painkillers and would have passed it off as a natural death, had it not been for that doctor. I know that because she made me buy three strips of painkillers just two days before Robi died.'

'What painkiller was that?'

'Tramadol.'

Lily Lahiri was correcting answer papers when the telephone rang. Only a few of her closest associates knew that she gave lessons in Math and English to schoolchildren of grades five, six and seven, in a discreet tutorial group that met at her house twice a week. Lily Lahiri maintained a car and two servants, had memberships in two clubs and occasionally travelled, but all that created a financial strain and she could use the extra cash.

'Lily here,' she drawled.

'Madam, I am Roy speaking.'

'Yes?'

'I was given your number by Nisha Bose.'

'So?'

'We have an excellent collection of Bangladeshi saris, pure cotton, intricate designs, gossamer-fine . . .'

'I am not interested.' Lily Lahiri banged down the phone.

She went for her bath, leaving the answer papers on the table. The full-time maid was on leave and the daily would be in any time. When she reappeared, wearing a printed kaftan with an expensive satin fluting that showed only a hint of raggedness, the doorbell rang. Lily Lahiri went to open the door for her maid. Two men stood on the doormat. They were short and stocky, each carried two black bags, and kept smiling.

Lily Lahiri's heart froze. She had never seen them before and wondered how they could have got past the security desk at the entrance. She thought of all the stories in the newspapers and wondered if she, too, was to become the subject of one of those stories.

The men had pushed in and shut the door. They were still smiling.

'Why did you hang up on us so rudely, Aunty? Didn't we say that we have some interesting things to show you?'

As if to illustrate his point, one of the men hoisted the bag on to a low coffee table. Lily's heart sank. His fly was unzipped and she turned her face away with a strangled moan. Was it to be the other thing too?

The bag was opened and out tumbled saris. Lily panicked, thinking the worst, and in that moment, she blurted the first thing that popped into her mind: 'Get out!'

'It's all right.'

'Leave at once.'

'Look at this sari, the colour of spring leaves!'

'How dare you!'

The men continued to pull out saris and strew them on the carpet, settling down comfortably, patting and unfolding their wares.

Lily Lahiri considered running out to the landing and ringing her neighbour's doorbell, but that would mean leaving the men inside which was, perhaps, what they wanted. What a mess! Where was her cell phone? She remembered it was in her kaftan pocket, for she had taken her phone in with her, in case the maid was too long at the door and could give Lily a missed call from her number.

With shaking hands Lily took out the phone and dialled Toofan Kumar. The phone rang and was disconnected. Poor Lily Lahiri could not possibly know that Toofan Kumar was at a meeting with senior bureaucrats over anti-government demonstrations scheduled to rock Calcutta through the whole week and had no time for Lily Lahiri.

The men were throwing saris on to the sofa. One of them asked her whom she was calling.

'Nisha, to find out if she really knows you.'

'Of course she does.'

The men were now giggling. 'Nisha is close to our hearts, we have a long association with that family, you can ring up and find out all you want to know. May we use your bathroom?'

Lily Lahiri, who was sweating with fright, signalled them towards the service toilet and dialled Bikram Chatterjee's number. The man with the unzipped fly had left. Lily walked to the window. A cool voice answered the phone and Lily quavered, 'Bikram Chatterjee, is that you? I'm Lily Lahiri, I had come with Toofan Kumar's reference that day, for god's sake help me, two men have entered my flat saying they want to sell Dhaka saris, they just forced their way in, no, I did not ask them to come, I thought it was my maid, I'm all alone, they might kill me, I can't even go to the lift and scream . . . it's . . .', here she gave her address.

Fortunately for her, Bikram knew the voice of genuine terror when he heard it.

Lily finished her phone call and looked around. The men were patting the saris, but this time they were folding them away and putting them back inside the bag.

'Really, Aunty, you shouldn't worry so much. Calling the police and all! Did you think we came to rob you, or tease you, or have a look around or a bit of fun?'

Pat, pat, pat went the saris. Bits of the tissue covering had rolled on to the carpet but the men took no notice.

The men stood up and smiled.

'Pity you didn't like the white sari with the black border. It would have suited your personality, Aunty.'

'Don't you have a chain lock, Aunty? Tell your daughter to get one for you from America.'

They bowed and nodded and smiled and left, pulling the door shut after them. The lock clicked in place.

Lily Lahiri stood shaking on the carpet, her heart pounding, her knees limp. She had never been so frightened in her life. Bits of tissue clung to the carpet. Lily felt tears pricking her eyes. She reached out to the sofa to steady herself and her hands brushed against something, a piece of paper, it had figures written on it, and something else in Bengali. Lily Lahiri fell against the sofa with the piece of paper crumpled in her hand, only dimly hearing the doorbell and her cell phone go off together.

Pilot 56A rumbled into the Diamond Point thana and the officer-in-charge got out with a sigh of relief. It was 6.30 p.m., hot, dusty, and even seeing off the inspector general's convoy had not improved matters one bit. Constables in various stages of undress lounging around the thana compound scuttled across the courtyard like distressed crabs at the officer's sudden arrival. The duty officer, engaged happily in killing mosquitoes with an electric exterminator that looked like a racquet, quit his enjoyable pastime to make a hasty salute.

The officer-in-charge groaned, ordered a cup of tea and switched on the air conditioner he had bullied out of a local tradesman. As he stood up to shut the window, he could see that the sweeper was drunk and weaving around the thana veranda with a commode brush in his hand. Damn the man!

He began work on a mountain of files that had built up relentlessly on the table over the last week. The inspector general's parting words had promised an inspection. If he only knew what it was to be in the thick of things and not just roost happily in the comfortable confines of a splendiferous city office! The officer-in-charge wailed to himself and attacked the mountain. His phone rang. It was his most reliable informer.

'I'm sending along a friend. Johnny. He might have something interesting to say.'

'About what?'

'Arms. Currency too, maybe. Interested?'

The officer frowned. Illegal arms and currency were too much of a bother to follow up. On the other hand, if he could pull off a few successful raids before the inspection, he could petition for a transfer closer to town. His wife nagged continuously about sharing a flat with his parents, and family squabbles were giving him sleepless nights.

'Okay. But you're sure about this, right?'

'I've never let you down, have I?'

The officer admitted that he hadn't.

The door opened and the duty officer entered. He said, 'A guy wants to see you, Sir. Says he has some information he can convey only to you.' Johnny was brought in, limping on a pair of crutches. He was short and stout, with long hair curling about his shoulders and he sported a moustache.

'This information is hot,' he announced without preamble, 'provided you don't give in to pressure and let the man out after a few days. His name is Babul and a deal's going down—arms. Usually, the stuff comes from the Northeast and from Nepal, but this time it is coming in on a fishing trawler. The main thing is, he's not to be let off.'

The plan was to keep watch on the railway platform where the arms were to be handed over. Once the exchange was made, Johnny would give the signal and the arrest could be made.

'Mind you, Babul must not escape by any means.'

The name Babul was completely unfamiliar to the officer-in-charge who had spent much of his time investigating local political party brawls and covering up for the favoured political party of the moment. The rest of the time was spent in looking after weekend murders—as he called them—call girls done in by their employers on the beaches following dirty weekends, or college girls killed by their boyfriends once the fun was over. Beyond the murders and the political warfare, was a steady stream of VIPs to be escorted to the Sunderbans resorts and back; members of the bureaucracy and the judiciary and film stars, all demanding pilot cars and fresh fish and armed guards and Sunderbans honey. Where was the time to find out what Babul really did?

Acting on Johnny's instructions, the policemen watched breathlessly as the train slid in to the station. Even before the train reached the platform, the blind beggars and musicians jumped off, followed by the pickpockets with the trip's pickings. Vegetable vendors crowded the platforms, carrying enormous baskets filled with brinjal and spinach, papaya and gourd. Over the years, Calcutta streets had begun to metamorphose at certain times in the morning and evening, into impromptu bazaars where the farmers sold their vegetables, fruits and fresh country eggs. The policemen watched with impatient eyes as the wares were loaded on to the densely packed suburban trains. These would make their way to middle-class neighbourhoods where, in the heat of the afternoon, the farmers would take time off for a nap, their stuff piled high under jute matting, so that Tara returning home from work would have to pick her way delicately between the vegetable mounds.

Johnny was in a corner of the platform, before a row of taps, glued to his cell phone which had been squawking for some time now. The policemen watched, hoping the mysterious Babul would bite.

Hard-eyed women in saris, college girls in dresses of synthetic fabric, hungry-looking suburban men in cheap trousers and scruffy shirts, farmers in loincloths, vagrants with black, torn shorts, fishermen's wives in ragged saris, children in patched skirts and boldly coloured tops—no, Babul didn't seem to fit anyone who tumbled in and out of the compartments.

Johnny suddenly moved towards the train. The engine let out a low moaning whistle before starting. A man wearing a white shirt and a pair of white trousers, carrying a broad black sports bag, leapt nimbly down from the train just as Johnny reached him. The train lurched forward. The waiting policemen struggled to reach the pair. It seemed as if all the world's fishermen and farmers' wives were thrusting themselves in their way. The train had begun to move forward slowly. At the same time, another man darted in from another part of the platform, rushed up to the man in the white shirt and began talking to him excitedly. Babul, momentarily taken aback, turned aside to look at this man. The policemen, throwing all caution to the wind, completed the last few paces with a wild cry and leapt upon the trio. Babul was netted at last and in the most inglorious way, under the shadow of a railway urinal by a couple of lowly police constables.

With him were Johnny, secretly triumphant, and the third man who looked as if he had just seen a vision of his own funeral. A ramshackle jeep swung into the Diamond Point thana and the officer-in-charge, astonished that his raid had actually worked out, waved them all into the lock-up and wondered what to do. He had just finished planning a weekend trip with his wife and child and the successful raid was a spoiler. He spent ten minutes placating his wife, then mopped his brow and got down to business.

He knew Johnny and guessed who Babul was, but stared heavily at the third man. Who on earth was this chump?

'Name?'

'Buro Das.'

'What were you doing there, talking to this man?'

'I couldn't find my cell phone and thought he had taken it. I want to charge him for theft.'

'Where did you lose your phone?'

'In the train.'

'But you have it now, do you not?'

'It was a mistake, I realized later on.'

'Are you sure you don't know the man?'

'I don't, Sir, do believe me. I came here to visit my friend who lives in the next village and I need to go home.'

Had the officer been attentive he would have realized that Johnny was trying to make a sign to him about something. Johnny, caught in the terrible position of pretending to be arrested without really being so, had an idea that Buro had been there for some other purpose. But the officer's head was too full of his wife and the cancelled trip, and the fact that the Additional SP and the SP would soon be in his small office and a hundred other cases would be dug up for perusal.

So he blinked tiredly and desultorily took down the false address which Buro supplied him and then let him go.

In a triumph of miscommunication, Bikram heard about Babul's arrest two days later, and about Buro's arrest and being let off, nothing at all.

When two men from the local police station arrived at Lily Lahiri's opulent flat, they found her sitting with a stung look on her face. Lily had, however, sufficiently recovered her composure to frown at their arrival and ask them to take off their dirty boots.

'You're late,' she said angrily. 'They could have killed me.'

'What happened, if you could kindly tell us . . .'

Without asking them to sit, Lily Lahiri related the events of those harrowing ten minutes.

'Is anything missing?'

'No, at least . . .'

Lily cast her eyes quickly around the room, even though she knew the men had not really been ordinary thieves.

'Have you ever seen them before?'

'No.'

'What about your maid?'

'She's washing the clothes, so you'll have to wait to see her,' said Lily ungraciously.

The older policeman, acquainted with high-society ladies and their ill-humoured servants, said that if that was all, they would go back to the police station, and if madam or her maid had anything else to report they could do so there.

'But you haven't even looked around,' said Lily pettishly.

'Our boots are dirty, as you say. Would you like to have them clumping round your rooms?'

The other man suddenly noticed the bits of tissue and the crumpled scrap of paper on the carpet.

'Did they leave that behind?'

'Possibly, it wasn't there before.'

He picked the paper up, one of which had a name that looked like S.K. Hassan on it.

'Did they give this to you?'

'Didn't you hear what I said? I ordered them out of my flat and rang the police up to make a complaint.'

The policemen glanced around the room and then, finding nothing better to do, left.

The paper travelled to Bikram at the end of the day along with a rather emboldened report, detailing the policemen's visit and inspection of complainant's flat.

Lily Lahiri rang up Parry Prakash's wife and outlined the incident in a rather embroidered report, ending with the policemen's muddy boots and how she would have to get her carpet dry-cleaned again.

# 16

'If you will allow me, Sir, I would like to take a shot at the Bose house once more.'

'Thank you, Raja, but that won't be necessary.'

'I'll be careful this time.'

'I just told you, don't bother.'

'But I want to, I must. I've never failed at anything and here I am, unsuccessful the one time the man who has saved my life has set me to do something.'

'Raja, go home, or wherever you sleep at night, if at all, and forget I ever told you anything.' Bikram wished he had never confided in Raja. While Bikram liked his irrepressible jauntiness, lately he was finding his informer to be a bit of a bother.

Raja himself was distressed by his failure and by Buro's discovery of him. He consulted his astrologer who assured him that the stars were beneficial and a long-awaited wish would come true. Then Raja looked up his telephone diary, thumbed through the names, settled on one and took the plunge. Montu Mondol had been set free on bail and was only too happy to help. He still remembered the Coke at the airport police station and cherished fond memories of Bikram. Montu looked at Raja with newly-found respect. 'You're his guy? Lucky! How often do you meet him?'

'Hardly talks to me, you rat. Picked me up at that Babul raid but let me off lightly. I want to do him a good turn.'

They discussed Babul and who might have turned him in and, more importantly, who was running the racket now.

Then Montu expressed his willingness to do what he could for Bikram.

'There's a posh house we have to watch. I tried it once during the day, but the whoreson who works there is too smart for me. I'll need your help.' Raja fumed as he described Buro. They drew up a sketchy plan, celebrated their partnership with a bottle of XXX rum and went home.

Montu considered his options. He could go as a salesman, a serviceman, a postman or a courier delivery guy. But none of the disguises was foolproof. Finally, he made a few phone calls to influential friends, strolled around to the club at the corner where the underlings of the local councillor played carom, made friends with the secretary, procured a copy of the electoral rolls for the upcoming municipal elections, promised help in securing votes when necessary, collected a sheaf of 'Vote For—' posters, cans of paint, paintbrush and set off for the Bose residence.

The durwan blocked his way. Montu explained patiently, 'All we want is to talk to your master.' He looked down at a piece of paper. 'Robi Bose, and ask him for permission to paint names of candidates on this outside wall.'

'You can't.'

'We'll wash it off after the elections.'

'The master's dead.'

'Shit, man, we're sorry. The mistress, then?'

'She's not at home.'

'Look, brother, times are bad, and the poor are getting poorer. People flock from the villages every day to Calcutta to look for a job and set themselves up on the pavement. Do you want a cigarette shop to spring up before your gate, or a ragpicker to start a dustbin here? Be wise, man, and let us in.'

The durwan understood and after a hurried discussion with someone inside the house, let them in. As the iron gates creaked open, Montu laughed. He had climbed higher and sturdier gates in his life. This looked like child's play.

'Are there dogs in the house?' he asked chattily. 'I'm scared of them, got bitten once and had to take injections in my abdomen.'

There were no dogs.

'Surveillance equipment, you must be having advanced and very modern security.'

'We have plenty,' said the durwan, 'inside the house.'

Not on your life, thought Montu, or I wouldn't be here.

'Could we set up some of my equipment here?' Montu pointed to the door of the durwan's outhouse. He fumbled in his pocket and took out a packet of expensive cigarettes. The durwan's eyes gleamed but he refrained from helping himself. No smoking.

Outside, were two or three of Montu's associates, standing and measuring walls and doing just enough to pass off as lower-rung party cadre.

Once inside, Montu lost interest in politics and began to admire the beauty of the garden and the shrubs there. 'What lovely flowers! Sunflowers too. I haven't seen them for quite some time.'

He was taken inside to Nisha Bose. She did not invite him to her patterned and cushioned drawing room but dismissed him from the door. Still, from the variegated plants in the background and the paintings on the wall, along with the expensive-looking rug whose edge he was standing on, Montu calculated the opulence inside. Curiously enough, he was not struck by Nisha's beauty. She stood before him in a dressing gown with dragon patterns on it and her hair was washed and smelling of cedar. Montu saw only the petulant droop of her mouth and her crinkled eyes, as if she had just turned away from the sun or had been scolded by her parents.

'No posters and no graffiti. I'll complain to the . . . Anyway, I'll have none of it.'

'We were just asking. No pressure.' He tried to look soothing and produced the electoral roll. 'Nisha Bose: age thirty-four; Robi Bose: age forty; Buro Das: age twenty-five; Mithu Das: age twenty-two; Gopal Tewari: age forty. These are all the people in your house. Anyone else?'

Beyond her he could see the veranda that ended tantalizingly in cavernous halls he itched to explore. House break-ins were always exciting, even though they were now the stuff of his infant years. He waited for the expected reply. None came. 'All right. No posters, not at all,' he parroted. 'But I need to confirm our electoral rolls to see if our records are all right. Sometimes people die, or move out and our records have to be updated.' He waited again for a statement but, as before, none came.

'Sorry to trouble you. I'll be off.' Montu ambled out of the veranda, waited for the door to close, then looked around. Here was an old house run in an old-fashioned manner. No dogs, no surveillance, two servants who were no better than stick figures and a middle-aged watchman with cable TV in his room. Montu could only imagine what he did after dark. Also, the boundary wall lay close to the kitchen and a convenient jackfruit tree grew close to it.

He turned his attention to the watchman. 'Why don't you join our club on weekends? We have good times there.'

'Never heard of it.'

'Of course you have. It's in the bazaar down the road.'

The durwan looked ill at ease. 'Political stuff's not for us. We do our work and mind our business.'

'But it's not always political.' Montu winked. 'We have video shows and all. Good booze, foreign. And discounts at local shops. Good connections to make there. For example, you need a new mobile phone. The one you have is a 2003 model.' The durwan's phone was trilling—an agitated Nisha was at the other end, wanting to know if that obnoxious man had left. Taking this opportunity, Montu escaped. He had enough to work on.

Raja and Montu returned at 2 a.m. Rain fell around them heavily, bringing with it the smells of wet earth and green leaves, but the two were unmoved by nature's charms. Wearing black raincoats over army camouflage colours, they hoisted themselves over the wall and into the garden. The kitchen window was unlocked and Montu, amazingly athletic despite his toad-like appearance, partly twisted his body in and looked around, then slithered back and shook his head. The pantry door was closed. They circled around, looking for doors and windows left open by chance, but the rain played spoilsport.

Rain fell thickly around them and stung Raja's scalp. He put his mouth to Montu's ear and said something.

'Okay,' Montu mouthed back.

They crawled back to the durwan's two-roomed house at the gate. One of the windows had come undone. It was banging against the iron grill each time a gust of wind blew. Montu steadied it with a dripping hand and peeped inside. The durwan was asleep, sprawled out on his bed. The mouldy smell of unwashed clothes mingled with the smell of rain and earth from outside. The room had been carefully cleared before he went to bed. No phone, no radio, no watch, because the window had been left open and the durwan, being a man of the world, had been clever enough to discourage petty thieves.

Raja pointed to a black object in the corner. Montu lifted his hands in question. As if in answer, a blinding flash of lightning lit the room and the two men saw the black bag simultaneously.

'Get it!' said Raja.

'But why?'

'Just get it.'

Montu rolled up his trouser leg and pulled out what looked like a small foldable baton from a holster strapped to his shin. The baton had been procured from a specialist's shop on the Bhutan border for a considerable sum of money and was just the thing for such occasions. Unfolded, the baton became a flexible tool. The grill was old-fashioned, two iron rods placed vertically, with enough space between them for Raja and Montu to carry out their task. Montu lifted one end of the baton and, with infinite care, slid the end of the strap over it. Then carefully, his brow furrowed in concentration, the sweat running down and mingling with the drops of rain, Montu eased the bag, inch by inch, across the room and between the window bars till it dropped into his hands.

'Go?'

Raja nodded.

The rain kept falling steadily and the pitted and rugged road was already filling with water. Raja kickstarted his motorcycle and Montu leapt on, clutching the bag. They roared into the pelting rain. In a little while, Raja stopped.

'What now?'

'I must see what's inside?'

'Now? Are you nuts? Let's get dry first!'

'Let's take a look first.'

They stood beneath a portico that jutted out on to the pavement. A wet dog watched them sourly. They opened the bag. There was nothing inside except a five-rupee coin, a dried-up flower and a plastic packet. They rustled the plastic packet and found it empty. They searched the pockets and found only a pen with the Kingfisher Airlines logo on it. In desperation, Raja kicked at the dog.

He deposited the bag the next morning before Bikram and sheepishly explained the circumstances of its arrival.

'Oh Raja, how could you?'

For once, Bikram looked as if he would burst into tears.

'We thought we could snoop around and find something. But the room was like a hermit's, no hidden booze, no money, nothing. Just this.'

'And once he finds the bag missing, he will know that someone was up to mischief in his room and will become even more cautious.'

Raja's eyes widened innocently. 'Should we take the bag back?'

Marvelling at Raja's faith in his own powers, Bikram swept the bag off the table hastily. 'It might still come of use, leave it.'

'Then we've done well?'

'I didn't say that . . .'

'But we have!'

With great effort, Bikram stopped his desire to laugh out loud and said evenly, 'Not bad.'

Raja seemed to wobble in what looked suspiciously like a dance step.

'But, don't discuss this with anyone else,' Bikram cautioned.

Smiling affably, Raja left.

Bikram slapped at a mosquito that was annoyingly orbiting his head and dropped back on his chair. He had opened the window and shut off the air-conditioning, but now the sounds of the cars and the smell of pee from outside his office demanded a return to his air-conditioned cocoon. I'm getting too soft, he thought. And fat, eyeing his waist critically. He decided to while away the time doing some push-ups.

At the first push down, his nose touched the black bag.

Damn!

He picked it up to throw it into a corner but then took a closer look. It was an ordinary black bag, like the thousands sold along pavements and at railway stations. A fake REEBOK label had been painted on at one end. The bag was empty but Bikram felt his way through the pockets carefully. A mischievous idea was forming in his mind. A black bag from Nisha Bose's house could always be put to good use. Something had been, no, was going on in that house, of that there could be no doubt. And if she had murdered her husband or one of the servants had done so, under her orders, this black bag could help set up the case. His long fingers encountered cloth lining and emptiness. He should have sent the bag for a forensics check up, that was a goof-up! But all that forensics would find would be Raja's and Montu's fingerprints. That duo was stupid, were they really capable of committing serious crime with such brains?

In desperation Bikram picked up the bag and shook it hard. A five-rupee coin slipped out and rattled on to his table. With excitement building up, Bikram patted the bag once again and slid fingers into various crannies. Through a hole in the lining he could see something white. Anxiously, yet with infinite gentleness, he pulled it out. It was a scrap of paper with tattered edges and the ink washed out to an almost indecipherable blot. He could barely make out a ten-digit series of numbers—94330-34, no, 54, was it 4 or 6? Bikram bent over the scrap of paper and reached for his cell phone. It was tricky, but it might work. He felt sure now that it would because, somehow, his luck had turned and everything would be all right from now on. Had Shona prayed for him?

While Bikram—assuming that the smudged figures on the shred of paper were telephone numbers—waited for them to turn into names and addresses, he was interrupted by Toofan Kumar on the telephone.

'You will have to step out of your cosy office now and then, you know, Bikram, and do some actual police work. There's a sit-in at an important road junction by the Association for the Rehabilitation of Municipality Sweepers displaced from their free lodgings at various city parks. Help the Regent Park police station regulate them.'

'But . . .'

'But, Sir! Manners, man, do I have to remind you who I am every time I talk to you?'

'But, Sir, Regent Park has many sub-inspectors. I mean, I might be having a few leads on some of the cases and, well, I am crime branch. Sir!'

'You will be zero branch very soon,' growled Toofan Kumar, 'if you don't . . .'

Aware that it was useless to waste his time arguing, Bikram held the phone away from his ears and rang the bell for the peon to ready his car. The receiver squawked and spluttered, then went still, then squawked some more. 'Hello hello, hello,' shouted Bikram confusedly, as if the connection had suddenly become unclear.

'Ullo, ullo,' bellowed Toofan Kumar.

Bikram hung up, then grinned, imagining the apoplectic fit that would ensue. Then he glared at his own reflection in the antique mirror Shona and he had purchased from a shop in the narrowest lanes of old Calcutta, and prepared to give himself up to the sweepers at Regent Park.

The call came through just as he was returning from his round. Bikram took down the details on a letter pad that sat on the corduroy flap of his car seat.

'Your speed amazes me,' he told his contact at the telephone office.

'And I'm amazed by the deterioration in your eyesight,' answered his contact grimly. Every one of the digits was wrong and we had to close down all operations and pore over your stuff. Even then, it could be two or three numbers, as we narrowed it down. Do you want them now?'

'Go ahead.'

'It could be Mr Naren Das, Shibtala Street, Chandannagore, or Sumeet Kejriwal, Canning Street, Calcutta. The third name and number which might fit in is that of Muhammad Apple Hassan, registered to an address in Ripon Street, Calcutta.'

'What?'

'I know, what a name! Apple today, Pineapple tomorrow, Banana after that, quite weird! God, how do you manage to retain your sanity, Bikram?'

Montu's interrogation had turned up a floating dealer called Apple Hassan, and Mr Dawson and Tara had hinted at drugs in the Bose house. So, a link between the two worlds of Sheikh Hassan and Nisha and Robi might not be entirely far-fetched.

'Anything else for me to do?'

'You've done enough, thanks.'

'How's Shona? We need her help for a pre-puja office bash. She promised me last time but you poked your nose in.'

'I won't, this time,' said Bikram and sounded as if he meant it.

'You'd better not, or no more apples and bananas for you, only nuts.' Cackling at his own joke, the officer in the telephone department rang off.

Raja, pacing up and down in one of the bedrooms of the Honey Grove Guesthouse, was beginning to lose patience. Negotiations had been long completed and payment was due, but the proprietor and his wife were being unnecessarily nasty.

'You're asking for too much,' began the proprietor's wife again. 'We can manage the cops on our own, without having to make payments through you.'

'In any case, we've had two from the local thana drop by twice already,' chipped in the proprietor. 'They hadn't heard of you and told us to throw you out if you came in here for stuff. It's their area, they said, and you are no one.'

Raja could feel his body quiver in rage. Play it cool, man, he told himself. He sat down on the bed and pretended to pluck idly at the scalloped bedcover. On the opposite wall was a poster of a naked white woman, who, bent over, her backside shining unnaturally, regarded Raja from between her legs. The proprietor's wife was quick to notice this distraction. 'Our girls can do that too, and even better,' she said. 'Forget this whole business and come down here once a month for a free session. Two hours, for you, with the choicest college girls. That's a deal.'

'You just went back on your earlier deal,' said Raja. 'And now you want to set up a fresh one. As for girls, this joint may not be open much longer if you don't pay up. Will you or won't you?' There was an authority in his voice that went beyond plain swagger and even the proprietors of the Honey Grove Guesthouse were mildly impressed. But they refused to relent.

'Now look here . . .'

'Yes or no?'

'We need to discuss some more . . .'

Then Raja's phone rang and he couldn't believe his luck. It was Bikram. 'Are you busy? Can you talk?' For once, Bikram had shed his mask and sounded excited.

'I am in a location at the crossing of Southern Avenue and Lake Road, Sir, but it's not important. Do you want me to go to your crime branch office or the police station?'

Out of the corner of his eye Raja could see the proprietor looking at his wife accusingly.

'I need both you and Montu, because it's about the bag

you got from that house. There was a lead there. Can the two of you bring over Sheikh Hassan alias Apple? Montu knows him. Don't frighten him, for heaven's sake, this has to be done very carefully, he mustn't go underground. Set up a meeting and let me know. You can make it the Prinsep Ghat again or, if he doesn't agree, a restaurant, I'll give you the name later on. Are you there?'

Raja was there, marvelling at this turn of events that would enable him to please Bikram and silence Honey Grove, two very delicate operations all in one go! He managed to keep his voice steady and say goodbye, yes, he would do whatever he had been asked and report back soon, then turned around and, pretending to lose all interest in Honey Grove, made to leave.

'What about your payment, Sir?' The proprietor and his wife had finished their hurried whispered consultation and now sidled up to him ingratiatingly.

'What about it? It's off, isn't it?'

'Not at all, that was a complete misunderstanding! Heh heh! If you were to get angry, where would poor people like us be? Forget the past, the present is all that matters, and this is what the present has to offer you.'

The proprietor's wife whipped out a large sequinned purse from a flashy bag and took out a wad of notes.

'I suppose they are five-hundred-rupee notes,' said Raja. 'I think I made it plain I only deal in hundred-rupee notes.'

'No problem, no problem. Get him what he wants.' The proprietor's wife turned angrily on the proprietor. 'You're always so disorganized, why do you keep him waiting, don't you see he's got loads of important appointments to keep with the police sahibs. You will put in a good word for us, won't you?' she whined.

'If your payments are regular and you remember to hike

them every six months, I'll try to remember,' said Raja
gleefully as the proprietor's wife's face fell.

Once outside he made a phone call to Montu, set up a
meeting and took a taxi to the appointed place. As he passed a
Kali temple he made the driver slow the taxi down, then raised
his right forefinger to his lips, his forehead, his lips again,
all the time whispering a thanksgiving prayer. It is all Mother
Kali's doing, he thought, that I, Raja, puny and weak, always
ill and suffering as a child, expected to die any day, unwanted
by all except my grandmother, am today Border Raja, king
of the Indo-Bangladesh border and proud friend of the best
cop in the state.

It was difficult running Sheikh Hassan, alias Apple, to ground.
Raja and Montu spun elaborate webs, tapped all their resources,
made umpteen telephone calls, spent a small fortune on taxi
fare and on running up and down the length and breadth of
the exhausting and overwhelming city. They met on multiple
evenings over bottles of Kingfisher beer and tikka kebabs,
argued and gave each other conflicting words of advice, broke
up quarrelling and then made up.

Then, on the third day, Montu was handed a consignment
to deliver to none other than Apple himself. Flushed with
triumph, he demanded Bikram's number from Raja.

'I'll tell him myself. No need for you to bother him.'

'Oho, jealous in case I get closer to him. In that case
I withdraw. This is a partnership, and I have a full right to
contact the policeman myself!'

'I'll tell him,' said Raja petulantly.

'Do, and he'll send you back to me in a trice,' said
Montu jubilantly.

Raja's heart was heavy with the struggle of having to share
Bikram with Montu but he knew there was no other way for

it. 'There is never any happiness when good friends and
accomplices fall out, so here it is, but you must promise to let
me in on every move,' grumbled Raja.

Montu suppressed a smile and solemnly promised.

The handing over of the consignment, usually done in
guesthouses and on railway platforms was, this time, to be
done in the Don biryani restaurant.

Montu sat at a table wearing a scarlet T-shirt and a cotton
jacket. This was his sartorial concession to the importance
of the occasion. All around him waiters rattled plates,
thumbed bills, shook bottles of dubious water and ladled up
enormous amounts of saffron-coloured biryani with chunks
of leathery meat. Outside, the trams trundled past and the
bus conductors shouted out the names of stops, all the time
urging new passengers in.

Montu sat serenely, betraying none of his inner nervousness.
The plan was this: Bikram and Raja, seated at different tables,
would join them once Apple Hassan arrived. After that, it
was anybody's guess what would happen. Montu hoped
Apple would continue to be the sensible man he seemed and
not create a fuss. Anything unseemly would put Montu in
a far pricklier situation than ever before. He would lose his
livelihood, the protection of his gang, would have to hunt
for another and would be completely at the mercy of this
policeman. Montu remembered his wife and his son, his
family, the rent that was outstanding, the tuition that would
have to be paid for, the medical bill for his mother that would
have to be dealt with and the whole sombre business of life
that clamoured for his attention. This Bikram seemed
sympathetic, but would that sympathy extend to these other
more urgent areas of life?

He tried hard not to look at his watch, but the minutes
went by, and the quarter-hour, and then a half-hour. At

a quarter past one, when the restaurant was at its busiest, a heavy man with a moustache and with eyebrows joined at the bridge of his nose, entered and surveyed the room warily. He was carrying a black bag on his right shoulder. Montu, who had seen Apple Hassan from a long way off, did not rise or show any sign that he knew he was there, for fear that this might be construed as a tip-off.

The man with the knitted eyebrows stepped into the restaurant and walked up to Montu's table. At the same time, a boy carrying a steaming hot plate of biryani towards the next table said, 'Side, side.'

Raja, who had risen at Apple Hassan's entry, dodged his way to the table and asked the boy, 'Where's my order? Why did you get this one first?'

'But I didn't,' the boy wailed. 'This is the first time I've heard of your order.'

A shadow crossed Apple Hassan's face. He tried to turn quickly around not noticing that Bikram had crept up silently and stood on the other side. And now, hemmed in by Bikram on one side and Raja on the other, Apple knew.

'What do you want?' he asked quietly.

'A chat,' said Bikram. 'And lots of information.'

They could not return to Bikram's office, with the phone calls and the curious clerks and the stream of visitors popping in every minute or so. You cannot extract confessions from a man amongst lovers in parks and gardens, and Apple Hassan could not be interrogated in a plush coffee shop in a city shopping mall. Working in the crime branch off and on for five years, Bikram had figured a couple of handy questioning zones of his own, where he could take his informers and trusted sources without anyone knowing. His favourite one was a small room that opened out on to a jetty on the river, the Boatman's Bay of Bengal Club, a tiny place fitted out with businesslike compasses and bunks and maps. Outside, the barges bobbed on the water and the tugboats hooted while, on the opposite shore, the warehouses stood empty with the new residential blocks towering behind them. In the distance, one could see the gleaming iron girders of Howrah Bridge.

Apple Hassan got out sulkily from Mistry's car and struggled in the hands of Sanjoy and Debu, the two security guards.

'Now, now,' said Raja. 'Be a good boy and don't give us any trouble. Sa'ab here simply wants to ask you a few things.'

Sheikh Hassan shot Raja a venomous look and a longer, more inscrutable look at Montu, at which the latter's disquiet increased. He hung back and beckoned to Bikram. 'If this gets out, and Hassan turns me in, I'm finished.'

'Have faith in me,' said Bikram. 'He won't touch a hair of your head.'

'He won't need to. Half a word here and there and I'll be dead before I know it.'

'Relax, Montu. Go out and have a cup of tea. There's a hotel nearby called Scoop, or you can try the tea at the bus stand, that's good too.'

'But you should not have any of that stuff, Sir,' said Raja unexpectedly joining them. 'Remember how you had a cup once after your walk at Eden Gardens and nearly died of a stomach upset.'

'How on earth do you . . .?' Bikram stared at Raja.

Raja winked. 'I do my homework well. Now here's Ghosh Sir. Right glad I am to see him after so long.' Raja bowed down before Ghosh, who was still trying to extricate himself from his car, in an elaborate gesture of pranam and was met with a cynical humph. 'Are you well, Sir? Have you forgotten me, Sir? At your service, Sir!'

'Still the same comedy show, I see,' puffed Ghosh, annoyed.

Ghosh entered the room where Bikram was already at work on Sheikh Hassan. In front of them was the crumpled scrap of paper taken from the bag Raja and Montu had filched from the durwan's room, the bag itself, and Apple's own bag which he was carrying today. There was also a packet full of white powder and a bundle of what had looked like paper but turned out to be currency notes. Bikram was doodling ferociously on a slip of paper while Apple Hassan sat in front as if carved in stone.

'And if I refuse?'

Ghosh looked around for a place to sit. Bikram said in a friendly tone, 'Then this officer here will explain what happens to you. Ghosh, Sheikh Hassan wants to know what happens to him if he refuses to answer my questions.'

'If that's hundred grams of heroin, he gets ten years, and if that's fake currency, he gets ten years more. Either way, we've got his bag and can plant enough evidence to put him out of the way for many years to come. Raja and Montu will swear in court to some other crimes, so, even if he can arrange bail on two counts, he'll have to keep arranging more bail and we'll keep convicting him. This goes on and, in the meanwhile, there's enough hue and cry in the media for some judge to come down really heavily on him and refuse him bail. If I were Sheikh Hassan, I'd take the alternative.'

'Very well,' said Apple Hassan shortly. 'I'll talk.'

# 17

'When Buro joined service at a hi-fi house in the city, he vowed he would never do anything stupid again. He had already got into trouble once before when he was an electrician's apprentice—couldn't restrain himself and picked up a brooch from a dressing table on his way out. Totally unnecessary, but that's Buro for you, thinks himself damn clever.'

They were still seated in the tiny room at the Bay of Bengal Club. Beyond, the plaintive chug-chug of the steamers, blended with the roar of the buses skittering towards Howrah, and was occasionally punctuated by the shush of the flush as someone used the toilet outside. Now that Sheikh Hassan had begun to talk, his sass came back. Hassan had a pear-shaped body and a look of undue ferocity because of the knitted eyebrows. 'Looking back, I now realize that Buro never had much luck with anything. His father died early and he had three sisters to marry off. Usual story, of course. I think he tried his hand at waiting in a tea stall, but the stall was burnt down in some election clash. He tried to ingratiate himself with the local panchayat but was too scared to handle a revolver, or so he told me. So he came to Calcutta and got too greedy too soon, as I just told you. After Buro went underground, following the brooch incident, a man from his village brought him along to me for some small jobs. I gave him a couple of roving assignments, occasionally ferrying an envelope, booking a room in a hotel for a client and such like, because I take my time over new chaps, especially drifters like him. I helped set him up, however, so that in a few months he found work as a masseur. Nothing much, about one hundred rupees a sitting, till he found better work at a physiotherapist's clinic, where he learnt his trade a little more professionally. He used to come and meet me now and then, grumbling about money and wanting better things to do. His mother was nagging him over the sisters and their marriages and he was unable to cough up the money. But he didn't want to join a factory in one of the cities either, as a common labourer. He wanted to become a contact man here but I said that life begins at the carrier stage, contact is level two, and he would have to make trips across the border with my stuff and slog it out before I upgraded him. But Buro was unwilling.' Sheikh Hassan sniffed. 'Always the softie who wanted quick and easy money. In a way, I'm happy to be here ratting on him today.'

'He stopped coming for about six months and I thought he'd gone off to Delhi or Mumbai. Then one day he turned up, very excited, wearing jeans and an expensive T-shirt. He had squirted perfume on himself and looked very happy and smug. I thought he had been taken in by some rival gang and he had come to preen before me, but that was not so. He said he had found employment in a rich household as a male nurse and the man's wife had the hots for him. I usually let these gawky youngsters ruin themselves without interfering, but Buro was such an ass I felt sure he would be entangled in something bad soon and would trap me too. So I took him aside and gave him words of advice, such as I have never done, and told him there would always be disaster if he tried to clean out the household or rape the mistress. Things are different in cities elsewhere in India. One can always pull off something there and have our organization help one go underground in Bengal, but it is impossible to pull off a caper in Calcutta and expect to hide in Bengal.

'Buro laughed, which I found very insulting, and patted me on the shoulder. He laughed at me, can you imagine, me, who has been in this business while he was still drinking his mother's milk and shitting on her lap!' Apple Hassan's lips curled at the remembrance of this indignity and he stopped talking.

'He boasted about drugs, I suppose,' Bikram broke the silence.

'Yes. He said the mistress of the house was fond of rough parties, with crack for the more daring and pills for the newbies and the not-so-brave. Buro had fixed up with the local pharmacy but they were asking for too much money and their supplies were irregular. Buro had it all figured out: he would set up a laboratory and manufacture the stuff, take over production and delivery, and become the kingpin in his area. Then I laughed at him, reminded him of some of the names he would be up against and some of the men with whom he would have to cross swords. But he was adamant. He asked me for an advance, which is a measure of his stupidity. I refused and he went away. He must have managed the money somehow, because I heard he had set up his lab and was doing some work there. And that's all I know, in the name of Allah, so you must let me go now.'

'The address, please.'

Bikram pushed forward a slip of paper, but Apple Hassan was cannier than he thought. 'I can't write, and can barely read. You'll have to take it down yourself.' He dictated an address in an obscure lane in a northern suburb of Calcutta which Bikram took down.

Then Ghosh stirred and felt in his pockets and took out a crumpled piece of paper, covered with tissue, of the kind that expensive clothes shops use for wrapping their merchandise. 'And now, kindly explain to us, Mr Apple

Hassan, why you go around terrorizing innocent ladies by forcing yourself upon them unannounced?'

'I don't understand.' Sheikh Hassan was the picture of innocent bewilderment.

'Who went to a flat owned by Lily Lahiri and frightened her so much that she was forced to call the police?'

Apple Hassan continued to be puzzled. 'I didn't do a thing like that, why should I? That's stupid.'

Ghosh roared, 'Do I have to knock you on the head to make you confess? Look at these scraps of paper left behind by you, or your men, with your name on them, at Lily Lahiri's residence a few days ago this month.'

Apple Hassan stared at the scraps of paper, then turned to Bikram. 'I swear by Allah, Sir, I had nothing to do with this. The sari business is a front. I would be a fool to commit theft or murder as a sari seller! This must be someone else!'

Bikram and Ghosh exchanged significant glances. 'I think,' said Bikram, 'you'd better review your business partners and underlings and find out how many of them are disgruntled. Clearly, someone was trying to trap you.'

Sheikh Hassan sat frozen.

'And now,' said Bikram gently, 'thank you for all your help, but I do have to arrest you.'

Sheikh Hassan looked up sadly and his eyes were pleading.

'No,' said Bikram. 'You can never turn informer; you know this as well as I do. Besides, you know the tricks of the trade, and will know how to wriggle out of this one, just when we need lots more information out of you. Not just I, but my colleagues in other departments as well. You're too well known to be simply let off like Montu.'

Sheikh Hassan, alias Apple, smiled. 'You know what?' he said. 'I'm almost relieved. If I can go out of circulation for some time now, I can work from jail and reset my network.

The minute I go in, the traitors will expose themselves and I can weed them out. And yes, it is my good luck that I have been caught by a DSP, Bikram Chatterjee no less, and not a lowly constable. Now at least I can hold my head high!'

Two mangled Tata Sumo cars bumped and pushed their way over a battered road. The little bylane branched off from the main road and they could barely squeeze themselves between tiled mud huts and scum-filled ponds.

Ghosh and Bikram were intoxicated with pre-raid adrenaline but tried hard not to show it. The house had been scouted out beforehand, its location noted and the constable who had done so, now sat in front issuing instructions, left, right, left again, down by the tree, right, alongside Jagabandhu Sweets, beside the Corporation School, beyond the Milon Sangha, yes, there it is, Sir, that old house over there, up behind the locked gate. The house stood alone, with no signs of habitation around it. It was 2 p.m. but all was sleepy and quiet.

Brakes screeched and doors were flung open. From the Tata Sumo at the rear, constables tumbled out and took up positions around the house, slipping and cursing as they went. Bikram walked calmly over to the gate, vaulted over it and disappeared inside. Ghosh, sweating and fuming, shouted at the constable beside him to break open the padlock and hurry. He looked around him. The house was old and shut and looked completely empty and abandoned. A narrow patch in front was overrun by weeds and bushes. The unmistakable crack of a pistol shot came from within the house. At the same time, Ghosh's phone rang. It was Bikram.

'Don't worry, it was just me, firing at the lock to open it.'

The line went dead. The constable rattled and pushed at the lock with his implements and Ghosh aimed a kick at the gate. Crash! The right section of the gate collapsed and Ghosh jumped back in surprise. He stopped and mouthed a silent thanks that the gate had not fallen as Bikram was jumping over it.

The front door was open. He's agitated, thought Ghosh, or he would never have made the mistake of firing at a door behind which people could be living. But there seemed to be no one inside except rats and lizards. The red floors were covered with weeks-old dust. A pair of chappals lay abandoned in a corner and a dirty mattress in another.

Ghosh moved cautiously to the next room. There were two iron chairs before a table with an aluminium top. On the table were three chipped cups, four cracked saucers, two dirty red flannel rags, a China teapot and a sheet of newspaper. There were also four bottles of locally made alcohol, empty and lolling forlornly on the floor.

The sound of footsteps sounded and Ghosh looked up. Bikram entered, looking a picture of misery. There were cobwebs on his shirt and collar and an ugly tear in his trousers where it had caught the rusted gate. He was pocketing his revolver and looked so dejected that Ghosh felt a twinge of pity for him. 'Beg your pardon, Sir, but I think you should check if you are bleeding or not. That gate was really bad. Perhaps you should take an anti-tetanus shot.'

He could have spoken to the table. Bikram collapsed on a chair and sat back, with his eyes closed. 'And all along I had visions of a sophisticated amphetamine factory, Ghosh, with Buro and his gang furiously cranking out the stuff. Do you think Sheikh Hassan deliberately misled us?'

'We misled ourselves, Sir, because we let our imagination run. We should have realized that it was not possible. Buro could never have set up on his own. Meth manufacture is sophisticated and beyond Buro. We knew all this, and yet persuaded ourselves to dream a bit.'

Bikram had been massaging his temples as Ghosh spoke, now he opened his eyes and stared at the ceiling. 'You're right, Ghosh, and we fell into a nightmare. But even the worst nightmares have an end and sometimes idle dreams do come true, but in an unlikely way. For look you, Ghosh, there, above me, I can see what may take us somewhere nearer our destination.'

He's gabbling, thought Ghosh. Had the strain got too much to bear? He followed Bikram's gaze, not knowing what to expect, and then held his breath.

Perched on the iron beams above was a shoe box.

Sanjoy and Lalbahadur, scouting around the interiors and flashing torches in a show of efficiency, were hailed by Bikram. 'Get that box down carefully.'

Someone found a high stool and dragged it in, while Sanjoy and Lalbahadur argued who would climb, till, after a bellow from Ghosh, both tried to climb it together. Finally, the box was brought down.

It contained ten packets of white powder.

'Not bad,' said Bikram. 'Not bad at all. This and that black bag Raja and Montu picked up from the durwan's house, together with Apple Hassan's testimony, should help us tie it in. Pick up those bits of cup and plate as evidence also and send them along for a forensics test. We are sure to find fingerprints that will match Buro's. The thing to do is to shape all the evidence tidily, organize it well and then present it to Buro. If we do it properly, he should crack and confess.'

That afternoon, two addicts who were sliding into cold turkey in the airport thana lock-up were in for a pleasant surprise. They were taken out of their cell into an adjoining room where two policemen, one fat and sweat-drenched and the other very obviously a senior officer, offered them a sampling such as they had never imagined in their wildest dreams.

Currency notes were rolled into columns and the powder laid before their bewildered eyes.

'Now tell us how it is.'

Addict number one, younger and newer, was at first apprehensive, but addict number two leaned over and whispered. 'Even if it's some kind of torture and they want some confession, take the stuff first before they jerk it out of reach.'

The heady fumes sank in slowly and the familiar tingling came back. Elated, they looked up with glazed eyes.

'Tell us, you fool, how it is. Is it good? Is it the real stuff?'

'Real good,' whispered one.

'Excellent,' mumbled another.

'How would you rate it on ten?'

'I don't have any money.'

'I didn't ask you to pay me, you shithead. I said, how would you rate it? Is it fake, or adulterated or genuine?'

'It's good stuff.'

The elder addict, more worldly-wise, knew he would have to make a few noises before slipping into torpor. 'It would fetch a good price in the market. Must have come in from Nepal or Bangladesh, it's got that right kind of blend about it. May we have some more?'

But the fat man was already gathering the powder back together. The elder addict watched him plaintively for a while and then slumped down beside his partner.

Bikram came home, washed, dabbed antiseptic on the wound which was throbbing malevolently and looked bad, then looked at his watch. It was 5 p.m. Another hour or so and Dr Geo Sen, having preached temperance and regulation all day, would be out to glut himself. He dialled Geo Sen's number and waited, three quick rings and then Geo Sen's carefully cultured voice, 'Yes, Mr Chatterjee, how goes it with you?'

'I need your help professionally.'

'Yes?' The voice sounded doubtful.

'I need an anti-tetanus injection and then a quick consultation. My physician is out of town.'

'Dear me, nothing serious I hope.'

'It was at a raid. I jumped over a gate and hurt myself.'

'What exciting lives you lead! Be here at 7.30 p.m. and I'll keep things ready for you.'

At precisely 7.35 p.m., Bikram presented himself at Geo Sen's chamber and was ushered into the sumptuous inner room, where he sat for ten minutes on a plush sofa inhaling the smell of cappuccino and leafing through the month's copy of *Cosmopolitan*.

At 7.55, Dr Sen bounded in. He was followed by a nurse looking natty in her uniform. The wound was examined and the nurse applied some ointment on it and covered it with a gauze bandage. Then she finished off with the anti-tetanus shot and coffee was brought in.

The doctor plied Bikram with cookies and leaned back, smiling. His smile indicated that he was not displeased with Bikram's visit. It was always useful to add a policeman to your list of contacts and it was clever of Bikram to have turned an acquaintance formed over an uncomfortable investigation into a friendship.

'How is everything?' The doctor was still beaming.

'Everything's just fine,' said Bikram sunnily. 'We are, in fact, putting the finishing touches to the Robi Bose case. It's probably all over by now.'

'Probably?'

Geo Sen continued to smile but Bikram could see that the news had startled him.

'Yes! The whole thing was very flat, very banal, in the end. Drugs.'

'What about them?' The doctor's lips were still stretched in a smile but a shadow had crossed his face. 'Robi dosed himself on an excess of painkillers, right? Isn't that what we all knew from the beginning?'

'Robi's drug overdose was very different from the other kinds of overdoses in that house. *You* can tell me more about it.'

'I can tell you nothing.' The smile had left the doctor's face and a cold fury had taken its place. 'Had anything been otherwise, I would have told the police obviously. You can't sit here in my office threatening me.'

Bikram shrugged his shoulders delicately and spread out his hands. 'I haven't said a thing and yet you're so agitated. I hope you really aren't hiding anything, because if you are there might be trouble. You see, even as I talk to you, Buro, Robi's trusted attendant, is being put under arrest. Very soon the newspapers will get wind of it. Once we start briefing journalists—you know how we policemen love to talk. We let out that Buro is confessing and mentioning names, and among them is that of a famous doctor. Do you think your cosy little practice can withstand the nosy press, digging deep into your past, your assets, your lifestyle?' Bikram took a deep breath, lifted the coffee mug, took a sip and watched the doctor who had gone absolutely quiet. The nurse knocked, entered the room and presented the doctor with a cordless receiver. 'Mr Tekriwal on the phone, Sir. He wants to have a word with you.'

The doctor raised his head brokenly and the nurse, with admirable insight, sensed trouble. 'I'll tell him you're in an important meeting,' she intoned breathlessly and scuttled out of the room.

'If I tell you what you want to hear, will you promise that I won't be dragged to court as a witness?'

'I cannot make any such promise, because you know as well as I do that a criminal suit, especially one of homicide, is too deep and entangled for one to make empty assertions.

However, once the charge sheet is given and the trial starts, it may be a long time before matters get to the stage where you will be required in court. The press will have forgotten the case by then and you can slip in and out of the matter anonymously. The time to be feared is now, and I can help you, if I desire, depending on my satisfaction with your responses.'

The doctor knew when he was beaten. But defeat somehow revived his spirits. Settling himself comfortably on the sofa, he began: 'I don't know whether Nisha did drugs in her youth or not, but I suppose she did, in a casual kind of way. Of course, she was too aware of her beauty to let anything harm her looks. Robi was a good catch, good because he was presentable and had a fair amount of money without being unnaturally overbearing and bullying. Nisha had a husband to fall back on and she had her little flings. But she always had them with men who could give her something material in return, not money, like an ordinary harlot, but an introduction to someone powerful, or a tip-off on shares, or someone who could dig out money outstanding to her. She had a succession of small businesses: designing, art gallery, travel agency, all those things where one can escape tax and make quiet money. Her house soon became a kind of intimate boudoir where a select group of clients could drop in for chats and services rendered in a genteel manner.'

'Were you one of them?'

The doctor went on speaking without a pause, as if he had not heard Bikram's question. 'Robi knew, of course, but never let on. At least I never heard of any big quarrel or accusations of infidelity. Perhaps it was the fear of scandal or that he was too much in love with his wife to give her up. His stroke could easily have happened, though, from all the strain and emotion, the rage at being constantly cuckolded.

'I don't know how the drugs started. They did party drugs,

cocaine and meth, and partook of the illicit pleasures of Proxyvon and alcohol cocktails. The women went for it more than the men. Nisha, perfect businesswoman that she is, began to charge a fee, especially for the use of her house. Then Robi became ill and Nisha was a free bird. And fortuitously for her, Robi's attendant appeared to have access to an almost limitless supply of drugs. All at once Nisha's life opened up to new possibilities. I warned her, time and again, about what she was doing, especially because she was now part of what was obviously a well-run racket, but she was too far gone to care. And her friends loved it—who wouldn't? There was now no need to hunt high and low for safe places to score from. I think the parties got wilder and the set of people became dangerous, with new entrants she couldn't have screened personally. So I began to distance myself from her. And the answer to the question you just asked is, yes, I was her lover once, but no, never in these circumstances.'

'Did she call you when the police investigation began and make any statement?'

'She was very angry about Sudip Pyne's obstinacy. She was scared, because she was sure that with the police all over the place, one of the servants might say or do something to arouse their suspicion. There had been trouble amongst the staff, I think, between Buro and her maid, I can't remember the name . . .'

'Mithu,' said Bikram.

'Yes. Mithu and Buro had been fighting over the drug profits. Mithu had also probably been stealing money and blaming it on Buro. Nisha was unable to control them and she had asked for help from Toofan Kumar, I think, and he sent you down.

'But Nisha was afraid and asked me for help, which I could not give, considering I had drifted out of her life for quite some time by then. I felt sorry for her but I couldn't say I told you so, though that was the most appropriate comment under the circumstances. And, Mr Chatterjee, that is all I know. I'm sorry I don't know whether Buro did his master in or Nisha, her husband.'

Bikram was finding the room and the speaker, including his tale, oppressive and disheartening. He was also conscious of the fact that, though the things that had been going on in the Bose house were easily established, he was in no way nearer to the actual hand behind Robi Bose's death. The day's activities had been wearying and his leg ached. Also, he was beginning to feel dizzy and at times the doctor's face seemed to come from some way off.

'Go home and rest.'

Bikram lifted his eyes and found that Geo Sen's face was swimming in and out of focus.

'You need a shot of Tramadol yourself, I think.'

Bikram mumbled something, rose and stumbled to the door. Exhaustion bore down upon him and the nurse looked curiously as he gripped the door and walked heavily to the lift. Traffic was thick, and they fought their way through the evening crowds and reached home at nine. Without bothering to eat, Bikram changed and dropped into bed like one dead.

Ghosh was sitting uncomfortably on a swivel chair in a room in the crime branch. The door flew open and Chuni Sarkar entered, followed by Sheena Sen, looking vivacious and inviting in her uniform in spite of the fact that it was close to midnight. Then a man walked in, his face downcast, wearing a pair of dark trousers and a grey checked shirt. His hands were tied at the wrists. Behind him trooped in two constables and two others whom Ghosh found familiar but could not place till he realized that one was the liftman and the other, the canteen superintendent.

'Leave,' he said pleasantly, then shut the door.

They stood ringed round Buro, the five of them—Ghosh, Chuni Sarkar and Sheena Sen forming the inner ring and the two constables, the outer circle.

Then the constables scraped chairs and set up water in glasses and Ghosh, avoiding the uncomfortable swivel chair, settled himself on an ordinary wooden one.

'Is the DSP coming?' asked Sheena Sen.

'No, I'll take the first round. Let's see what happens,' said Ghosh.

Chuni Sarkar began the proceedings. 'Why were you resisting arrest, pretending you hadn't murdered your master? Yes, we know, and we have witnesses in the house who will swear that you did.'

Buro, surveying the floor, looked up and there was fear in his eyes. 'What witnesses?'

'That's not for you to ask. Now confess and we'll get you a competent lawyer who can state your case properly in court and help you. You slipped an overdose of painkillers and tranquillizers into his Horlicks, didn't you?'

'I didn't, Sir, believe me.'

'Who stole petty cash in the house? Think well before you say you don't know because we have one reliable witness who swears she saw you do it.'

Buro's eyes glazed over with terror, the kind of look Ghosh had seen in many eyes.

'Mithu! I knew she would,' whispered Buro. He slid down to the floor in a heap. Ghosh frowned. Chuni should have allowed him to sit.

The constables rushed and dragged Buro to a chair. Water from one of the glasses was sloshed over him and he came to,

shaking his head and spraying droplets over Ghosh and Sheena
Sen. Ghosh took out his all-purpose handkerchief and wiped
his face and neck, then took over.

'How long have you been doing drugs?'

'I don't know what you mean.'

Ghosh leaned over to a drawer and carefully took out one
of the packets they had found in the shoebox.

'We know everything. Sheikh Hassan, also known as Apple
Hassan, has been arrested and has confessed. Shiv Ram Prasad
Tewari, the guy to whom you made payments, has also ratted
on you. You're in for a long haul with us, Buro, so you'd better
come clean and tell us all about the murder. We'll see what we
can do after that.'

'I didn't murder Robi Bose, I swear I didn't.' Buro's voice
quavered. His hands were still tied at the wrists, he lifted them
as best as he could and attempted a namaste. Tears rolled down
his cheeks. Sheena Sen took out a piece of gum and put
it delicately into her mouth. Chuni Sarkar smiled, leaned
forward and aimed a sharp blow at Buro's shaking hands.
Ghosh's cell phone rang. He looked at the screen and his
heart sank. It was his wife.

'Don't wait up for me, I'll be late,' he said, hoping
fervently she would be too displeased to continue the
conversation further.

'And how will you get in? Like Superman, through the
window? Don't you know that it's the guard's day off and
there's no one to open the front door?'

Damn, thought Ghosh. He said, 'You go to sleep and
I'll wake you when I reach.'

'You will sleep in the park if you are a minute later than
1 a.m.,' said his wife and slammed the phone down.

The cross-examination was proceeding along expected lines.
Chuni Sarkar read the charges again and Sheena Sen repeated

them, embroidering them with what Mithu had told her. But Buro's defence was unyielding. He hadn't murdered Robi Bose and knew nothing of what had killed him. It was a frame-up. For what? He didn't know, couldn't think, he implored them to set him free. Ghosh looked at his watch. 12.30 a.m. Perhaps, with luck, they would wear him down soon and he could go home. But the minutes crept by and 12.30 a.m. wound on to 1.15 a.m. and to 1.30 and, horror of horrors, 1.45 a.m. Buro's face took on a ravaged look but he stuck resolutely to his guns. The consolation was that, midway, he admitted to knowing Apple Hassan and Shiv Ram Prasad Tewari, so Ghosh knew they could gradually close in on the drug angle. But what about the murder? That was the case at hand and if they couldn't pin it on him, the weakest link, they would have to start all over again.

At 2 a.m, Chuni Sarkar opened the window and stared out moodily. What a bother! There was only one man who could break him down and that man was happily dreaming in bed, perhaps with that starlet girlfriend of his! If only they could leave off and go home too. He could hear Ghosh droning on in the background. Sheena Sen joined him at the window.

'It's no good,' she said. 'Only Sir can do it. Let's call it off.'

They both shot a quick look at Ghosh who looked haggard and worn out too. 'Why don't you make the suggestion?'

'All right,' said Sheena Sen and slipping up to Ghosh, said something in low tones. Ghosh listened, then nodded. The three clustered at the window and looked out to where a dog was scratching itself at the deserted ATM booth and a sentry paced down to the urinal.

'The lock-up might actually help,' said Chuni Sarkar. 'I'll bunk him with a difficult partner who can ruffle him. Maybe the bird will sing.'

Buro was led out into the night air, hot and stifling, and he looked up once at the great big moon that hung over the leaves of a pipal tree. The guards were angry at being kept awake so long and shook and dragged him roughly to the van and half kicked him into it. The van roared off and Chuni Sarkar followed angrily, determined to give the oaf a cosy cellmate for the night. Ghosh stepped dejectedly into his car and wondered if his wife would be merciless enough to create a scene at 2.30 a.m. for the neighbours to enjoy.

## 18

Bikram was awakened at 7.30 the next morning by the insistent buzz of his telephone. It was a journalist. 'Has the Robi Bose case been solved? I heard that the crime branch arrested the culprit last night from the Bose residence. His personal attendant, who confessed to murder almost immediately at headquarters. What are your comments?'

Bikram tried to sit up and felt a violent throbbing in his leg and in the arm in which he had been given the injection. He tried to see the time through the mosquito net but the room was too dim for him to make out the clock. When he spoke, his voice sounded hoarse. 'I don't know, because others have been working on it last night. You'll have your answer once we produce him in court today.'

'Will you be handling this case personally?'

'We all are.'

'Is it true that if you are unable to produce a conviction on this one you might be transferred out of crime and to a remote district?'

'From where did you get that one?'

'Sources,' said the reporter cagily.

'Tell me more?' asked Bikram chattily.

'Is there any suspicion against any other servant of the household?'

'Staff would be a better word, I think.' Bikram was trying to raise the mosquito net and hoist himself out of the bed, which only made the pain worse.

'Is there any other statement you would like to make?'

'What's the point? You will, in any case, fabricate all kinds of statements and attribute them to me. So you'd better get to work.'

'At least you should thank me, Bikram! You didn't even know about the confession.'

After the journalist had hung up, Bikram phoned Chuni Sarkar. 'When did he confess?'

'He confessed nothing, Sir. This one will take some time.' Briefly, Chuni Sarkar outlined the course of events of the night before.

'Well, we'll have to hurry up, because the press have got the story wrong, as usual, and might force our hand.'

'It's not just the press, Sir, but others too.'

'Hmm, yes. Has he rung you up?'

'Not yet.'

'Can you do me a favour and give him a preliminary report, exactly as you outlined it to me just now? If you do it well, he might not be too nasty.'

'As you wish.'

Chuni Sarkar, who wanted desperately to stay on in his present posting, would have loved not to make this particular call, for reporting to Toofan Kumar was like playing a nerve-racking game of passing the parcel, and this time the parcel had dropped in his lap.

Bikram limped through his shave and bath, rummaged in his cupboard, swallowed a muscle relaxant, and read the morning papers. Nothing in them yet! Then he nervously switched on the television and zapped through a few news channels and 'breaking news' banners. Nothing there either! With a feeling of relief, he dressed with something of his old fastidiousness, matching clothes and shoes perfectly and cringing in pain now and then, before leaving for the office.

At 11 a.m., he rang up Ghosh. 'Where are you?'

'At home.'

'Why? I thought you had taken Buro to court?'

'Not I. If we do all the work, Chuni will have nothing to do.'

'Let me know when he's been brought back. And set up a meeting between the three of us, I'd like you to be there too.'

'And Sheena Sen, I suppose, since she was there too.'

'If you must,' said Bikram unkindly.


At 2 p.m., Bikram, Chuni Sarkar and Ghosh assembled in the same room to which Buro had been brought the night before. Sheena had been called off on another assignment but promised to hurry down as soon as possible.

Bikram spent exactly fifteen minutes with a bedraggled Buro. He must have had some tough luck with his cellmate for he only cried, pleaded innocence and begged for freedom. He also stuck steadfastly to his original line of defence. Yes, he had been associated with drugs once, but he had not murdered Robi Bose. When Bikram gave up, he found the others waiting for him. A look at his stony face told them what had happened.

'This affair is at a complete deadlock,' said Ghosh mournfully. 'I had hoped that this Buro would confess and put an end to it but it seems like there's no end in sight. What are we to do now?'

'Think,' said Bikram.

'Of what?' objected Ghosh.

'Of everything, which is what we haven't done till now,' said Bikram. 'We have only been running around hopelessly from one dead clue to another.' Bikram stared at his fingers, then embarrassedly fished a mini notepad out of his pocket and opened it. Ghosh tried to peep in but could not see much. At any rate, what there was seemed to be handwriting rather than pictures. No drawings, thought Ghosh. He must have been really distressed.

Bikram cleared his throat and began. 'Suspect number one was, as we all agreed, Buro. Obvious motive, robbery, but nothing was missing. Deeper motive, hired by someone else, probably the dead man's wife. Had means of procuring poison, had all the means of tampering with drinks—either earlier in the drawing room or later on in the dead man's own room or when the food was being made in the kitchen. Evidence, links to gangs, was a petty criminal himself. Mithu the maid says he stole money, which presents an additional motive in that Robi Bose may have challenged him over it.' He waited, and when no one said a word, went on. 'The second suspect is Tara Bose, the cousin. Obvious motive, gains control of the house by removing Robi Bose. The widow has an inheritance too, but the girl may not have realized that. Deeper motive, has had a quarrel with Robi, feels insulted and humiliated by the way he and his wife treat her, loses her head and kills him. Means of procuring poison: purchased medicines herself and has done so in the past. Often went and kept the deceased company, so no one would keep too sharp a watch on her. Evidence: she too has abused prescription drugs and I myself have seen drugs and alcohol in her own house.'

Since this sounded indelicate and suspicious, he hurried on to his third point.

'Number three. Nisha Bose, the third suspect, had the easiest access to her husband, to his food and drinks. Motive: to get rid of someone who was becoming increasingly burdensome. Evidence, resisted a post-mortem from the outset, insisted that the death certificate be given and her husband's death be passed off as natural. Also, was a pusher herself, and possibly a user too. Which brings us to an additional motive—that her husband found out and threatened her with action and she took the easiest way out.'

Bikram finished but the other two continued to stare dully at the wall.

Finally Ghosh stirred. 'Can we leave out the people at the party now? We did prepare a list, but I don't think it's been followed up. Where is it, Chuni?'

'In my office,' said Chuni Sarkar shamefacedly. He had forgotten all about the names and addresses of the men and women at Robi Bose's house on the night of his death that had been so painstakingly prepared by an assistant sub-inspector and then dumped unceremoniously by Chuni in a brown envelope in his drawer. No one had followed up on them because of the unspoken hope that the case could be solved without such a large and complicated investigation.

'But why leave it in your drawer if the case is being dug up here?' asked Ghosh maliciously. 'I suppose you haven't looked a single person up from that list?'

'Of course I did,' lied Chuni Sarkar vehemently. 'Half were travelling and the others were not available when my men called on them. And after that, well, I do run a police station, you know? If it was that important you could have asked one of your own men to take over.'

'Very well, let's first look at what we've got,' said Bikram, heading off the quarrel. 'Forgetting the wild-card entries like mysterious party guests, who do you think did it?'

Again no one spoke, till Ghosh and Chuni Sarkar began together. 'Buro,' said Chuni Sarkar at the same time as Ghosh said, 'Tara.'

'Why?' said Bikram looking at Ghosh. 'Why settle on Tara?'

Ghosh shifted uneasily. 'I don't have any definite proof, obviously. But the girl seems too self-sacrificing and meek; today's girls aren't really like that. I'm sure she was suppressed, no, what they call it, repressed, and took it out by bumping off her cousin. With the money she'd inherit after selling off the house she could have got any boyfriend she wanted.'

'But Robi wanted to settle her claim in any case, so why take the trouble to murder him?'

'She wanted her share as a matter of right, not a claim settled by her father and cousin. Besides, she also didn't think the death would be suspect. A sick man dies in bed and everyone thinks it's expected. No one expected a nosy Sudip Pyne to turn up as he did!'

'What about Mithu the maid and the durwan?' asked Chuni Sarkar. 'Can they be exonerated?'

'Yeah. And what about the tailor and the masseuse and the electrician who came to fix the fuse and the man who walked by outside their house the evening before, talking on his cell phone at 7.56 p.m.?' Ghosh asked his question in a wretched voice. 'Chuni! We'll never get anywhere at this rate!'

Then he turned to Bikram. 'What about your ideas?'

'I haven't any,' said Bikram truthfully. 'To tell you the truth, this kind of domestic murder isn't quite my thing. Give me a political crime or rape or robbery any day.'

'That's nonsense,' said the faithful Ghosh. 'You excel in crime work of every kind. So?'

'We each go our own way,' said Bikram. 'Chuni goes back to Buro and you can interrogate Tara Bose since you have some misgivings about her.'

'And you, Sir?'

'I'll take the last slice on the plate—Nisha Bose.'

At 5 p.m. Tara was called by the doorman at Wisdom Press to the pantry.

'There's something important.'

'Such as?'

'Your cousin's murderer has been caught. Look, there he is coming out of jail, no, wait a minute, the court. He's been remanded to police custody.'

Tara followed Buro's familiar figure which now looked strange and almost unreal on television. She remembered his insolence and barely camouflaged contempt each time she visited Robi's house. Now here he was, stricken with fear and shame, looking away from the camera as it panned over his face.

The reporter's voice declaimed breathlessly on the death of Robi Bose, the suspicion on the durwan and the maid, and the fact that the police had finally arrested the attendant. While the voice-over, mixing fact and fiction, created an eerie account of Robi's final moments, the camera showed the Bose house, their garden, Mithu peeping out from behind the gate and a single shot of Nisha wearing sunglasses and driving away in a car with tinted windows.

'Is that your sister-in-law?' It was Anju, Tara's friend and colleague, asking the question. 'Wow, she's quite something.

Tara turned away and returned to her desk with her mind in turmoil.

She thought for a moment, then picked up her handbag and took out her telephone book. The number was there, nestling protectively in the middle, copied out once in her own handwriting but also preserved in the original slip which he had given her. She picked up the phone and dialled. There was no answer. Tara retried, then gave up and thought some more. She returned to the telephone book and hunted for Ghosh's number without any success. Finally, she called the pantry attendant and asked him for what she wanted. The man was excited at being part of a drama that had potential to merit the attention of prime-time television. He said, 'My cousin works in the government. You want the number of a Mr Ghosh of the crime branch, right? The one we saw on television just now?

'Yes. I had his number but I seem to have misplaced it.'

'No problem, I'll get it in a minute.'

The man was as good as his word. Tara quickly dialled before she had time to change her mind.

Ghosh sounded hurried and annoyed when he picked up. On giving him her name, however, there was a grim silence.

'I've just seen the news on television. It couldn't have been Buro,' Tara said.

The line was so quiet that she thought Ghosh had hung up.

Actually, Ghosh was trying to work out where he could interrogate Tara. 'Would you like to talk about it?'

'Yes,' said Tara.

'You can come to our office at about 7 p.m. and tell us what you want to say. I will hear you out.'

'Won't Mr Chatterjee be there too?'

'No, he's out on some other work.'

'But I want . . .' Tara stopped herself in time. Ghosh groaned inwardly. This was an emotional tangle he could have well done without! On the other hand, she might have a vital clue.

'I'll call back later, when you're not so busy,' mumbled Tara miserably. She had bungled it. What must he think of her?

Feeling sorry for her and angry with himself for not thinking on his feet, Ghosh softened his tone. He had a fifteen-year-old daughter at home and had a good idea about girls and their infatuations. But then again, he was a careful man and wary of Bikram spending too much time with young female witnesses. So he said, 'If there is anything important, you can tell me now. After that we can meet some other time and I'll promise to get Bikram Chatterjee along.'

'No,' said Tara, tears of shame stinging her eyes. 'I can tell you over the phone. Robi had only one drink which Buro mixed for him. He couldn't have put in anything without my seeing him. It is highly unlikely that the stuff was mixed in his food because Robi had only boiled vegetables and toast with margarine for dinner. And as for his Horlicks . . .'

Ghosh waited.

'I mixed his Horlicks for him,' said Tara in a voice that combined sullenness and defiance. 'In which case you should let Buro go and arrest me.'

Bikram drove up to the Bose residence once more and looked at the bougainvillea and the sunflowers, the smooth whitewashed walls, the narrow patch of grass. The iron gate was shut again and the durwan was nowhere to be seen. Opposite, a television van with the name of the channel scrawled picturesquely on its sides straddled the pavement and half the road, and forced cars to travel single file.

He had forgotten the members of the press, who now rushed up to him. His leg hurt, his throat hurt, his mind rankled and now this!

'Have you come to make further arrests? Any new clues to follow up after the confession?'

'No comment!'

'Why not?'

'There will be a press briefing soon and the inspector general or the SP will brief you.'

'But you are the investigating officer; why not say a few words now?'

'Go away,' said Bikram testily. He stood fiddling with the locked gate when one of the reporters said, 'The durwan's been absconding since morning. You'll have to climb over.'

And gift a first-rate picture to you, thought Bikram. All his hopes of catching Nisha Bose and her household unawares vanished. He would have to give notice and wait for someone to open the gate. Bikram climbed back into his car and turned back the way he had come.

He got Mistry to stop the car as they rounded the bend, then climbed out. One of his guards was in uniform while the other was in civvies. Bikram motioned to the uniformed one to follow him and cautiously crept back. The TV van blocked the road and just as well. Bikram crept along the road, head down. At the house just before the Boses', he stopped and rattled the gate. A man wearing the uniform of a private security agency opened the gate slightly and peered, then stared at Bikram and his uniformed guard.

'Let me in,' said Bikram. The gate opened further and Bikram and his guard pushed in.

'Who are you?' demanded the sentry.

'Shut up,' said Bikram and left Lalbahadur to deal with the man.

He walked quickly to the wall on the left and continued along it. The wall was high but manageably so. About a third of the way down, Bikram found what he wanted—a reduction in height and, on the other side, he could see Nisha Bose's backyard with the kitchen and the jackfruit tree at the far end.

'Lalbahadur!'

He came running, followed by the scandalized sentry clucking and fussing.

'Get me over, my leg's giving me trouble.'

As Lalbahadur hoisted him over, Bikram told him to go around, get the car and park before the Boses' gate. Then he scrambled over the top.

He took the kitchen entrance because he knew that would be open throughout the day, as kitchens are wont to be, even in a house that has seen death and disaster. He could hear the murmur of voices. His intention had been to loom up behind them and catch them unawares but his foot struck the door and set it shuddering open. He looked in and found the durwan and Mithu staring at him open-mouthed.

He walked in nonchalantly and said, 'Keep quiet and go out in front. Move now. Into the pantry and the dining room. Yes, not a word or you two will be the ones to be arrested after Buro.' On an inspiration he added, 'There's a swarm of policemen covering your house anyway. Where is she?'

'In the bedroom.' It was Mithu who answered. The maid looked at the stairs and looked away and Bikram could tell she was frightened.

'Which one, hers or her husband's?'

'Her own.'

'Switch on the fans here and in the drawing room.' He turned to the durwan. 'Go and wait in your room at the gate and let my car enter. Close the gate at once because there are reporters outside.'

He took the steps two at a time, which was difficult because of the heat and his bad leg. The house was hot and he was perspiring freely. He heard the slow whirring of the fans as they started up and cranked noisily, which was why he had asked for them to be switched on, so as to camouflage his footsteps. Let me not blunder, oh Shona, pray for me, he said to himself. Then he softly tried the door handle and entered.

He stood in the middle of the room lined with mirrors and he randomly thought how he felt like the character played by Bruce Lee in the movie *Enter the Dragon*. He tried not to look at the split and fractured Bikrams that moved backwards and forwards from the mirrors but was momentarily transfixed by them, for Bikram could never go by a mirror without looking at least once. Then he looked around at the bedroom.

It was empty.

From the bathroom came the sound of running water and he hoped Nisha would come out fully clothed. While he was considering his next move the bathroom door opened and Nisha Bose came in. She was wearing a scarlet housecoat and her feet were bare. Her hair was tied in a ponytail and there was a white patch under her nostrils. Nisha Bose was bleaching her upper lip.

When she saw Bikram her hand flew up to her face and smudged the bleach, then she opened her mouth to scream but shut it without a sound. 'Hello,' said Bikram. 'May I sit down?'

'Your sense of humour is delicious,' said Nisha Bose. 'Deliriously delicious! Fantastically so! Did you arrest my maid and durwan as well and walk into an empty house?' She had recovered herself almost immediately and was as winsome and self-possessed as ever.

'They let me in,' said Bikram. 'They were happy to do so, and there was no unpleasantness. Would you like a sponge to dab it off?'

Without waiting for an answer, he took a white sponge pad and handed it to her. Their fingers met for a second and both looked down. Her skin was cold against the heat of the day, and Bikram could feel his skin crawl. Then he turned round and sat on a chair and motioned her to one before him.

'So, what can I do for you?' Nisha's voice was steady, with no hint of surprise or discomfiture at the way in which he had entered her bedroom or the reasons behind it. She seemed to be relishing the scene.

Bikram took a deep breath for courage. 'It's Buro. He's been talking. About you and your . . . friends here. And the parties you had. What can you tell me about that, Mrs Bose?'

'Nisha, call me Nisha.'

'Very well.'

'May I call you Bikram?'

'If you answer my question, yes.'

'How many men have you got hidden behind the door to take down every word?'

'Go ahead and check for yourself.'

'I will.'

Nisha slipped to the door and opened it while Bikram watched her in amusement. She returned and stood before him.

'Turn out your pockets.'

He did. There was a monogrammed handkerchief, three pens, a small pocket notebook and his revolver.

'You came armed?'

'I can leave the gun on the table if you want?'

'That might make you more desirable, yes.' Nisha's eyes twinkled.

Bikram slipped open the chamber and took out the cartridges, then laid the revolver down on a small table crowded with magazines and other odds and ends. With the revolver on top, the room looked more and more like a Bond scene. Then he put back his handkerchief, arranged his pens in his pocket and held out the notebook open at a page.

'Does this name sound familiar to you?'

'Sheikh Hassan, alias Apple, of the Dhoor Syndicate? It's all nonsense and drivel to me!'

'It's related to the question I asked you but you sidestepped. Buro has been talking about rave parties at your house. Do you deny that?'

She looked at him, laughing, and said, 'Of course I deny it. Buro might have been feeding my guests something but that was without my knowledge. All I did was to step up the music and set the food and help my guests have a good time. Buro was in charge of arrangements. I would be busy looking after Robi, and had very little knowledge of what Buro actually did to make my guests comfortable. He may have pandered to their whims now and then. How would I know?'

'And you think he murdered your husband?'

'That's what you say, Bikram.'

'What do you think, Nisha?'

'He must have. I trust the Indian police. When they say something, I believe it.'

'Did you kill your husband?'

Her voice was still calm, edged with satisfaction. 'What a shocking thing to say! Do you know how widows are treated in our society? Can you even imagine how much I loved him? It is sad to see wonderful men like you tainted by the muck you handle every day to even think of dirty things like this.'

'Buro might say you did!'

'Let him, by all means.' She sounded almost bored now. 'The testimonial of a shady drug-dealing beggar! I'll hire the best lawyer to defend myself if anyone should dare proceed against me.'

Bikram sat very still. There was nothing more he could do. He had come here with an unformed idea in his mind, a kind of vague certainty that if he could get Nisha Bose alone he could charge her with her husband's death, catch her off guard and see if he could get a confession. That was why the stealth, the need to catch her unprepared, take her by surprise. But the woman was almost inhuman in her composure. She sat before him, her eyes a-glitter, easily elegant in her housecoat, teasingly rendering Bikram's plans to nought and sparkling in the knowledge that she was unassailable.

'Are you done?' She broke in on his thoughts. He looked up and into her face, gleaming softly in the electric light, a sculpted perfection seated amidst the shambles of her kingdom.

'I've finished,' said Bikram. 'There's nothing more for me to do.'

He rose to leave. The carriage of his body suggested a great, tragic defeat. His eyes turned into pools of sorrow, running over with the anguish caused by the hopelessness of the case and the pain in his leg that was now radiating to his lower back. He reached forward to pick up his revolver.

'Wait,' said Nisha and put her hand over his. Her touch was light yet firm and her nails, coloured in a delicate shade of pink, rested alluringly on the back of his hand. 'Don't go!'

He lifted his eyebrows in question.

She turned to her cupboard and hesitated a moment, plucking nervously at the lapel of her housecoat, then suddenly, having reached a decision, opened it and flung open a box.

Bikram slipped the cartridges into the revolver and put the revolver in his pocket. At the same time, Nisha found what she was looking for and turned round to meet him. Her eyes carried a clear, direct, almost savage look. 'You came to get something out of me and so you shall.' He reached forward for the piece of paper that she held out. She held on to it tightly and looked at him. Their eyes met and the stillness in the room became unbearable. Suddenly, a crow cawed on the other side of the slatted windows and the tension snapped. Bikram shook his head almost imperceptibly and tugged gently at the paper. Nisha Bose sat down on the bed with her head bowed. It was a piece of paper torn out of a notepad that had *Nisha Bose* printed on the top in beautiful calligraphy. Underneath was the text, written in a shaky, unformed hand.

I am responsible for my own death. I can't take this life any longer. Nisha has no time for me and spends it with others who can give her what she wants. But I know all about her and the things that go on downstairs and in the other bedroom when they think I am asleep. Whoever you are, doctor or policeman, please don't let them get away! But spare Nisha, she was helpless in their hands, my poor little doll!

Robi Bose

Bikram read it through once, then again, and looked helplessly around him.

'If you want samples of Robi's handwriting, Mithu can get them for you from his room.' Nisha Bose's voice was hard.

Bikram looked at the letter and pursed his lips. He remembered Buro's frightened face, cornered by an unforgiving system for a crime he had not committed. Then he looked at her, and the anger in his heart was tempered by a twinge of pity for this woman whose almost pathological self-centredness had wrecked her whole life.

He asked, as kindly and gently as he could manage, 'Where did you find this?'

She sat quietly for a while and then began quickly, as if she did not trust her own voice. 'It was by his bed, when I came up that night. I had drunk a little too much and, had . . . had . . . a little something else. At first I thought he was sleeping. I usually don't look in at night, but that evening Tara had been in, suddenly, without my having called her in, and I was worried that something was on. I tiptoed in and found that piece of paper and tossed it aside. Then I found that the bedcover was in a mess and the room smelt. I called Buro, picked up the piece of paper and read it and my world crashed. I could hear Buro coming up the stairs and I didn't want him to know about it. I stuffed it into my pocket. Buro came in and looked hard at Robi and then at me. I'll never forget the expression in his eyes. Then he came and stood beside me, very close, too close, and smiled.'

'Did he accuse you of anything?'

'No, but the way he smiled, as if I had killed Robi! God, I wasn't too sober, and then that evil man standing there. I felt so messed up, I completely lost my head. That's when I came to my room and hid the letter. I had an idea that a suicide meant the police and I was scared of what Buro might say and do. So I decided to keep quiet and pass the death off as a heart attack.'

'And after Sudip Pyne came it was too late to produce it?' Bikram's voice was as gentle as possible.

She shuddered and said, 'Yes. I was too far gone by then.'

'You could have shown it to him.'

'I was scared, thought I could shoo him away and get in another doctor through a hospital administrator called Chopra, whom I knew well. Anything to stop the police from coming to my house.'

'What about the bedcover that was changed?'

'That was Buro's idea. He said that if the sheets were switched and the new one looked cleaner, then the next doctor who came in would easily swear to death by cardiac arrest or something and let us go. I pointed out that people who have a cardiac arrest or a cerebral stroke do vomit and froth from the mouth, but for some reason he went ahead and changed it and hid the old sheet. Perhaps he did it deliberately, to make the death look suspicious and make things difficult for me. We were like cats in heat in that house, circling around one another, not trusting anyone or anything, plotting and planning all the time.'

'Why didn't you show me the note on my visit after that? You could have saved yourself some trouble.'

There was no answer. She sat looking impassively ahead.

'Was it because you had an idea that it could now be used to your advantage? To implicate others, perhaps? Tara, or Buro?'

She shot him a quick disapproving look and became quite still again.

'With Tara out of the way on a murder charge you could dictate terms to her father, who would, no doubt, be a broken man by then, and gain full control of this house. And with

Buro out, you could get rid of someone who was beginning to be difficult. You could, in fact, kill two birds with one stone.'

There was silence and then she said emptily, 'What else could I do?'

'Are you happy now?' he asked her.

She pondered for a while, then lifted her face, and said, 'Actually, I am, yes.'

Bikram looked gravely at her but she pretended not to notice.

Then her face broke into a smile and she said mischievously, 'But I'd like to tell you something I've never told anyone else. For the first time in my life I'm feeling sorry for someone. Would you like to know whom?' She leaned forward and brought her face near his till it was only inches away. When she spoke he could see her even white teeth and the finely chiselled bones of her neck. Her hair smelled of mountain flowers.

'I can't imagine.' He answered slowly, with a hint of irony in his voice.

'You!'

'Because?'

'Because you cannot charge me for possessing drugs, for taking them or peddling them! If you try, I'll get Rory Ganguly to defend me. I have money enough for that, and he'll tear your poor accusations into shreds. I'll say that Buro did everything. Buro tied up with my friends, unscrupulous beasts that they are, and used the house of an invalid and his innocent wife for his dirty activities. And finally, there was no homicide! The death was a suicide, with a perfectly justifiable suicide note, which a poor, panic-stricken wife could not remember to hand over, but that is hardly a crime. Am I right, Bikram?'

Bikram put the paper in his pocket, turned around and went to the door. Multiple Bikrams looked at him from the mirrors that lined the walls. At the door, he turned round and looked at her. Nisha Bose had let her hair down and was stroking it gently with a faraway look in her eyes. She was a vision—a beautiful woman standing temptingly in her bedroom. Bikram saw a broken woman in her mid-thirties who would have to find a new keeper, a new livelihood.

He said, 'You've lived life dangerously for some time now, and you are getting away with it. And yet, be careful, Nisha. I'll be keeping an eye on you. Don't do anything . . . rash . . . again. Your luck might run out the next time.'

Then he ran down the stairs, ignoring the piercing pain that now stabbed his back, and went outside into his car. 'Mistry, Lalbahadur, the two of you can take a bus or walk home. I need to drive.'

He rang up Ghosh.

'Location?'

'Looking for you, but your phone was switched off, so I thought I'd take a look at the Bose house. That Tara girl frightened me badly; she actually challenged me to arrest her as a potential suspect. She seems to be on the verge of a mental breakdown.'

'Where are you now?'

'Near the Silver Mall, stuck at a traffic signal.'

'Can you see me in my car near the signal?'

'No, wait a minute, yes I can! What a coincidence! You're driving,' he added dubiously.

'Come and join me, I have news to give.'

The lights had turned green but Ghosh ignored them, stepped ponderously out of his car, asked the driver to make a U-turn and follow Bikram's car, then walked over.

Ghosh clambered in and looked at his companion. A funny look crossed his face.

Bikram selected one of the pens from his breast pocket and handed it to Ghosh.

'It's that new camera and tape recorder we got from Delhi last week. I couldn't check it midway through but if you go through the footage, you'll know what happened. But,' he hesitated, and suddenly looked at Ghosh pleadingly, 'don't think ill of me; I had to do it that way. I hate playing with emotions but she would have never confided in me otherwise.'

The agitation and perplexity in Ghosh's mind increased. To cover his disquiet, he said, 'Has she confessed?'

'Read this.'

Bikram gave him the suicide note. He pressed the accelerator and the car jumped forward, changed lanes and almost mowed down a motorcyclist overtaking from the wrong side.

Ghosh read it and looked up. He looked shaken.

'Is it real?'

'Yes,' said Bikram shortly. 'Later you can check with the handwriting analysts. She hid it so that she could fix either Tara or Buro. Even one out of the way would have settled at least one front of her turbulent life.'

The car was now on a flyover and Ghosh could feel the wind whistling in his ears and see the billboards flashing past. Below, at the intersections he could see the traffic stuck in irregular jagged lines. 'She could have been arrested also.'

Bikram overtook a car that, in turn, was overtaking another and, for a moment, all three were frozen, crazily hanging upon the flyover.

'She took a risk,' said Bikram, adding, 'some are like that. They like to live life in the fast lane.'

Ghosh's phone rang. It was Chuni. He put it on loudspeaker and a breathless voice filled the car and struggled with the traffic noises for attention.

'We've got it, Sir. It's all over!'

Ghosh's heart jumped.

'Is he dead?'

'No! He has confessed! We crushed him so completely that he has confessed, not just to the drugs and all that but also to the murder! It's all right, don't you see? I couldn't get the DSP on the line so I told Sheena Sen and she's informed Toofan Kumar. The press meet is at 8.30 p.m. in his office but the journalists have already started swarming in. Buro killed Robi Bose because he was threatening to call in the police over his drug deals.'

Ghosh disconnected the line and stared at the pen camera recorder in his lap and at Bikram by his side.

Bikram had pulled the car over to the kerb. They both said nothing for a while and then Bikram suddenly shook his head, put it down on the steering wheel and started laughing.

'Ghosh, can you take over? I need to go home.'